ABSOLUTION

BY JENNIFER LAURENS

Grove Creek Publishing

A Grove Creek Publishing Book
ABSOLUTION
Grove Creek Publishing / October 2010
All Rights Reserved.
Copyright 2010 by Katherine Mardesich

Cover: Sapphire Designs
http://designs.sapphiredreams.org/
Book Design: Julia Lloyd, Nature Walk Design
ISBN: 1-933963-82-2
$13.95
Printed in the United States of America

For Rebekah

ABSOLUTION

- BOOK THREE -

ONE

"*What the hell do you want?*" The man boomed from the doorway.

I was unable to squeak out a sound, much less answer his question. Black spirits slithered like snakes up his shoulders, wrapping around his neck and gut, winding down between his legs, covering his gray suit. I'd seen evil before, been so close darkness had almost submerged me, but this infestation was acute. My body trembled. I broke out in an icy sweat.

"Is Krissy here?" Thankfully, my friend Chase was by my side. Thankfully, Chase couldn't see the evil writhing on Krissy's father or he'd be speechless. Like me.

The burly man scowled. "She can't come to the door."

Chase cleared his throat, pushed up his silver-rimmed glasses. "I respectfully disagree with your statement, sir. Krissy called and told me to come over."

The rugged skin on Krissy's father's face flushed scarlet. "And I'm telling you my daughter is not available."

"But—"

The door slammed in our faces. We stood in stunned silence staring at the thick, weather-worn wood.

"Wow," Chase blew out. "He's not the friendliest guy in the world, is he?"

Now that a slab of wood stood between us and the creepy crawly black spirits harbored on Krissy's dad, I breathed. My knees still shook. "Yeah."

"What should we do?"

Though part of me wanted to flee, the part of me that cared about my new friend Krissy—timid, quiet Krissy—didn't want to leave without making sure she was all right.

"Maybe she's waiting for us." I started around the circular structure—the only house I'd ever seen that was round. The shape made the house nearly as odd as its occupants.

"Her dad will have us arrested for trespassing, Zoe. The last thing I need is another run in with the cops after that party."

"That's probably the reason he doesn't want us talking to her. She's in serious trouble after what happened to Brady."

"True." Chase stood back, his gaze sweeping the exterior of the odd-shaped house. "But the likelihood of her going to jail is zero. I mean, she had a party at her parents' house while they weren't home. That's not grounds for incarceration."

Chase was a *Law and Order, CSI*—crime show—geek. I had no doubt he'd already staked a gamble on the outcome of the fateful events at Krissy's party.

"Brady hung himself at the party," I added. "And died."

"Still, it was an accident." Chase's concerned scan swept the house. "We should do *something.*"

"I agree, but what?"

"I don't know."

"She *did* call you, right?" I glanced at him, two hesitant feet behind me as I continued around the perimeter of the house. "Right?" Hopefully, this wasn't some scheme of Chase's to hang out with me. He knew we were just friends. He knew my heart belonged to Matthias and my life, at this moment in time, was caught up in Weston.

"Yes, she called." Halfway around the building his stride matched mine.

I stopped and stared at the windows. All were covered with white pull-down shades. No sign of anyone peeking out from behind them. "What did she say, *exactly?*" I asked him, my eyes going from one window to the next.

"She said, 'I need to talk to you. Can you come over?'"

⇒✦⇐

2

My gaze shot to Chase. "She didn't ask for me?"

He lowered his large brown eyes.

"Are you serious? Chase, that was a girl being a girl. 'I need to talk to you' means come over, I want to hang out. It means, I think you're a hottie. It means pay attention to me."

Chase's Adam's apple bobbed. "It does?"

I stormed back the way I came. He followed.

"I'm sorry. After the funeral, I thought she was in trouble. She sounded scared on the phone."

Brady's funeral had only been hours ago. The image of Albert and Brady's spirits there, Brady's wicked soul stirring his mother's anger into the vengeful act that influenced her to pull out a gun and shoot at Weston still hung in my mind. My brain replayed Brady's vengeful words, *'You always had to be number one!'* A hiss from the other side of the grave that only I had been able to hear, stung my spine. The piercing anger on Mrs. Wilcox's face as she'd locked her ruthless gaze on Weston and pointed the weapon and pulled the trigger. That's when I'd stepped in front of him. Not thinking about myself. Gut reaction. Matthias appeared. Glorious, powerful, Matthias. He'd lifted his hand, caught the bullet in his palm and the shell disintegrated on contact. Pandemonium had broken out.

When I'd finally left the cemetery, Brady's casket still straddled the open grave. I shuddered, a lonely ache rambling through me. Was there peace for the wicked?

I clicked the remote key for Mom's burgundy minivan and the doors unlocked. Chase stayed at my back.

"You really are going to leave?" he asked.

I opened the driver's side door. "Of course. I'd look like a retard crashing what Krissy probably hoped would *become* a date."

"A date? After today?" Chase's brows arched. "Do girls want to go on dates after a friend's funeral?"

"Some girls." I was reminded that just because Krissy and I shared a class and had chatted a few times, I didn't know her very well. Her social about face last week at the party had inadvertently contributed to Brady's death. At the funeral, she'd appeared eaten alive by guilt.

"What if she needs help? You saw her dad."

"Just because her dad is Mr. Rottweiler doesn't mean that he has anything to do with Krissy not coming to the door." In my heart, I doubted my own words. After seeing the evil crawling all over Krissy's father, I was certain the man had everything to do with why Krissy hadn't shown.

Chase gripped the door with urgency. "Maybe we should go to Starbucks and… figure it out."

Chase was clueless about girls. Most of the time his naiveté was endearing. Other times, like now, it bordered on annoying. But the hopeful grin on his face nudged aside my exasperation. And I could use the relaxing sauna of scent Starbucks offered. I glanced back over my shoulder at the round house.

Was Krissy okay? Foreboding roved inside of me, even though I tried to push it aside.

The front door opened. Her father appeared, looking every bit as angry as when he'd stormed across the snow-covered grass of the cemetery to retrieve Krissy from Brady's funeral. Now, he advanced like a grizzly ready to attack.

"Where is she?" he demanded.

As he neared, the ground beneath my feet trembled, shooting fear up my legs and throughout my body. Black spirits spun around his head, twisted and slithered along his limbs and when he opened his mouth, a flock of the translucent creatures flew out, joining the others congregated on his body in a disgusting celebratory display.

"Where is she?" He brought himself to the minivan and peered through the glass of the backseat. "Krissy!" He slid open the side door, dipped inside. "Krissy!"

My heart pounded out of control.

"She's not here." Chase sped around the front of the minivan and halted at the front passenger door, keeping a three-foot distance from Krissy's dad. "And it's not okay for you to search somebody's car without their permission."

4

Krissy's dad's spun around, his eyes bulging. "I'll damned well search what I want when my daughter is missing." He took off to Chase's car and tried the door. Locked. He glared at us, then crossed back to the minivan and pounded his fists on the windows as he peered through the tinted glass.

"Krissy!"

"She's not here, sir. We came looking for her, remember?" Chase said. I glanced around for Matthias. Nothing. As bad as this guy was, I obviously wasn't in mortal peril, or Matthias would be here.

Krissy's dad seethed. His slit eyes fastened to me and he marched my direction, stopping too close. The infestation of black spirits so overwhelming now, I could barely see through them to his face.

My mouth opened but no sound came. Chase inched close to me, his face tight as his gaze stayed with mine.

"If I find her anywhere near either of you, or that you're lying to me, I'll contact the police."

Chase snorted. "And tell them what? 'My daughter was hanging out with some of her friends, arrest them?' That's not going to hold up."

The man slid his furious glare to Chase. "Kidnapping will hold up."

Chase laughed. I couldn't believe his nerve. But then, he couldn't see the wild evil jumping, gnashing and screaming in silent pleasure on the man's body. "Let's go, Zoe." He took my elbow and led me around the hood of the minivan to the open driver's side door.

Krissy's dad marched across the front lawn, through his open front door and slammed it behind him.

"What a psycho," Chase mumbled.

I got inside the car, my hands shaking as I reached for the steering wheel.

"That was the worst case of black spirits I've ever seen," I muttered through a shudder.

Chase looked at the closed door of the house. "Really? Worse than what you saw at the funeral?"

I nodded, swallowed. "There wasn't an inch of his body that wasn't…

infected." I shook my head, shuddered. "Disgusting."

"The man's obviously got an anger issue."

"He's got more than anger issues." I was certain now that whatever plagued Krissy probably met my previous assumptions of some kind of abuse. I was more determined to find her and help her. I hoped, wherever she was, her guardian was by her side.

"You gonna be okay?" Chase's voice softened, his gaze flicking from my hands to my eyes. "Want me to drive you home?"

"And leave your car here for that weirdo to destroy?" I shook my head. "I'll be fine. Take your car and get out of here."

"Yeah, good idea." Chase studied me a moment. "You sure you don't want me to follow you or something? Non-stalkerish, I promise."

I smiled, took a deep breath and tried to erase the vision of Krissy's dad covered from head to toe with evil from my mind. "That's okay. Let me know if you hear from Krissy."

"You do the same," he said. "I can't imagine where she'd go."

"Yeah."

Silence.

My heart tore for Krissy. Where was she? She had one outfit she wore: her maternity-style denim jumper with that white long-sleeved tee shirt and her ankle boots. And one retro camel coat.

I hoped she wasn't pregnant… that was unthinkable.

"I gotta run," I said, hoping to find her somewhere. "Call me if you find her."

"I will. You too." Chase shut my door and stood back. I sent him a wave and drove, my gaze scanning the streets. If she'd only called Chase a few minutes ago, and she'd made the phone call from home, she might not be that far. I tried her cell phone on the off chance she had it with her, but I only got the stock phone carrier answering message.

Night's darkness swallowed the sky now, and white flakes began to fall. Krissy. Out alone. I said a silent prayer in my heart that she'd be okay.

I drove around Pleasant Grove for an hour, up and down Grovecreek

Drive, winding street after street. I even stopped at the high school, got out and jogged the open perimeter of the campus, calling for her on the off-chance she'd think to hide out there. My voice echoed back. A creepy shudder iced my spine. Part of the school remained locked behind a chain link fence. No way was I going to climb over and search for her.

I drove home heavy-hearted. Home looked warm and welcoming, with golden lights shining from each double-hung window. Love waited for me there. My family. Safety.

Luke's blue Samurai was parked out front. He wasn't usually home this early, but I was glad he was. Maybe, like me, the long day with the funeral had taken a toll and he yearned for the completion of home, too.

After parking Mom's van in the garage, I went inside. I was smacked with an invisible boulder. Albert. I froze.

TWO

The sound of Mom's sniffling trickled from the kitchen. A door slammed—Dad's office—the glass French doors had a fragile sound when they closed—or slammed. Abria's squealing, upstairs. Her fists against her locked bedroom door. A thump. Two.

My heart raced. "Mom?"

"What?"

As I crossed the family room towards the kitchen, my gaze flicked the area for Albert. Drawing closer to Mom, the vibe of weighty energy intensified. She was kneeling on the tile floor in the center of what looked like a misguided contemporary art piece of splattered and drizzled chocolate, amber syrup and white cream.

I didn't need to ask who'd caused the mess. Mom had no doubt found Abria playing in the contents of the refrigerator. Abria loved the smooth texture—not to mention the taste—of any syrup. We'd often found her 'painting' walls, floors, and table tops with Hershey's chocolate, maple syrup and caramel ice cream topping if we didn't hide the bottle in the back of the fridge.

"Let me help." Cleaning took my mind off Albert for a millisecond. He was here, somewhere, his menacing presence layered my body with the impending heaviness of being buried alive. I grabbed a roll of paper towels, wet them with hot water and joined Mom in wiping up the sticky goop.

"I asked Dad to check on her because I was upstairs folding laundry. Of course, he was working and got distracted just long enough for her to do this."

"I'm sorry."

"If he'd gotten up for one second. *One second*...." They'd argued. Ugliness still hung in the air like pollution. Weighty darkness pressed around me, closing in with suffocating presence.

Paper towels sopping with gook, I gulped in air, stood. Albert's ice-green eyes met mine from across the kitchen. The pleasure in his grin sent fury through my bones. He leaned casually against the pantry, his black suit popping out in contrast against the white door behind him. The noose-tie he wore proudly around his neck writhed with the tortured souls he'd conquered and enslaved.

My skin flushed with anger. "Get out!" I shouted before thinking. I looked at Mom, who stared up at me with a frown.

"Excuse me?"

Albert laughed and crossed his arms over his chest, his sleek black suit shifting in designer-like ease with every move he made. "You should have seen them going at each other, Zoe." His voice slit my skin. "They're getting the hang of arguing. But then, hostility only needs the gentlest fertilization to ripen in most people."

I bit my tongue.

"Are you going to help me or not?" Mom demanded.

"Yeah, give me a second."

"See how fury feeds?" Albert floated closer. I stepped back, my heart pattering against my ribs. "Like cancer. Devouring until it consumes everything in its path."

I swallowed a lump. *Oh yeah?* I shot him a glare and made a beeline for the stairs. His hideous laugh trailed me and seemed to nip at my heels as I took the stairs up two at a time.

I unlocked Abria's door and snatched her into my arms, enjoying a luscious feeling of victory. *Let's see how long you stick around now, psych-job.*

I skipped down the stairs and Abria giggled in my arms at the jiggling movement. "That's right, baby. You laugh all you want."

Albert's gaze fastened on the two of us the moment we were in his line of vision. He'd moved into the family room, fifteen feet away from the kitchen. He jerked upright. A stony expression flashed and held his face paralyzed shock. The faintest howling screams lifted into the air around him—and I realized the voices came from the noose of souls tied around his neck—their cries screeching like fingernails scraping a blackboard.

Abria went still, her blue eyes on Albert.

Albert turned his face, closed his eyes and dissolved.

I squeezed Abria to my chest. My racing heart finally started to slow. "Good girl," I whispered against her hair, kissing her.

"Goo gir," she parroted.

"Did you see him?" I held her chin so that I could look into her round, blue eyes. "Did you?"

"Di ju."

I set her on her feet, and she ran into the kitchen where Mom was cleaning. I jumped and tackled her. Abria screeched. My knees ached coming into contact with the cold tile. "No you don't," I grunted.

"Why did you bring her down?" Mom barked. "Take her back upstairs. I'm too angry to be around her right now." She scrubbed harder.

"Sorry." *But there was this evil guy here and I had to get rid of him.* I carried my sister back up the stairs. Abria knew where we were headed, and started head-banging my chest in protest.

"I know, I know." I tightened my grip so she wouldn't wriggle free and race back downstairs for more syrup. "But you made a huge mess and we have to clean it up. Then you can go down."

"Go-dow! Go-dow!"

Soft voices seeped out from underneath Luke's closed bedroom door as I passed. I stopped, listened. Abria's pleading drowned the quiet conversation. I crossed the hall to her bedroom and set her on the floor. "I'll be right back honey and we'll take a bath."

"Ba! Ba!" I could hardly bring myself to shut the door in her eager face but if I didn't, she'd go bug Mom. I brought the door closed, my heart squeezing. I held my finger to my lips. "Shh." *As if that'll work.* Abria's autism didn't allow her to pick up on social cues of any kind, let alone most common commands. I closed the door, her chirps continuing on the other side.

I knocked on Luke's door and the voices silenced. The door opened. Luke had changed out of the slacks, shirt and tie he'd worn to Brady's funeral earlier that day.

"Z."

"What's up? You okay?"

He nodded, glanced around, then motioned for me to enter. Abria still chirped from behind her closed door, "Ba! Ba!"

I entered Luke's bedroom and took in a breath of incense. His sunset-colored lava lamp cast an orangey glow onto the boogie boards and skating posters hanging on the walls. Luke moved aside and I stopped. Krissy sat on his bed, head bowed. Her dated camel coat soggy and stained with mud splotches that also stained the hem of her denim jumper—the same clothes I'd seen her wearing earlier at Brady's funeral. Her red-rimmed eyes lifted to mine.

Luke shut the door and stood beside me. "I found her on State Street, hitchhiking."

Krissy lowered her head, averting her eyes.

"Chase and I went to your house looking for you," I said, sitting next to her on the bed.

She wrung her hands.

"It's cool, Krissy," Luke said. "Zoe won't snitch."

Luke and I had made some strides for him to say that, and I couldn't help that my lips lifted into a little grin.

"What happened?" I asked her.

She remained silent. Luke shrugged and tweaked his face as if to say he didn't know anymore than I did. I reached out and laid my hand over her wringing fists. She went still. Suddenly, her shoulders buckled. Soft sobs followed.

Luke stepped back, shoving his hands in his front pockets. Krissy crumbled against me, her sobs growing into howls. I put my arms around her and patted her back.

"Shh, it's okay," I said.

Luke fidgeted, his hands scraping his face. He glanced at the door, as if anticipating Mom walking in to see what was going on. "Keep it down," he whispered. Krissy's cries lowered a few notches.

"Talk to me," I said.

Krissy's weeping slowed to hiccups and snorts. She sat erect, wiped her nose with the sleeve of her coat and kept her gaze focused on the denim fabric of her jumper crushed in her white-knuckles. "I can't go home."

"Okay," I said.

She looked at me. "I'm serious. I can't go home."

"You don't have to."

"What will I do? I don't have anywhere to go."

"Do you have family here?" I asked.

"An aunt up in Ogden. My mom's sister."

"Want me to call her?"

"No! No one can know!"

Silence. *No one can know... what?*

A tap on the door froze us all. "Uh, busy," Luke piped.

"Is Zoe in there?" Mom.

"Yeah, be right out," I said.

"I thought you were going to help me." Remnants of frustration clung to her tone.

"I am. I will. Give me five minutes."

"I'll be done in five minutes," she growled. Her heavy footsteps pounded down the stairs. Surely Albert hadn't come back. I couldn't possibly handle him *and* Krissy.

"Five minutes?" Krissy's voice was meek.

I patted her hand. "I'm not going anywhere. Now..." I moved closer and latched my gaze with hers. "Tell me what happened."

Fragile moments stretched through papery silence. Her face shifted like sand beneath a violent wave, emotions tearing at her. She took a deep breath. "I can't." She jumped to her feet, edgy. "I need to go."

> ✳ ⋲

"Where are you going?" I joined her.

"Yeah, it's freezing outside," Luke added. "And you're like all wet."

"I don't care."

"Hold on a second." I touched her elbow. Her eyes lifted to mine, empty. Lost. "You just said you can't go home, and you don't have anywhere to go. So…"

Krissy took a deep breath. "I was kidding." Her face remained pale and her expression dead. "Can you give me a ride home?"

Luke and I exchanged glances.

"Zoe!" Mom.

Krissy's defeated gaze dropped, as if she didn't have the strength or courage to continue to fight anymore.

"You can either wait for me to take you, or Luke can take you." Krissy's father's menacing threats hissed through my head. Whoever took her home would have to drop her a block away from her house for their own safety.

Krissy's shoulders lifted.

Outside the bedroom came the slam of a distant door, thumps and Abria's screaming.

"Zoe?" Mom again, her voice ratcheted up five tense notches. "Can I get some help here? Joe? Luke? Anybody?"

"I'm trying to work!" Dad yelled from his office downstairs.

Static discomfort jumped into the silence Krissy and Luke and I now shared.

"I should go," Krissy whispered.

"Well, I'm trying to get some help," Mom shouted in reply to Dad.

"I'll go help Mom." Luke headed for the door.

"Come on." I tilted my head in the direction of the now-open door. "I'll give you a ride."

Luke tossed me the keys to his Samurai and I grabbed them mid-air. "In case they're too into it to let you drive one of their cars." Then he disappeared.

"I'm sorry." Krissy's eyes watered. "This is my fault. I shouldn't be here."

"How is my parents' argument your fault?" I whispered as she and I

13

slipped into the hall.

Abria's laughter came from her bedroom, mixing with Luke's bass voice and Mom's crisp tone. "What's Zoe doing?" Mom asked. "She was helping me and vanished."

"Um. Not sure," Luke said. "But I can get Abria dressed for bed."

Abria squealed.

"Quit jumping on the bed, it's not a trampoline!" Mom's exasperated tone followed Krissy and me down the stairs even though Mom was in Abria's bedroom.

Slam. The glass doors to Dad's office clattered. My heart stammered. The heavy foreboding I'd felt before when I'd been near Albert seeped at me from the living room, Mom's pristinely clean sanctuary because no one but guests were allowed inside. Albert sat stretched out on the ivory couch, one arm along the back, legs crossed, his black-suited form like ink spilled on the unadulterated fabric.

His grin sparked fear and anger inside of me. I came to a halt. Krissy stopped by my side.

"Zoe." His creamy voice—the familial tone—always reminded me of Matthias. "Did you think I was done here?"

If I spoke to him, Krissy would think I was insane. Compelled to defend my home, my family and everything I held dear, I glared, retorts bursting like fireworks in my brain, needing my voice.

"What?" Krissy whispered. Out of my peripheral vision, she followed my gaze to the couch, which I was certain to her was empty.

Albert waited, grinning. "I liked her *party girl* look better," he finally said, though his eyes never left mine. A shudder rambled along my spine.

I took a deep breath, shoved Luke's keys at Krissy and kept Albert locked in my locked vision. "Take Luke's keys and get in the car," I said. "I'll be right there."

She hesitated, but took the keys, her gaze darting from me to the living room couch I was so intensely focused on. Quietly, she went out the front door, shutting it behind her.

Dad sat inside his office, on my left. I didn't verify with a look, too afraid and wanting to keep Albert in my sights, but I wondered if he saw me staring into the living room. He'd think I was nuts.

"Get out," I hissed.

"Zoe, that's hardly the way to treat a guest." Albert gestured around the room, but his steely blue eyes never left mine.

"Yeah, well, I didn't invite you."

"Ah, yes. But I enjoyed a fruitful visit with your parents."

"You can't stay." I inched closer, so my voice wouldn't carry and rouse Dad. I glanced over my shoulder at him; he was glued to the computer, the icy blue light of the monitor reflecting on his stressed face. My mind scrambled with my options.

"What are you going to do, go get your sister every time I show up?" Albert sat forward and clasped his hands.

"If I have to."

"You can't wear her around your neck like a cross or a clove of garlic, Zoe." He chuckled. "As if something so puny could actually repel me. No one—not even Abria—can protect you from me."

His words sent fear rumbling through my soul. He was wrong, he had to be. Matthias said evil couldn't stay in the presence of an innocent, like Abria. And I had Matthias. Where was he?

"Looking for Matthias?" he asked.

My heart thrashed inside my chest. Albert couldn't read my thoughts, could he? "I can get rid of you myself, loser." Anger pulsed in my blood stream.

I crossed to him, body shaking, fury rising like a tornado inside of me. I stared down at him, at the wretched noose tie. The twisted pale remnants of souls locked in a hellish prison—on display for the world to witness was utterly humiliating. But the faint screeching and howling that trickled into the air from their bondage sent me into a comfortless round of shudders. "Get out."

Albert rose from the couch to tower over me. His angled face turned rock hard, his eyes leveled me. I shrunk. I realized my anger and frustration were products of his influence. I had to resist the overwhelming urge to leap on him and tear his head off.

I can do this, I can do this, I can do this. I closed my eyes for a second, searching for calm, remembering Matthias' words: evil can't have a place inside unless it's invited. Albert may have come into the house with my parents' argument, but I was kicking him out. Right. Now.

"You can't dismiss me, you're too weak." Albert's voice slithered into my head. My eyes snapped open. His face was inches from mine.

"I'm not weak." I tried to tamp out the anger smoldering inside of me. Why was it so hard? I'd always had a short wick, and standing this close to a flame wasn't helping.

I stepped back, hoping distance would help. I didn't even see Albert move. With my next breath, he was chest-to-chest with me, his submerging evil so dense my knees knocked. I thought I was going to crumble to the floor and lie helpless at his feet.

"You see?" Albert whispered.

"Zoe?" Dad. I hadn't heard the office doors open, hadn't sensed him in the living room but here he was. His brows creased. "What's going on?"

Albert never took his eyes off me, an eerie, stripped-naked feeling I couldn't be rid of.

"Someone's here." Dad's tone was irritated, and he tipped his head in the direction of the front door.

I glanced through the front room windows. Two headlights beamed at the house from the driveway. Luke's car remained dark and parked at the curb. I didn't see Krissy's silhouette inside. Where was she? I hoped she hadn't split.

The doorbell rang, followed by an angry pound. Albert's grin spread wide.

Dad crossed to the front door and swung it open. Krissy's dad filled the frame. Covering his body, a pack of wild black spirits crawled and writhed in their usual silent but frightening frenzy of malevolence.

THREE

"I'm looking for my daughter, Krissy." He peered past Dad, saw me and his eyes slit. Six black spirits leapt from his torso to his shoulders and jumped in a horrific dance.

"I'm Joe." Dad stuck out his hand but Krissy's Dad ignored the gesture.

"Peter. Is she here?"

"Do you know where she is?" Dad asked me.

Krissy's father glared past Dad, scanning the house. Dad stiffened. "If Zoe says she's not here, she's not."

"We've looked everywhere for her," Peter barked, spitting a black spirit out of his mouth. The creature joined the revelers on the top of his head.

"Amateurs," Albert whispered in my ear. Goosebumps rippled my skin.

Albert nodded in the direction of the wicked spirits. He lifted his hands in the air and suddenly, the beings infesting Krissy's dad came to a halt, their soulless eyes shifting to Albert.

What's he going to do? I had the fleeting hope Albert would dismiss the hideous creatures, but he wasn't Matthias. He encouraged trouble, not disseminated it.

Albert glided toward the door. Peter's chest rose and fell beneath his shirt and long, black coat. His face pinked. As Albert drew closer, the wild spirits became crazed, their mouths opened in silent screams, their wiry shapes jumped and skittered, translucent eyes hollowing.

Albert lifted his right hand and sliced the air. The pack swirled upward in a whirling black effluence that shot out the front door and into the dark night.

A shudder raked my skin. Albert sent a dazzling grin at me over his shoulder and then slid into Peter. He stepped over the threshold, his ferocious glare locked on Dad. "I want my daughter."

Dad stepped forward, shoulders erect. "Hold on—"

"She's here, dammit!" Peter's arms shot out. I gasped. He tried to grab Dad's forearms, but Dad's fists fastened to the man's shirt and he shoved him against the sidelight.

My heart raced. Krissy's dad let out a muscle-ripping growl, his eyes blackening with hate. Albert's ghosted image lifted in and out of the enraged man, Albert himself caught up in the attack. Peter's arms reached, flailed, but could not adhere to Dad's flesh and bone. My hand covered my mouth, stifling a scream.

With surprising ease and total control, Dad held Peter against the sidelight.

Upstairs, Mom appeared, staring with wide eyes from the balcony.

"I think you should go," Dad said between clenched teeth. He released the man and his hands slowly dropped to his sides.

Krissy's dad panted. "If I find that your daughter has lied, you'll both answer to me," he boomed.

"Is that a threat?" Dad's voice rose. His hands fisted.

I joined him, and touched his stiff arm. "Dad, he's not worth it." *I'm talking to you, Albert.* What did it matter? Albert couldn't hear my thoughts.

"I've got half the Pleasant Grove police force out searching for her! You'd better not be lying to me."

"Don't come to my home and threaten my family," Dad snapped, stepping closer to Krissy's dad.

My hand tightened around his arm. "Don't. He's dangerous."

"You damned well better believe I'm dangerous," Peter seethed. "If it wasn't for you and your partying friends, she'd be at home. Now, I've got social services breathing down my neck!"

"I had nothing to do with Krissy's party," I shouted. "I tried to talk her out of it!" What was I doing, arguing with this whack-case?

I pulled Dad's sleeve, but he resisted. "Go. Now," he said, reaching for the door. He started to close it, but Peter slapped a palm against the wood with a thunk.

"If you see her, you tell her to call me immediately."

Dad slammed the door. "For a minute I thought there would be blood."

"What in the world?" Mom's voice was breathless coming between her fingers poised over her mouth.

"The weirdo," I muttered, glad he and Albert were gone.

Dad dragged his fingers down his face, leaving white stripes over taut skin. "What a day."

"Yeah." Between the funeral, Krissy, her dad and Albert, my body and brain overflowed with stimulation. I needed sleep, and the urgency sunk into my being with the weight of lead.

Dad glanced upstairs. His tight features softened when he saw Mom. Then his green eyes met mine. "Have you seen Krissy tonight?"

I swallowed a lump, nodded.

"You must have a good reason for not mentioning that to her father."

"Yeah. She came here upset, said she couldn't go home. Something's up but she won't say what it is."

"Where is she?" Dad glanced around.

"Not sure. She left right before her dad came."

"Well," Dad sighed. "At least we weren't lying to the man then. We didn't know where she was. If you do see or hear from her though, Zoe, tell her to call her dad. Let's avoid any complications. That guy is dangerous."

He started upstairs, wearily taking them one sluggish step at a time.

Abria, dressed in my old *Friends* t- shirt raced from her bedroom to Mom and Dad's bedroom with Luke chasing after her. Mom met Dad on the landing. Mom stopped, so did he, and their eyes spoke a silent message that brought another wave of fear through my chest. Would they argue again? Abria giggled from inside their bedroom. Luke's frustrated tone followed, "Time for bed, Abria."

I went out the front door with my soul weary, closing it behind me, and jogged to Luke's car. A soft glow of light radiated from the backseat—the illumination surrounding Krissy's guardian. Krissy lay in the passenger seat, the chair reclined. She jumped when she saw me. I opened the door and got in. I wanted to say something to him. My eyes connected with his and he gave me an acknowledging nod. I barely nodded back, so as to not draw Krissy's attention to the fact that I was communicating with someone she couldn't see.

"My dad's gonna kill me," she stuttered out a plume of white breath in the chilled air.

I held out my hand for the keys and she plopped them into my palm. "Why is he so mad?" I turned the engine. "Is it still about the party? I mean, I understand. But he has to believe that Brady made his own choice that night."

Krissy shifted her gaze out the window, the blue light of the moon casting cobalt ice over her frightened face. I cranked the knob on the heater to high and cold air blew, throwing my body into a fit of shudders.

I pulled the car onto the street and headed toward Krissy's. She remained silent. I glanced through the rearview mirror at her guardian. "It's going to be okay," I told her. "You're not alone—"

"Right."

"I'm serious. You have me and Luke and Chase."

Tears slid down her cheeks, glistening tracks in the moonlight.

"I'm in serious trouble, Zoe." Her voice was tattered.

"Everything will work out, you'll see." I hated it when Mom and Dad told me that, and here I was saying the same thing. But I honestly believed everything would now. I understood that our human efforts were not solitary in this life.

"The thing is," she sniffed, faced me. "I'm not sorry I had the party. I wanted to do it. And it was cool, you know? It's just that I shouldn't have dared Brady."

"Even if you dared Brady, he didn't have to take you up on it. And he and Britt brought the alcohol. They gave you the weed."

"Which I didn't have to take," she said.

"You're right. We all make mistakes." I glanced at her guardian in the mirror, our eyes meeting. His kind smile soothed me. "And we all learn from them. Just don't get all hopeless on me, okay?" Was he here because she was going to try to hurt herself again?

"Thanks," she whispered. Our eyes met, then I focused on the road again. *How can I comfort her? How can I make her see that we all make dumb choices but nothing is unfixable?*

"You sure there isn't something I can do?" I asked.

She shook her head.

"Call me any time. I mean it."

"That's what Luke said," she sniffed. "He's a nice guy, isn't he?"

I nodded. "I'm glad he found you tonight." With a father as seemingly controlling as hers, was she aware of the inherent dangers of hitchhiking?

"Yeah."

I drove onto her street and she sat up, her hands wringing in her lap. White fear turned her face stony.

The street was quiet. When we neared her round house, I didn't see any police cars as I expected. One light shown through a white, pull-down shade upstairs.

"You'd better let me off here. I don't want him to see your car."

"Luke's car is not exactly anonymous," I joked, hoping to see her smile. Her wide-eyed gaze was too focused on her home to notice my jesting tone.

I stopped six houses down from hers and she opened the door with a shaky hand. She got out, and her guardian was already behind her, his ivory light softly ebbing comfort into the night air around them.

He smiled at me, nodded. "Thank you."

Had I done enough? My soul reached out to her in such a way I nearly leapt from the car to walk alongside her. "You sure you want to do this?" I asked. Krissy peered at me, her brows drawn in a hard line across her forehead. "There are places you can go, Krissy. Safe houses. If you want, I can help you—"

"No." She shook her head. "That'll make things worse. I've got to go.

Bye, Zoe." She shut the door and headed in the direction of the round, wood house.

I remained in the idling Samurai. Whatever Krissy faced, I took some relief from the fact that her guardian was by her side. I could also make an anonymous call to Child Services. Better to be safe than sorry, Mom always said. I watched Krissy walk in a bubble of light, her guardian by her side.

Once I shut the front door of home, I rested my back against the smooth wood and let out a sigh. *Peace, at last.* My bones felt leaden beneath weary muscle and flesh. I couldn't wait to hit the mattress. I'd only been gone fifteen minutes at most, and the lights still burned on the main floor. A scattered few shone upstairs.

Mom and Dad's voices jagged out from beneath their closed bedroom door. My heart picked up speed. The foreboding I thought had gone with Krissy's dad was back.

I looked left into the darkness of the living room. Empty. Right—into Dad's office. Empty. Heart hammering, I crept through the arched hall that lead to the family room and kitchen. Nothing. The idea that Albert had taken residency in my home terrified me. But then, Matthias had warned me that life would be difficult. That Albert would be relentless in his pursuit of my soul.

I headed upstairs, passing Luke's bedroom. His door was open and I peered in, found him standing just inside, staring out into the dark hall in the direction of the master bedroom.

"How long have they been arguing?" I whispered.

He joined me in the doorway. "Since you left. I hate this."

And because Mom and Dad rarely fought, their arguments brought everyone in the house to a standstill—everyone except Abria of course. Light gleamed beneath her bedroom door and I heard her prattling inside.

"Did something happen to start it?" I asked Luke.

He shrugged. "I put Abria to bed and the two of them were in there going at it. I heard some stuff, but, you know… I didn't stay and listen."

Darkness pulled me in the direction of their bedroom. Splintering fear shot through my body. I reached for the doorknob.

"What're you doing?" Luke whispered, following me.

I held my hand up to silence him. Luke still didn't know I could see evil. Now wasn't the time to drop that bomb. I wanted to help my parents if I could, as carefully as I could.

Dad's voice was low and hard, mixing with Mom's high pitch, the two tones reeking of sarcasm, and snapping with ugliness, specific words muffled through the closed door. Flushed with fear and frustration, I blew out a breath, turned on my heel and marched to Abria's room.

"I just put her to bed, don't wake her," Luke hissed over my shoulder. We both knew putting Abria to bed didn't mean she actually went to sleep. I opened her door.

Abria jumped on the bed like a gymnast, glee on her face. Matthias stood ready to catch her.

My breath caught at the sight of him: radiant purity. A vision of beauty and peace that stilled my worried soul and lifted me on eyesight.

Behind me, Luke stuttered, "Oh, wow…it's him."

Luke's milk-white face and open mouth reminded me that he still wasn't used to seeing Matthias. At least he hadn't passed out like the last two times he saw him. I tugged Luke through the door, shut it and faced the man I loved.

"Zoe." Matthias smiled.

"Hey." I didn't care that my voice sounded insipidly happy to see him. *You're beautiful,* I thought knowing full well Matthias would overhear. My love for him was no secret. *I feel so much better knowing you're here.*

That's why I came.

Abria giggled, jumping higher. And higher. Her head nearly hit the ceiling. Matthias swept her into his arms and hugged her. "You little monkey. Careful."

"Man, this is so wild," Luke murmured.

"Plenty wild," Matthias said, tapping Abria on the tip of her nose.

23

"Wild little monkey."

"Monkey," Abria said, clear and crisp.

Luke and I exchanged glances of surprise. Any time Abria spoke coherently was a time to celebrate; most of her communications a garbled mess of sounds without clarity. Matthias' touch not only comforted me and Luke, but from Abria's consistent reaction to being in his presence, something about him loosened Abria's tongue, enabling her to speak.

I almost forgot why I was there. This time, I'd get rid of Albert by myself.

I headed for the door. Matthias blocked it. How he moved so fast was part of the miracle of who he was. I didn't question or doubt, but was still amazed by his angelic powers. His clear blue eyes looked earnestly into mine.

You weren't kidding when you said Albert was relentless.

Matthias nodded. *He is powerful and dangerous.*

"I know. But I got rid of him twice already. I can do it again."

"Bearcat." The corner of his lip lifted.

Tempted as I was to let him kick his father out, I didn't want Albert thinking I was a pushover. I had respect for forces both evil and good, but I relished the opportunity to force Albert out of our house. Even knowing he'd come back.

"Where are you going?" Luke eyed me.

I opened the door. "To kick some seriously wicked butt."

I took off down the hall, adrenaline pulsing courage through my veins. "Can she do that?" Luke's query brought a grin to my lips in spite of the fear jangling my nerves at the thought of confronting Albert.

"She's a sassy little sheba," Matthias replied. "She can do anything she wants."

Exactly.

My parent's voices boomed from behind the closed door, like an angry pianist taking his frustration out on the keys, inharmonious chords belting into the air.

"We trusted her!" Mom.

"We can't be sure she's still drinking." My heart plummeted to my feet. They were talking about me.

I came to an abrupt halt. Why didn't Mom trust me? How could they think I was still drinking? I thought we were miles past that.

"I can look at her and tell you she's on something," Mom hissed.

I thrust open the door. Mom and Dad stood facing each other at the foot of their four-poster bed. Mom's arms were crossed tight over her chest; Dad's hands set immobile on his hips. Albert lay in the middle of their bed propped on his side, as if watching a sick reality show on TV. A grin split his lips upward. Every frustrated, confused thought I had about my parents' perception of me flew out of my system at the sight of him.

The instant I entered the room, his grin widened. "What? No Abria?"

My speeding heart caught on my breath. I ignored him.

"Zoe!" Dad's body tensed. "Your mother and I are in the middle of—"

"I know, I'm sorry." I dug deep for the calm I'd felt seconds ago in Matthias' presence. "I heard you guys arguing. I wanted to help."

"You don't barge into a private conversation, I don't care how much you want to help. You knock first," Dad boiled.

"Okay, you're right. Sorry."

Their taut faces stirred with wariness, unasked questions and frustration.

"I know I've been acting weird lately," I said, stepping forward. "I need to tell you something."

Albert shifted on the bed.

Fear flashed on Mom and Dad's faces. As if their minds raced with the worst news, a truth they hoped had only been yet another nightmare neither wanted to experience over again their bodies seemed to brace.

The mood in the room had a definitive shift from high burn to rolling boil. "I'm not drinking."

Mom folded her arms over her chest. "You were listening to us?"

"I couldn't help it, you guys were yelling."

"Since when is it okay for you to listen at our—"

"Let her say what she wants to say, Debbie."

Mom's eyes blazed. She stiffened, arms tightening across her chest.

I took a deep breath. Noticed that Albert's brows now drew in a line across his face. The day had been long, rough and it seemed as though conflicts would never end.

"I'm not sure why you think I'm drinking again, but—"

"How about the fact that you randomly talk to yourself," Mom said. "Like you have countless times lately. You think we aren't going to notice?"

"Debbie," Dad broke in.

"What? You told me she was in the living room talking to the couch just a few minutes ago."

I scrubbed my hands down my face. "Okay, okay, I have been doing that, yes. But I haven't been drinking or using or anything like that."

"Then what is it?" Mom cocked a hip. Her arms remained folded. Would they believe me? I had to tell them something. They waited, their stares cutting into me.

Albert sat upright, his face paling.

"I…"

Weston had believed me. Luke, too. But he'd also seen Matthias. How would they take news of their daughter telling them that she saw spirits? Not only saw them, but interacted with them?

Was in love with one?

I didn't need to share that little piece of information.

"Okay. This is… hard for me to express, so hang on. I… something happened to me before the accident. I… saw…" *They'll never believe me. They'll think I'm a freak. I can't do this to them. Yes you can. You can do this.*

I sucked in a long breath. "I saw a heavenly being in the car with me before the accident."

Mom's eyes widened. Her arms gradually loosened from the tense grip they had around her body since I'd burst through the door. Dad blinked, but his expression remained steady and I knew Dad was close to understanding and believing what I was telling him.

"He was there to comfort me." Speaking of Matthias shifted my nervous tone to awe and respect. "He was real. As real as you and me. He's... I know it sounds outrageous, but... he's a guardian angel."

Silence.

Thinking of Matthias sent an extra measure of strength into my being, a palpable comfort I felt from head to toe. I closed my eyes, overcome.

When my eyes opened again, I found Mom and Dad focused on my face, their expressions stunned. Did they see the change? The light? Neither spoke for a few long seconds.

Albert was gone.

Relief and hope filled me.

"Can you tell us what happened?" Dad's voice was barely above a whisper. I was sure he believed in such things as guardian angels. He had a firm belief in God. Maybe it wasn't too much to hope that he believed me.

Another deep breath. "Well, before the truck hit me, I saw him. Sitting in the seat—the passenger seat. He told me not to be afraid. And I wasn't. You have to understand that you can't be afraid when he's around because it's impossible. He radiates this... this comfort and peace and joy and it's the coolest most powerful feeling in the world and it takes you over. I mean, not takes over but the power is so real there's no denying it. There's nothing like it in the world. It's absolutely—"

"Zoe," Mom blinked hard. "Are you sure this didn't happen after the accident? Maybe you had a near death experience or something."

I'd definitely had a near death experience. "Mom. Yes. I had a near death experience. I died. This happened before the accident."

More silence. Not heavy, not angry. Ponderous.

"Why didn't you tell us?" Dad's voice was soft.

Now, their expressions were wounded. "I wasn't sure you'd believe me. What happened to me was so miraculous, I..." My heart swelled and tears filled my eyes. "It's special to me. I'm sorry. I was dealing with a lot. Recovering—"

"I understand." Dad held up a hand. "You're right."

More silence dragged by.

27

"I know it's a lot to think about. But it's real. It happened. Since then, I've seen him again. He's... he's Abria's guardian angel."

Mom's hand flew to her mouth. Her blue eyes grew wide with—shock? Did she think I was lying and had gone too far? Dad didn't move. His even expression only became more alert, his eyes piercing me as if probing for a lie.

I could go off on a tangent, trying to prove what was true, but I remained silent. Waiting. Hoping their hearts were open enough that Matthias' presence could work its way in, that the undeniable, tangible feeling would leave them as convinced as if they could see him for themselves.

"You're serious," Mom whispered.

I nodded.

When neither of them said anything, panic scratched its way up my spine. If they didn't believe me, I'd be seeing a psychiatrist at the very least, sent to a mental hospital at the worst.

I kept my gaze on my parents, but turned my head toward the open door. "Luke!"

"Yeah?" His voice came from Abria's bedroom.

"Come here, will you?"

"K." I heard Abria's bedroom door close.

"Luke knows about this?" Mom gasped through her fingers.

Luke appeared, his gaze flicking from me, to Mom and Dad.

"I told Mom and Dad about Matthias," I said gently. His eyes grew to saucers. The dense air surrounding us became prickly.

Luke shoved his hands into his front pockets. "Um... yeah. She's telling the truth."

Another gasp from Mom. Her fingers closed over her mouth, sending the skin on her face around her hand white.

"Luke's seen him too," I said.

FOUR

"Well done, Zoe, well done." Matthias's glowing countenance lit the dark hall outside Mom and Dad's bedroom.

My limbs sagged, drained of the last bit of energy. Admitting to my parents that I saw Matthias lifted a weighty load from my shoulders, leaving me deeply relieved. I wasn't sure how things would be in the morning, but I was pretty sure they'd have plenty of questions.

I dragged myself to my bedroom, more than ready to say goodnight to the longest day of my life. Matthias' face grew sober, his blue eyes steady on mine. "I'm sorry."

"For?" I flicked on the light and entered, wobbling from exhaustion. Matthias' strong hands braced my shoulders. His strength filled my being, racing through my arms, core and legs.

"My father…" He studied my face, a crease forming between his brows. "His efforts are wearing you out. Zoe, you're a brave, sassy bearcat." His lips lifted in a slight grin. His finger tapped my chin. "But he's very powerful."

"I'm getting that. But he can't overcome a mortal, right?"

Matthias' fingers tightened on my shoulders. His eyes crinkled in a smile. "Smart and sassy, a deadly combination. You're ab-so-lute-ly right. Evil can't overcome you unless you allow it to."

"So, I have nothing to worry about, because I will never let that loser take me. Never."

A shadow crossed his face. I reached up and wrapped my fingers around his wrists. "I'm sorry, I shouldn't have called him a loser."

His hands slipped down my arms. He sighed, and slid his hands into the front pockets of his lightweight linen-white slacks. A dull ache echoed from my heart out into my limbs. Matthias' pain. I was still getting used to our deep connection that enabled me to feel his hurts, see his memories, feel him as though we were one.

I took his hand and shut the bedroom door. I had hopes of him staying with me, and the vision flashed into my head of him holding me in his arms while I slept. My heart pattered. *Uh-oh.* The drawbacks of your guardian angel being able to hear your thoughts could be humiliating, embarrassing and recklessly human.

I was beat and was about to collapse from fatigue. Could I help it if I wanted to cuddle with him until I fell asleep? Matthias' amused gaze shifted for a moment, meeting mine, and my bouncing heart lodged in my throat.

Cuddle?

Don't listen to me. I'm loopy right now.

As if bricks weighted my arms and legs, I crossed to my bed and flopped, stomach-down, onto the bedspread, my limbs spread like soggy noodles. My eyes closed the minute I smelled my pillow.

"You've had a day." Matthias' voice poured over me like an invisible blanket. I closed my eyes.

The bed shifted when he sat beside me. His light caress on my head soothed any residual anxiety from the day into sweet nothingness. *Thank you.*

You're welcome.

Matthias' touch skimmed to my shoulder, tracing lightly to my hand, the electrifying effect shooting tingles through me. I opened my eyes. His were locked on mine, as if waiting. He lifted my hand to his lips and brushed a soft kiss across my knuckles. A flock of hummingbirds flew through my system, shooting flutterings from my fingers to my toes.

I wet my lips, and when I struggled to sit upright, was reminded by my fatigued muscles that I needed rest. Ignoring them, I remained sitting up.

"Are you going to stay?" My voice rasped.

Matthias spoke against my knuckles. "Your wish is my command, remember?"

A tired laugh scraped out of me. *I wish.* "No, I mean, will Albert be
back?"

Matthias lowered my hand to his knee and covered it with his other
hand. His gaze sobered. "I'm certain he'll be back. He doesn't need sleep, Zoe.
He hopes to wear you down, catch you at your weakest."

"Great." I let out a yawn. "Then I'd better catch some z's. It's what—"
I glanced at the clock on my bedside table, "—only midnight. It's early yet." I
teased. "Should I sleep with boxing gloves on?"

"I'm quite serious."

"I know you are." I forced my lowering eyelids up. "I'm being careful.
And I took care of him tonight. You said yourself I did well. Now that my
parents know about you, well, it should be easier, right?"

He nodded.

I sent him a lopsided grin. "I ain't no pushover."

Matthias reached out and his fingers pushed back a strand of hair at
the side of my face. My head rolled into the palm of his hand, my eyes closed
again. Beneath me, the mattress shifted. He moved closer, wrapped his arms
around me and we settled against the headboard.

Is this what you want?

I nodded, snuggling against the easy rise and fall of his chest, immersed
in his heartbeat—a lullaby that carried me into slumber.

My eyes opened to darkness. I lay still, gaze darting around my
bedroom for what had awakened me. Used to being ripped from sleep—most
of the time because Abria was stirring in her bedroom—I usually got up,
checked on her, and fell right back into rest.

This time, dread filled the air. I threw back the covers, shivering. Stood.
Muscles moaned for more rest. Was someone in my bedroom? *Stop this you
spaz. You didn't invite evil, so it can't be in your bedroom.* But the doom fogging

the air was potent, coming from behind my closed bedroom door like some looming apparition straight out of a nightmare.

I glanced at the clock. I'd slept for two hours? My muscles dissolved into wavering weakness. I couldn't face Albert like this. I didn't have the strength.

But where was he? What was he doing?

I couldn't leave my family to his whims. They may know about Matthias, but they still had no idea how powerful Albert was.

Hands shaking, I crept to the door and cracked it open. Hot, muggy terror filled the hall—like choking invisible smoke. No light came from beneath Abria's closed bedroom door. My parents' bedroom was likewise dark.

A faint glow seeped from beneath Luke's door. Each step I took drew me closer to the invisible fog of darkness I was becoming familiar with whenever Albert was in the vicinity. Nausea rushed up my throat, mixing with vibrant fear.

He's waiting for me.

My cold, clammy hand wrapped around the knob. *You have to see what's going on, Zoe. You can't leave Luke alone with him.*

Praying for strength, I closed my eyes. *I can do this. Matthias said I can, and I can.* And if I was in mortal danger, he'd be here.

I opened the door and a powerful whoosh of evil pressed into me, as if I'd walked into the fiery steam of hell. The force sucked breath away, sent me back a step. My limbs vibrated as the invisible yet potent force shocked my system. My eyes latched on Albert, pacing back and forth in front of Luke who sat on the floor, his back propped against the side of his bed, his head buried in his hands.

I advanced into the room, afraid Albert had hurt Luke somehow.

"There she is." Albert grinned, his eyes sparkling into slits. "Did I wake you?" The familiar cadence of Matthias' voice—genetically gifted from Albert, now used as sincerely as a New Orleans voodoo doctor—again threw me off balance. "I certainly hope you were having delicious dreams, Zoe."

"You're disgusting," I sneered, moving closer to Luke.

Luke jerked his head left and looked at me as if he hadn't heard me come in. On the floor around him was a bong and the makings of a mind-blowing smoke session. But I didn't catch the musky-sweet scent of marijuana in the air.

"I know," Luke's voice was shredded, worn. "I'm a complete loser."

I knelt next to him. "I wasn't talking to you." I touched his arm. "Did you relapse?"

He shook his head, scraped his fingers down his face, his gaze on the drugs. "I'm trying not to."

Albert's grin had faded, and he watched with keen interest. "Good," I said to Luke, shooting Albert a glare. "I'm glad you haven't used. Want me to take this out of here?"

Luke took a deep breath, his gaze never leaving the bag of green grassy flakes lying at his side. "No."

Albert smiled. "That's my boy."

"Luke." I reached for the weed and Luke snatched the bag into his possession before I could grab it. "Come on, let me take it so you won't be tempted."

"I'm... I'm still deciding, Z."

"The ambivalent heart is so much easier to turn than the resolute," Albert said. "Perfect choice, Luke."

"You have to decide not to use." I gripped his sleeve, reached for the bag, but he held it behind his back, his face sharpening with anger.

"I didn't ask you to come in here," he snapped.

"Ah, now we're rolling." Albert rubbed his hands back and forth. "A little momentum. Just what I needed."

"You shut the hell up!" *Crap.* I was letting Albert get the best of me. I closed my eyes, took a deep breath.

"No, you shut up," Luke's voice raised a notch. He stood, stuffing the bag into the front pocket of his jeans. "And get out. Why do you always come in here? I didn't ask you to come in here."

I shot to my feet. "Please," I forced myself to slow. Think. *One, two, three, four, five, seven, ten.* I blew out a breath. "Okay, you're right. It's your decision."

"Save me the lecture," Luke snickered.

"No lecture." I softened my voice, pictured Matthias's serene face in my head. I closed my eyes, partly to see Matthias more clearly, partly to block Albert out of my mind. "Matthias was right about you," I said, opening my eyes and smiling at Luke.

Albert stopped pacing. Luke's eyes held childlike curiosity, and a glimmer of hope lifted my heart.

"He told me you were strong enough to get through this on your own."

"He did?"

I nodded. I crossed to Luke, the move causing his baby blue eyes to widen. His hand protectively went to the pocket where he'd stashed the weed.

"I'm not going to take your stuff. This is your thing. Your choice." I wrapped him in a hug. His body went stiff, bringing a grin to my face. Seconds stretched by. Finally, his arm went around me and he patted my back lightly with one of his hands.

"You're not crying are you?" he asked.

I squeezed him tighter, amazed that, as children we had hugged each other willingly, often in fun and games as well as real caring. How had the years spread our physical displays of affection so far out of reach? Now, more than anything, he needed to know my love for him was still inside of me.

"No, I'm not." I eased back and grinned at him. "I love you, you know that, right?"

He nodded.

"Isn't this precious." Albert's hiss slithered into the air around us. I didn't look at him, didn't allow his menacing presence to penetrate the love in my heart for Luke.

"Yes, it is," I said, keeping my gaze on Luke, fully aware that he would wonder what I was talking about.

"Is what?" he asked.

"It's true that I love you." I took his hand, stepped back and swung it in the air between us then let go.

"His heart isn't fully convinced," Albert's voice snuck into my ear. So close, a knot formed in my throat. Still, I didn't give him the satisfaction of looking at him. He moved into my line of vision, inches away.

"Nice try, but you can't read thoughts like Matthias can."

"I never said I could," Luke said.

"I—I know. I wasn't—um—forget it. What brought this on, anyway?" I gestured to the pipe lying on the floor.

Luke shifted feet, shrugged. "Just stuff."

"Krissy?"

Luke's mop of blond hair swished when he shook his head. "Nah."

"The funeral?"

"Yeah. It's hard, you know? Sometimes I wonder why I can see Matthias. I mean, you... you're... special that way. But what am I?"

"Nothing. Absolutely nothing," Albert slid close to Luke's ear. My heart pattered.

"Somewhere inside you believe in yourself." I stepped closer. A fight between belief and disbelief thrashed over his young gaze. "Count it as a gift and don't try to figure it out. Just hold on to it."

"Oh, by all means analyze," Albert hissed in Luke's ear. I ground my teeth to keep from spouting off at him. *Control, control, control.*

"I don't feel..." Luke hemmed. "Worthy of something so..."

"And you aren't." Albert zigzagged behind Luke. "You're nothing. Absolutely no—"

"You are worthy." I grabbed hold of Luke's sleeves in my clenched fists. "Close your eyes."

"Z—"

"Do it." I tugged. His dark blond lashes fluttered against his cheeks. "Picture Matthias." Albert's movements behind Luke started to slow but I didn't take my eyes from Luke's face. "The light he carries with him. See it. Picture it. Feel it."

Gradually, Luke's troubled countenance began to lighten. Albert, watching keenly, slowed to a stop. Still, I ignored the curiosity nibbling at me to look at him and stick my tongue out. The tension drawing Luke's face taut released like a sail free in the wind.

"Do you feel it?" I asked.

Luke nodded slightly. "Yeah. It's amazing, isn't it? He's amazing."

"He's perfect."

Albert's laugh filled the air. "He's far from perfect. He's deceiving you, Zoe." He floated to my right, hanging close like an annoying gnat. "Just like he deceived other women in his life."

My heart pinched. I bit my lips to keep from snapping back.

"Ask him." He leaned close. "Ask him about the women he savored while he was mortal."

My fists clenched. "You sold him out to pay a debt! Your own son! You're pond scum. A freaking leech."

Albert cocked his head. *What? He's pretending like he didn't condemn his own son to death?* The air around Albert drew tight. He fixed himself directly behind Luke and stared into my eyes. My heart faltered, I was sure it would stop. The screams of the souls tied in the noose around his neck seeped into the air. Their stretched whiteness writhing in torment nearly stole my fixed gaze from Luke's, but I remained focused.

"Z?" Luke's voice was quiet. He glanced left and right.

"It's not you," I said to him. "I'll explain later. Don't freak about it, okay?"

"Um. If you say so." Luke dug into his front pocket and pulled out the weed. His arm extended, and he took my clenched fist. My hand relaxed, and he squeezed the bag into my palm.

"Get rid of it for me."

I closed my fingers around the crispy mix and nodded, relief filling my soul. I glared at Albert, whose face remained dark with displeasure.

"Is Matthias here?" Luke asked with another glance around.

"No."

"Didn't think you'd talk to him like that." Luke crossed to his bed and crumpled onto the bedspread. "I'm wasted."

The sweet peace of sleep called to me. I wanted this day to be over. Wanted to be done with Albert forever. But Albert stood unmoved, so alert and irate I didn't dare leave Luke's bedroom.

I locked my knees, held the weed tight in my fist and refused to budge. Silence crept into the room. Time crawled on. I wasn't sure how many minutes went by, but soon Luke's deep snore filled the air. *Good, he's asleep. Safe.*

Albert circled me, his pace the slow drip of thick, diseased mucus. His piercing gaze punctured my heart with fear.

"The beauty of being immortal," he began, "is you never need rest. You can tease and tempt and taunt as long as you want to."

"You're not immortal, retard," I snarled. "Matthias is immortal. You only *think* you're immortal."

Albert threw his head back in a hearty laugh and continued to circle me. "Is that what Matthias told you? That boy was always a good storyteller."

"You're the one who bought the story," I whispered between teeth. "You think you have a body, but you don't. You're nothing but a psycho-ghost-leech living off old memories and feelings because you screwed up."

"I like getting under your skin."

"You're not under anything," I spat, "except the delusion that you have something you don't."

"I've no delusions, Zoe, darling."

His circling made me dizzy, so I turned in tandem with him, every now and then checking Luke's sleeping form. "So, you like being owned, is that it?" I snickered, livid momentum building in my blood, forging my weary muscles to alertness like beaten soldiers called back to the battlefield.

"You're mistaken."

"No, you're mistaken. Matthias isn't taking orders from someone who won't deliver on his promises. He's smarter than that. Must have gotten those genes from his mother."

Albert stopped. His eyes narrowed just enough to signal fury. A fury I would have missed if I'd blinked. Around us, the air shimmied. My heart flipped in my chest. Is he going to kill me now?

Matthias?

Nothing more happened.

Good, I nailed him. I wanted to slap him. Beat him over the head with a baseball bat. Hang him by that ridiculous tie from the ceiling.

What the?! I couldn't believe how carried away my thoughts were. I had to stop the anger, or I'd be no better than Albert.

"Give yourself to me now and this will end."

I shook my head. If I wanted to be rid of him, I had to keep my heart pure. Then, he'd have to leave, wouldn't he? Wasn't that why he'd left my parent's bedroom earlier? The heavy tiredness settling again into my body, dragging me south, shouted I'd better do something fast, or I was going to knock off right there.

I collapsed to the floor, leaned my back against Luke's bed and sighed. "Leave." Matthias had used the word and it had worked to dismiss Albert. Maybe I could, too.

Albert towered over me, studying me. His face was impossible to read, and, I was too tired to try. Would he wrap that noose around my neck and drag me to hell with him? Matthias wasn't here, so I figured the answer was no.

Then what was happening?

I looked up at Albert, my eyes growing heavier with each weary blink. He remained alert, his eyes fastened with mine.

"Leave," I slurred, sleep clawing through me. I thought of Matthias, picturing his serene face, feeling his calming spirit weave through me. In my weary state, the comfort so completely overcame me that I closed my eyes for a moment—just one—to rest, and when I opened them again, Albert was gone.

FIVE

Someone tapped my shoulder in that annoying way that made me want to scream at them to stop. I didn't want to move. I was comfortable. Sort of. My neck hurt. And my back. I was lying on a fluffy blanket, thank you. I needed more sleep.

"Z?"

My eyes opened. Luke's cocoa Berber carpeting was in my mouth. I lay on my side, neck tweaked, legs twisted like a pretzel. I sat up.

"You slept in my room?" he asked, amused. He had boxers on—ones with fried eggs and ham—and his hair stuck up like an old dried floor mop. He let out a yawn.

"I guess I did," I groaned, glanced around. No Albert, thankfully. I stretched, bringing out a myriad of pops from joints and limbs. "Man. What time is it?"

"We need to head in a half hour." He twisted his back and it cracked. "You'd better jam."

I jumped to my feet and scrambled to the bathroom. I didn't have time to shower, so I ripped off my flannel pjs and cami, sniffed my armpits—no stink, yay—sprayed ten squirts of perfume, then yanked on a fresh pair of underwear, new bra, lavender long-sleeved tee, jeans and threw my hair into a sloppy ponytail.

My reflection in the bathroom mirror made me cringe: thrown together, and that was being kind. I scrubbed away smeared makeup and quickly reapplied some concealer, blush and bailed on any eye makeup. Too time intensive.

The light on my phone blinked incessantly alerting me that I had messages. None from Weston. I tried not to let that bug me, but it did. One from Chase.

u ever hear from krissy? i didn't

My fingers raced over the keyboard: *yeah tons to tell u*

I grabbed my backpack and grimaced thinking about the studying I hadn't done—with Brady's funeral and the chilling events that had followed me into the wee hours of this morning I'd hardly had time to catch two hours of sleep much less study. *Oh well.* I skipped downstairs and out the door to Luke's idling car.

Luke eyed me. "That's a record for you." He backed the car onto the street, and the little automobile shuddered in the frosty air. A white sun tried to pierce through clouds over head, but it wasn't getting the job done and a layer of ice coated every surface, sparkling like sheets of cellophane and diamonds.

"What a night." I tipped the passenger-side mirror down, peering at my tired green eyes. *Should have brought mascara with me.*

"Yeah."

Was Luke sorry I'd encouraged him to not relapse? "I'm proud of you, bud."

"Where'd you put the stuff?"

"Like I'd tell you." I snickered. But his face remained stoic as he stared out the front window at the street. "I know it's hard."

He scrubbed his jaw.

A subject change was in order. "Thanks again for picking up Krissy. I didn't know you two had a class together."

"We do?" he asked.

"That's what she said."

"Huh. She's pretty nice. I don't know."

"She is."

"What do you think is going to happen to her?" he asked.

⇒ ✢ ⇐
40

"Nothing legally. But that doesn't change how bad she feels about all of it. It's obvious she's scared."

"It was an accident," a tinge of protest was in his tone. "I can't see her getting reamed for something that wasn't really her fault."

She was already getting reamed—by her father. Even though I still didn't know details, I couldn't dismiss the worst possible scenarios from flashing in my head. My stomach churned envisioning her dad with his swarm of evil. Brady's death might not have been her fault, but Krissy had admitted to me—graveside no less—that she'd egged him into hanging longer.

Luke reached over and turned up the heater. "It takes a while for it to work," he said.

"I know. Thanks."

At school, Luke pulled the Samurai into a slit of a parking spot. Other students screeched into the lot alongside us. Luke and I got out and joined the throngs trudging up the drag toward the buildings.

I caught glances, and wondered if people were looking at me because Brady's death was still fresh on everyone's mind.

Inside, signs had been posted: GRIEF COUNSELORS AVAILABLE IN THE OFFICE. The tone quieted as students passed the signs. Would Britt be here? Or would she be at home, hung over?

Luke and I parted ways and went to class. During second period, my gaze searched reflexively for Britt. She sat at her desk, black spirit perched in eerie stillness on her shoulders, its back arched.

Britt glared at me.

I crossed to my desk. Out the corner of my eye, her head, and the head of the creepy crawler on her back, turned in sync with my movement.

I sat. My gaze swept my fellow students, but their dipped heads, distracted faces or otherwise bored expressions left me unsure that anyone but me sensed the parasite. Mr. Bringhurst's voice droned on. I couldn't tune into his lecture, not with Britt and that thing's attention locked on me.

Don't let it get to you.

Britt's eyes were latched on mine in a heavy, primal dark stare that, if I

41

allowed it, would scare me. Threaten me. Cause me to shrink. But I'd been in the presence of worse. I wasn't a wimp.

A thousand memories of Britt and me flashed through my head: parties, sleepovers, drives with blasting music, hours shopping together, even more hours opening our hearts to each other.

My heart softened to putty. I wished things were different between us, that we could be friends regardless of what had happened between her and Weston.

For all I knew, Weston would have nothing more to do with me, anyway. After the weird turn of events at the funeral, Weston had told me he needed some space to think.

I can't compete with an angel. His words trickled into my thoughts and I closed my eyes for a second, recalling his voice. A pang of longing echoed through me. I missed him. The humanness of him. The mortal comfort and companionship he provided. His dark chocolate eyes. The way he made me feel wanted. Needed.

I opened my eyes. Britt hadn't moved. The black spirit crouched on her back hadn't either, its sinewy, slickness shimmering, then turning matte, like the ocean surface shifting beneath the force of wind. Its blank, black eyes never blinked, just stared.

She and I had hung together like conjoined twins for so long, I attributed the look of dull emptiness on her face to the stark realization that she finally understood how alone she was.

Britt crossed her arms over her desk and buried her head. The creature on her back remained fixed, as if it didn't care that she was miserable, that she'd moved. And I was certain it didn't care. The vibe of evil oozing out into the air from the direction of where Britt sat was like the scent of death— uniquely pungent, strong and morbid in its determined demise.

Death had its grip on Britt's soul. That was the bottom line. *Evil is death.* The thought that my former best friend was dying inside and she probably didn't know it, at least not that she was capable of admitting at this point in her life, sickened me for her.

What could I do?

I texted her.

im sorry about everything i wouldn't hurt u, u know that

I feigned interest in the lecture, faked taking a few notes but glanced at Britt. She sat up, dug into her hoodie pocket and pulled out her cell phone. She read the text and her nails tapped out a reply.

My cell vibrated.

but u did hurt me and i can never forgive u 4 taking wes
come on, britt, we're better than this

The filmy surface on the creature shimmered, then shifted to matte, then shimmered, the motion building in speed.

screw u, zoe Britt jerked her messy hair of head my direction, sending me a worn-out glare.

I slapped my phone shut.

The black spirit on her back stood on its legs mouth opening and closing around onyx fangs. Britt burst to her feet, her crazed glare on me. "I hate you! You can't have what you want so you take it from other people."

"Miss Walker, what is going on?" our teacher demanded.

The class rustled. Stared. Britt remained standing, breath heaving in and out. She pointed a finger at me, her skin blanching red from her neck up to her forehead. Her mouth opened, and two black spirits oozed out, joining the female resident on her back. Together, they whirled around Britt's head, torso and legs, their mouths gnashing, talon limbs stimulating. "You'll pay for this!"

"Miss Walker!" Mr. Bringhurst's voice boomed. "You need to sit down. Now."

"Go to hell," Britt ground out. She grabbed her backpack, swung it over her shoulder and marched to the door.

"Miss Walker—"

"I'm leaving!" Britt shouted. The partying creatures on her back leapt and swirled, their mouths agape, fangs gleaming. The door slammed behind her.

My day was starting well.

At lunch, I caught Weston at his locker. He was alone, pensive. Our gazes met across the busy hall as we stowed books. At least I didn't sense complete rejection from him. His was a more contemplative expression, filled with confusion unmasked by candid admiration.

I bit my lower lip, and kept my gaze on his. *I care about you. I hope you see that. I hope you believe that I care about you a lot.* Too bad Weston couldn't read my thoughts like Matthias, he'd feel better and I'd feel better.

He seemed to weigh the unspoken message I was trying to give him during the time we spent studying each other, then he shut his locker and continued down the hall, in the direction of the parking lot.

Lunch. Alone.

I hadn't spent lunch alone since my first year of junior high. I fought insecurity worming its way into my system. *It's just lunch and I don't have to care that I'm here at school instead of jumping into a car and heading to the Purple Turtle or some other place to hang. Who needs to be seen, anyway?*

I grabbed an apple from the ala carte section of the lunchroom and headed out of the building and into the warming winter sun. Snow blanketed the ground, but I found a dry iron bench and sat, content to be alone with my thoughts.

I bit into the apple and crunched the flesh between my teeth.

"Wow, you never stay around for lunch." Luke sat down next to me.

"Yeah, well. Things change. I don't have a car, remember? It's pretty hard to leave when you don't have a ride."

"What about Brittany? Or Weston?"

"Britt and I aren't hanging anymore and Weston needs some space."

"Well, you want me to drive you somewhere? That's not all you're eating, is it?"

"I'm okay. What about you? Where are your friends?"

He sat back, shifted his backpack from his back to his lap and sighed. "They're around. I don't know, I'm sick of them."

My insides leapt for joy even though I remained calm and took another bite. "It can be like that, yeah."

"I gotta have something to eat. I'm gonna go to the drive thru at Wendy's. Want to come?"

"Sure, why not."

We stood and strolled across the snow-caked grass toward the drag, where cars were filling with students eager to race off to the lunchtime offerings a few blocks away from the high school.

Luke and I got into his car and drove through the buzzing parking lot toward the street. "Hey, isn't that Krissy?" Luke asked.

Sure enough, Krissy, dressed in her denim jumper, hair in standard ponytail mode was walking alone in the city park adjacent to Pleasant Grove High School. Luke pulled the car close to the curb and tapped the horn. Krissy looked over.

Luke rolled down his window. "You wanna come?"

Krissy stopped. Her sober face lit just enough to nearly break my heart for her. Regardless of her brief moment dancing round the raunchy pole of high school partying, she was still an innocent. Maybe even a victim.

She started in our direction. I patted Luke's shoulder. "Nice."

His gaze never left her, but he nodded, his baby face softening with compassion.

Krissy got in the backseat and Luke drove on.

"Thanks," she said, her voice timid.

"No problem." Luke's gaze flicked from the street to his rearview mirror so he could see her.

"Your hair looks great up *and* down," I observed. Before the party, she'd been brave enough to try wearing her hair to her shoulders. Once. She had gorgeous, thick sandy blond hair and I figured—like everything else in her life—her return back to the ponytail was her father's idea.

Krissy's eyes dipped to her lap.

"So, how's it going?" I asked, perching so I half faced her.

Her shoulders lifted. "Okay, I guess."

Is your dad less of a whack job? I couldn't ask that, even if I wanted to. "What happened when you got home last night?"

Krissy avoided my gaze. "Not much."

"Your dad was really upset."

"He likes to know where I am. All the time," she said.

"Ours likes that, too," I added.

"Yeah, but I don't always tell him where I'm going," Luke put in.

"Parents want to know because they love us," I said. Krissy's dad may have different reasons, but until I knew for sure, I had to give her some hope.

She remained looking out the window. I remembered when she'd been so excited to go to lunch with Weston and me, being seen hanging with us was a boost to her social status.

"Wendy's okay with everybody?" Luke asked, his eyes on Krissy through the rear view mirror.

"Sure," I said.

Krissy's forlorn gaze didn't move. "Okay."

Wendy's was tucked into a Chevron gas station, the convenience store-slash-eatery a perfect spot for kids to hang, eat and watch for hotties any hour of the day. The parking lot was jammed with the lunchtime high school crowd. I scanned the parked vehicles for Weston's silver truck and saw it parked to the side of the building. My nerves hummed. Should I go inside? I didn't want him thinking I was stalking him, pressing him to move faster than he was ready in a direction he was hesitant to go.

How retarded are you? You like him. He likes you. Nothing is wrong with caring about what he does.

Inside the restaurant was just as busy. Laugher and shouting flew over the voices of employees calling out orders, the scent of French fries and grilling meats stirring my empty stomach into a rumble. I searched the hive of diners for Weston's chocolate hair.

He sat eating lunch at a table surrounded by a handful of guys I recognized from the football team. Once, Brady had been Weston's best friend, but the boys parted ways a few months back when Brady's partying style had gone over the top for Weston.

Weston's demeanor had gone from partying jock to pondering student. Even now as guys around him laughed and joked and made fools of themselves by being loud and obnoxious—Weston ate his lunch with a straight face, tuned out.

Part of me wanted him to see me, another part wanted to turn around and get out of there. I might have, too, if one of his buddies hadn't noticed me. The jock's jovial expression flattened. His elbow went into Weston's side.

Weston's head jerked up. His eyes met mine.

Luke, Krissy and I moved forward in the line, closer to the cashier. My brain muddled with Luke and Krissy's sporadic conversation. Thrill soared through me now that Weston knew I was there.

"You want something?" Luke asked.

"No thanks," I muttered.

"Uh, I was asking Krissy, Z," Luke chuckled.

"That's nice of you," Krissy said. "I don't have any money."

"Don't worry about it," Luke offered.

Weston rose, and my jagging nerves drew tight.

"Oh, no, I can't—" Krissy said.

"Let me get you something," Luke insisted.

The guy ahead of us moved aside to wait for his order and we stepped to the counter. I didn't hear what Krissy and Luke ordered, only their voices mixing together as they spoke to the cashier. My focus was utterly on Weston, weaving my direction. He slid around bodies until he was next to me, then stared into my eyes. He ticked his head toward the exit.

"I'll be outside," I tossed over my shoulder to Luke.

I followed Weston out the door, savoring his scent, watching the way his shoulders moved when he parted the crowd.

He held the glass door open for me and we went outdoors. He stayed at my side then, and our steps turned into a stroll in the direction of his silver truck.

"I've been thinking about you," he said.

Relief threatened to spill prematurely inside me. I held it in place, in case he was about to drop the *it's over* bomb. "I'm not here to force you into talking to me. I came with Luke for lunch."

"I'm not being forced," he said, rubbing his hands back and forth as if he was anxious. "I thought all I needed was time away from you. A break. To think about stuff. You know?"

I nodded, bracing myself.

We turned the corner of the building. His truck, clean as a showroom gem, glistened under the frosty noon sun.

"I didn't sleep last night." He scrubbed his face. *Oh no. Here comes the dump.* He stopped at the side of his truck, reaching out an arm, placing his hand on the side. His dark brown eyes met mine.

"Neither did I." I was sure his lack of sleep had nothing to do with being haunted by an evil spirit or admitting seeing an angel to his parents.

"All night I thought about you," he said. "About Matthias. As weird as everything is, I don't care. All I care about is being with you."

I wrapped my arms around myself, hoping Weston wouldn't see my body shake with adrenaline and joy. "It's a lot to… understand. I get that."

"I'm not going to try and understand it. If I think too much about it, I start getting weirded out, so I'm not going to think about it. Does that sound wrong? Maybe I'm weak or… or stupid for not wanting to figure it out. But… I trust you."

Matthias had told me plenty of stuff I couldn't understand. Stuff I'd had to accept and trust.

I reached out and laid my hand on his bicep, the contact causing him to go still. "I'll talk about whatever you want to talk about, but I won't push or anything like that, okay?"

The trust in his eyes humbled me, and dropped another weighty cloak of responsibility on my back. I was okay with that. I wasn't afraid of what it meant.

Weston slipped his arms around my waist and drew me against him. "I need to hold you," he whispered. Warm tingles raced through my body.

48

I returned the embrace. "You feel so good," he laid his head against mine, sighing.

He felt good too. I closed my eyes, relieved to have a friend. Mortal comfort and companionship.

The roar of an engine and the screech of tires over asphalt trumpeted through the air. Weston and I jerked around to see where the sound came from. Britt's white Mustang barreled toward us.

SIX

Weston's arms snatched me, yanking me away from the side of the truck. We flattened ourselves against the building.

Britt's Mustang screeched to a halt, barely missing Weston's truck.

"She's insane," Weston blew out.

Britt burst out of her car and wobbled over. The same dark spirits I'd seen in class earlier still leeched her body, stimulating her.

"You!" She pointed at me, swaying like a blow-up punching toy. "You stay away from him."

"You're out of your mind," Weston hissed. "You're drunk."

"'Course I'm drunk. 'S her fault." Britt lunged at me, but tripped on her platform shoe and crashed onto the pavement, coming down flat. Patrons slowed to watch. Britt didn't move.

Weston and I exchanged glances.

I inched forward. "Britt?"

Gawking passersby annoyed me. Britt remained flat on the filthy gravel.

"What the hell was she doing?" Weston twitched from head to toe, his face red as blood.

"She's pissed, dude."

The voice stopped my heart. Brady appeared behind Weston. He leaned casually against the building, one leg bent and propped up, his arms across his chest. Like Albert, he was dressed in black, only his ensemble wasn't the designer-like suit Albert wore. Brady looked like one of the Beatles in his tight black pants and snug black turtle neck.

"What are you doing?" I demanded.

Weston's angry gaze flicked from prostrate Britt to me. Brady laughed, and came away from the wall, strolling until he stood directly behind Weston's shoulder.

"She almost killed us!" Weston shrilled.

"That's what you deserve, loser," Brady hissed into Weston's ear.

"Yeah, well, she didn't." I had to cool Weston down. "Don't be mad, okay?" Weston knew I saw evil spirits, but he'd freak if I told him Brady was here. I voted to tell him after the fact. I had to get rid of Brady first.

"You're defending her?" Weston almost screeched.

Brady grinned and circled Britt, stopping at her ankles, his lusty gaze traveling up her bare legs to her hiked-up mini skirt. "Nice."

Control, control, control. "No. I just don't want to fight with you."

"Oh, please fight." Brady clasped his hands at his chest as if begging. "Please."

Shut up! I thought.

"Now what?" Weston shifted, set his hands on his hips.

My mind scrambled. "Let's get her out of here."

"Forget it. She did this to herself."

"Does she need some help?" A construction worker dressed in insulated overalls, stained overcoat and knit cap stopped, along with his ogling buddies, all of them trying their best not to stare, fighting the gravitational pull of Britt's hiked skirt.

"It's okay," I waved them on, hoping they'd split. They hemmed, then continued into the store.

I didn't want to go anywhere near Britt with the swarm of evil circling her like vultures honing in on the dead, and Brady's presence added to the mayhem. What gave him the right to hang around, anyway? *I hope he's not going to make a habit of showing up every time Weston gets mad. That's all I need.*

"We should put her in her car," I suggested, then bent down, reaching for Britt.

"And then what? How about we leave her here. She deserves a reality check."

"We can't leave her in the middle of the parking lot," I said, tempted by the suggestion. "It's freezing out here."

"I'm not touching her." Weston's hands lifted in surrender. I didn't blame him. But he couldn't see the black spirits and Brady hovering. Britt remained on the ground, dead to the world.

"I'll drive her home if you put her in her car. Let's go." I jerked my head in the direction of the Mustang. The gathering crowd thickened. Somebody asked if they should call a doctor and Weston sneered. I told the Samaritan-lady we had everything under control. Still, it wouldn't be long before management noticed what was going on and called the cops.

Begrudgingly, Weston slipped his arms beneath Britt and pulled her to her feet. He guided a limp, mumbling Britt to her waiting Mustang. I opened the passenger side door and he put her inside, then pried her arms from his neck. She blubbered into a crumpled heap. He closed the door.

Brady wagged his brows and morphed into the back seat of the Mustang. My mouth opened to shout at him, but I snapped it shut.

Weston rounded her car, as if he was going to be the one to drive her home. I raced around the back, meeting him at the driver's side door. He glared. "What are you doing?"

"I'll drive. You're too angry." With Brady *and* those black creatures in the car, who knew what would happen?

"I can drive without letting my feelings interfere," Weston whispered with a look around at nosey onlookers.

My fingers on his chest, I grinned and lightly pushed him back. "You'd trust me to drive your truck? I didn't think so. I'll drive Britt home."

He pinched his lips, as if fighting a smile. "Guess I'll follow you."

I really didn't want to get in the car and be locked in such a small space with those disgusting creatures and Brady. Swallowing a nervous knot, I dipped into the driver's side, and closed the door.

"Aw, I want Weston to drive," Brady whined from the back seat. My hands shook as I wrapped my fingers around the steering wheel. "It'd be just like old times."

"You're not getting anywhere near him, loser," I said, anger bubbling beneath my skin.

Brady let out a howling laugh. Britt stirred, her head lolling from left to right.

"You've always been kind of dense, Zoe. Don't know what Weston sees in you. Oh, wait, yes I do. An easy score."

My fingers tightened around the wheel. Disgust rolled from my stomach up my throat that I'd ever let Brady touch me, let alone once thought he had any decency inside of him.

Brady's attention shifted to Britt, lying semi-conscious in the seat next to mine. His stare grew dark. Britt's black spirits appeared oblivious to my presence, even though they seemed to be aware of Brady. They turned their heads his direction every now and then, eyes flashing, glimmering at him. Still, the three of them remained wholly concentrated on stimulating Britt.

"Man she was a wild ride," Brady's tone held nostalgia.

"You're sick."

"No, I'm dead, and I'm damned mad I'm dead, or I could be banging this slut right this very second."

"Oh, that's right," I snorted. "Kinda hard to do when you don't have a body anymore."

"I'm sitting here aren't I?" Brady ran his hands down his arms.

"Yeah, but what you're feeling isn't real. It's just a memory. Sucks for you, Brady."

A flash of fear crossed his face and his palms skimmed his thighs. Relief replaced the fear. He leaned forward, but the car didn't shift at all from the movement, proving to me that Matthias was right about evil not having a body. How had Brady not noticed?

"Pull the car over and I can show you how real I am."

I was ornery enough to bait him. "Why should I pull over? You want Britt? Take her."

His eyes widened for a flash, then slit. "I knew you weren't all that. See, you like to watch, don't you?"

I couldn't wait for him to realize he didn't have a body. All those racing male hormones were nothing more than ghosts, or in his case, goblins.

In a blink, Brady was straddling Britt. His hands roved her body and his tongue grazed his lips. Fascinated, my eyes darted from the road to Brady. What was he feeling if not Britt's flesh? I was astounded. Speechless. Shocked.

The creatures jumped up and down, rallying in silence.

Britt coughed and gasped, then jerked upright, eyes wide. Had she felt Brady?

"Ohh, baby," Brady oozed, his hands continuing to explore Britt, in spite of her oblivion. When Britt's gaze met mine, the creatures' movements slowed. The three parked themselves in eerie stillness on Britt's head and shoulders, their hollow eyes staring at her as if waiting for her next move. Only their talons shifted.

I swallowed.

Brady's strained countenance remained intensely focused on Britt, sending my body into a wave of uncontrollable shivers. "Come on," Brady growled when she didn't respond to him. His eyes grew wide and he lifted his hands, looked at them in wonder.

Britt lunged for the steering wheel. She grabbed hold, causing the car to swerve. My heart stammered.

"What the hell?" Brady screamed, shaking his hands, as if they were asleep and the action would awaken them. "What. The. Hell!"

"Britt stop." I shoved her back.

She rammed her fist in my cheek. The car jerked when my face took the impact of the blow. I straightened the wheel and jammed my elbow into her head. The black spirits danced and leapt. Britt fell back against the seat in an unconscious heap. Breath raced in and out of my chest.

Light filled the car and Matthias appeared. He wasn't sitting, he was simply there, between the front seat and the back, his presence powerful and unyielding to anything physical or otherwise in his way. The black spirits on Britt's back stood upright, their soulless eyes rounding, their fleshless forms shimmering, then turning matte when their attention locked on Matthias. They leapt and jumped, mouths opening and closing in soundless protest. Matthias raised his hand in their direction and they vanished.

He set his penetrating gaze on Brady and horror filled Brady's astonished face. I sucked in a breath. Brady dissolved.

"Your friend is out of sorts."

"He's not my friend."

"I'm speaking of the young lady."

I glanced over my shoulder at Matthias, now sitting in the backseat.

"I'm glad you're here," I said. "Sheesh. She's nuts," I mumbled, touching my sore jaw. "Between her and Brady, I wasn't sure what I was going to do."

"That Brady's a smarmy fellow, isn't he?"

"Smarmy, sleazy—you name it. I hope he's not going to be showing up all the time now." I crammed my hand into my hair. My gaze latched with Matthias' through the rearview mirror. My heart sunk. "Is he?"

"I told you, the fight for souls is relentless."

My cell phone vibrated, and I fished it out of my pocket. Weston.

"You okay?" His voice was strung with worry. "What happened? I saw her attack you. What a freaking psycho. We should have left her in the parking lot. Looked like she was trying to kill you."

"She probably was." I glanced at Britt out cold in the seat next to me.

"You should have let me drive."

"And take a chance she'd try to hurt you? Forget it. See you at her house."

"I don't like this, Zoe."

My eyes met Matthias' through the rearview mirror.

"She's unconscious now. I'll be okay."

Weston sighed audibly. I snapped the phone shut, returning my attention to Matthias in the backseat. "Would she have killed me?" I asked.

The sparkle in his eyes disappeared. "Her mind is not her own."

"Yeah… I know."

"And already you've forgiven her. That's my bearcat."

"Forgiving's easy when you're around," I smirked.

"You would have forgiven her even if I wasn't here," his smooth voice dripped truth into me. I didn't like the way Britt chose to live, but I wasn't taking her assaults, both verbal and physical, to heart.

"She needs help," I murmured.

"She'll get it."

I marveled at his certainty. "I'm taking her home no matter what the consequences."

"She won't see it like that at first, but someday, she will thank you."

I sighed. "She'll hate me."

"Better she gets help than she loses control and ends up in an early grave, condemning herself."

"Condemn?" *That's a strong word.*

Taking the life of another is not something to trifle with.

Is your father... condemned?

A long silence drew between us. Matthias's gaze remained with mine—strong and undeviating. "It's not over yet."

"I can't believe you still think he can change. I don't know, he's pretty far gone if you ask me." Immediately I wished I could retract my observation. Though I found it unfathomable, Matthias still loved a man who had sent him to his death, ending his young life of twenty-one years over an unpaid debt.

"Would you ever give up on Luke?" he asked.

"Of course not, but Luke's not a murderer."

"You believe there is good in Luke deep down, don't you?"

"Yeah, of course. I've seen it."

His gaze drew sharp. "As have I... seen good in Pop."

Matthias had shared with me a handful of his memories—both happy and sad events that flashed into his mind, part of the fascinating miracle of him being my guardian. I'd slipped into Matthias' conscience and *been* Matthias, reliving moments between his father and him—even his death, a stark, horrid moment that still wracked me with shudders.

"And you forgave him."

"That doesn't mean there isn't a price to pay. In Pop's case, he chose to lose himself to evil regardless of my forgiveness."

I swallowed, glanced in the rearview mirror. Weston's silver truck was right behind me. "He came back last night."

Matthias' disapproval of Albert blasted out in the car in invisible force, filling the space. He remained silent.

"After you left I found him in Luke's room. Luke was close to relapsing. I did what you did. I told him to leave."

"There's no magic in the words, Zoe. It's the strength inside of you that gives you power." Matthias leaned forward, his presence whooshing through my being like a gust of soothing wind. My breath caught.

"Wow. I like it when you do that," I said.

"So, you're telling me you don't need me anymore?" he murmured.

"No way am I telling you that." I turned on Britt's street, my heart sinking that Matthias would leave soon. Maybe if I kept talking about his father, he'd stay.

I took my foot off the gas pedal and the car slowed. I avoided Matthias' blue eyes in the rearview mirror.

It doesn't matter that you don't look at me. Your thoughts are mine.

Dangit! Heat rushed my neck and cheeks. "I can't help that I want you around," I mumbled.

"You've got me when you need me."

"I want you even when I don't need you though." I sighed. "That's the problem."

"Well," Matthias' voice softened. "The feeling is mutual."

"What do you say I dump Britt, take her car out on the freeway and drive it off the nearest overpass?" I teased.

Matthias frowned. "Not funny."

Britt's red brick house came up on the left. Her dad's pearly Escalade sat in the driveway. Her mouth hung open, drool leaking down one side onto her chin. Smudged, black mascara had dried in blotches on her pink cheeks. My jaw started to ache. I rubbed it.

"Does it hurt?" Matthias asked.

"A little."

He reached forward and his fingers grazed my jaw, drawing away the pain like a mist evaporating beneath the sun.

Thank you.

My pleasure.

I parked and turned off the engine. "Now what? You cast your spell on her and she's out like a light."

"A spell?" he said with a smile. "I'm no magician, Zoe." Matthias lifted his hand, his long, elegant fingers stretched out six inches above her head.

"Way better than a magician." I was awed that Britt now stirred.

Matthias withdrew his hand. The parting look of yearning in his eyes melted my insides. "Till we meet again." He leaned forward and I braced for a kiss. His warm lips pressed against my cheek.

My body swirled in deliciousness. "Good bye."

"What the hell?" Britt bounced upright, blinking, taking in her surroundings.

Matthias was gone.

"You brought me home?" she demanded. "You really are a snitch."

"Whatever. You'd be face down in the parking lot of Wendy's with your fancy thong on display if it wasn't for me."

"Shut up." She closed her eyes, and gripped her head and leaned back on the seat.

The front door of her house opened and her father, tall, with sandy blond hair like Britt's, marched toward us. He wore a sleek power suit in soft dove, a periwinkle shirt and red tie. The hard lines of his face prepared me for anger. But his gaze was on Britt who, upon hearing the pound of his stride, opened her eyes. She cursed under her breath and shrunk in the seat. "Thanks a lot, loser," she growled.

Mr. Walker yanked open the passenger side door and fumed. "What is going on, young lady?"

"Um, Zoe gave me a ride home because—"

"Because you're drunk?" He reached in and hauled her to her feet. "The school called."

Britt wrenched free, her face flushing red. Her gaze darted over her shoulder at Weston getting out of his truck. "I'm not drun—" Britt heaved, the yellowish liquid spewing onto her father's expensive suit in sticky chunks.

I killed the engine and got out of Britt's Mustang.

Mr. Walker jerked his head toward the open front door. "Wait for me inside."

Britt hunched her shoulders and glared. Then she stomped across the slushy grass to the front door. Weston joined me, shoving his hands into the front pockets of his jeans.

Mr. Walker's head bowed for a moment. He observed the vomit on his slacks, sighed and lifted his gaze to mine. "Thanks for bringing her home."

"Of course." I handed him Britt's keys.

Mr. Walker's countenance reminded me of my parents' then, filled with sorrow and bone-deep disappointment. My heart ached and I looked away. I wanted to tell him things would get better. I believed they would because Matthias had told me they would. They'd gotten better for my family. Deep down, Britt had good in her. She'd just lost touch with that.

"It'll be okay," I said.

His expression remained uncertain. "She needs help. I found three empty bottles of Vodka in her bedroom. Three. How does that happen?"

A million ways. Distraction. Ignorance. Trusting too much. Not seeing signs.

"It doesn't matter now," he said with a sigh. His eyes turned to the house. "I'm sending her to rehab."

I bit my lip. *Britt will hate that.*

"Thanks for being a good friend, Zoe." Mr. Walker patted my shoulder. He gave Weston a genial nod and, once again surveyed himself. He shook his head and crossed the front yard, into the house.

Guilt weighed down my heart. I'd been a drinking, partying cohort with Britt long enough that I felt partially responsible for where she was today: on her way to rehab. That could so easily have been me. The truth was humbling.

I climbed into Weston's truck and shut the door. The warmth of the heater chased away the chill of truth clinging to my bones, but the ache in my heart was untouched. I stared at Britt's window as the red, sheer curtains were pulled closed.

"Hey." I felt Weston's gentle caress on my shoulder. "You okay?"

I nodded. "She's safe now."

"Yeah." His hand lingered on my shoulder but I kept my face turned toward the window. Finally, his hand left me, and cool air replaced where his warmth had been.

The engine of his truck rumbled to a start and he drove.

"Don't feel sorry for her," he said. "You did the right thing."

"I know. It's not easy, though." I looked at him. "Her dad's going to send her to rehab."

Weston sighed. "She needs that, Zoe."

"Yeah."

"She'll come out of it."

All I could think about was the finality of Britt being gone. I wouldn't see her at all. Not even in her drunk, disheveled state—the one she'd lived in the last few months. I'd hoped that we could finish out our senior year together like we'd always planned: prom, parties, and graduation.

"She'll blame me for everything she's going to miss," I said.

"Her choices landed her here. Don't do this to yourself."

"Have you ever felt at all responsible for what happened to Brady?"

Weston scrubbed his jaw. "Maybe. A little."

We didn't talk on the rest of the drive back to school. No doubt he was trying to deal with Brady's death, and his part in it. Even though neither Weston nor I had stayed at Krissy's fateful gathering, we'd helped her plan it—Krissy had begged us to help her have a party, even though we'd both warned her that parties can get out of hand.

Now, Brady was dead.

SEVEN

I sat in journalism like a ghost. I stared at my computer, even edited a few articles in my queue, but I had a hard time focusing. I kept seeing Brady. Every time I thought of him, my stomach threatened to retch. He scared me. I didn't like that he had shown himself. Again. Why hadn't he gone—and stayed put—where all the miserable souls go? Why did I have to see him?

"So, fill me in." Chase planted himself in a chair next to me and studied me from behind his glasses. "What happened with Krissy?"

"Luke found her on State Street and brought her to our house."

"Just like a stray cat?"

"A stray abused cat. She was really upset." I told him about the tense, emotional Krissy, sobbing, refusing to return home then reneging and going home anyway, no matter how we tried to talk her out of it.

"She's so scared she can't think rationally," Chase deduced. "Sad."

"Sad. Sick. Ridiculous. I'm going to call Family Services and leave an anonymous tip."

"Yeah," Chase brightened. "Great idea. Still, be prepared for the fact that she might deny everything. Sometimes victims are so afraid, they won't admit anything's wrong."

"At least someone will go over and investigate. Maybe that will give her the time to get far enough away from the situation to see it like it is."

"That's probably what she doesn't want to see. Think about it."

I didn't like thinking about Krissy's circumstances.

"I heard about Britt and the parking lot."

"You did?" Nothing spread faster than a twisted story about another person's misery.

"Heard she almost killed you and Weston with her car."

"Yeah, well, she wanted to."

"Also heard she was drunk," he said. "Why didn't you guys call the cops?"

"I don't want to see her in jail. She needs help. Now, she's going to get it—her dad's sending her to rehab."

Chase whistled. "How would it be?"

"Being almost smashed by a drunk driver? Or being sent to rehab? Gee, I don't know, let me think on that one for a while and I'll get back to you," I snickered.

"No," he blushed. "How would it be to be Weston, and have crazy chicks willing to kill for you? Man, that guy is a stud."

"Don't say that too loud," I whispered, teasing him. He glanced around to see if anyone had heard him. "You aren't serious. Chase, that's not love."

"I'd like to try it."

I chuckled. "Okaaay." I clicked the mouse and closed Windows for the day. I wasn't getting anywhere and staring at lame stories wasn't helping matters.

Chase looked like he was sitting on eggshells. "What?" I asked. "There are girls who like you. Come on."

"Not the ones I want."

"After everything you know about Brit, you still want her?"

He stared at me, so long that I bit my lower lip. His gaze dropped to my mouth for an uncomfortably long moment, then lifted to my eyes again. "Not just her," he said.

Uh-oh. The shrill bell announcing that class was over did nothing to break Chase's concentration. His eyes remained riveted to mine. "Zoe, will you go to prom with me?"

My mouth opened but nothing came out.

"I figured if I asked you now, I'd beat Weston to the punch."

"Well, yeah, you beat him all right."

Chase slapped his thigh. "Yes!"

"Chase, you know Weston and I are… seeing each other, so I can't accept your invite, even if you did beat him at asking me."

"Oh, man." His right leg flopped straight out.

"Come on." I leaned over and side-hugged him. "We're buddies, right? Maybe we can double."

I drew back and he slumped in his chair. "Who am I going to go with? I suck at dancing, and you're the first girl who's ever said more than ten words to me."

"That's not true."

The right side of his lip lifted. "Okay, I'm exaggerating. But you'd be fun to go with."

"I'm really honored you asked me."

He snorted. "Honor. What a pile."

"Hey, girls appreciate honorable guys."

"I'm done being honorable. I want to have fun. Hey, maybe I could ask Krissy. You said she kind of likes me. What? What's that look on your face mean?"

"She's kind of into Luke right now, I think."

Chase blew out a breath. "That was fast. Not that I have anything against your brother, he's cool. But… man, I guess I gotta move faster. Is there a secret handshake or something I'm missing?"

I laughed. We stood, and I gathered my backpack and slung it over my shoulder. Chase crossed to his desk and did the same. We walked out the door together.

My cell phone vibrated and I dug it out of my pocket and grinned.

"Weston?" Chase asked, noting my smile.

I nodded.

"Guess I can hold onto the slim-to-none chance that you and he will have a fight or break up or something."

"Chase!" I playfully slugged his bicep before he went on his way.

want a ride home?

yeah b rite there

I slipped the phone back into the front pocket of my jeans just as I passed a poster, decorated in blue sky and billowy white clouds, for this year's prom: Paradise on Earth. I couldn't suppress the grin on my lips.

When Weston and I pulled up next to the house, Luke's Samurai was parked out front and, through the foggy glass of the back window, I made out two forms sitting in the front seats.

"Is that Krissy?" I asked.

Weston parked behind Luke's car and turned off his engine. "Looks like it. They a thing now?"

"They went to lunch together today," I said.

Weston hopped out, rounded the front of the truck and opened my door. "Thanks."

His hands went to my waist and held me in the opening. "I don't want this to be over." His voice was low.

My insides sparked. "You want to come inside for a while?"

He nodded, relief easing the pensiveness in his face. His fingers tightened at my hips and he moved in close, forcing my legs apart so his body was flush with mine. His arms wrapped around my back.

"I want to kiss you," he whispered.

Right here? Right now? Luke and Krissy could see us if they turned around. I glanced over. They seemed preoccupied in conversation.

Weston's warm lips coursed the side of my turned neck. Rivulets of heat raced beneath my skin. I closed my eyes; met his ready mouth with my own. His hungry hands roved my back. My fingers dove into his hair.

"Let's go inside," he said. "I'm your slave."

He shut the door we started around the truck.

I took his hand and led him toward the front door, passing Luke's car. Both Luke and Krissy, in the middle of talking, looked over. Krissy's lips curved up a little and she dipped her head. Luke waved.

I waved back, then continued to lead Weston inside. I whipped out my cell phone and texted Luke:

careful her dad's a psycho remember
yeah k

Weston's brown eyes stroked me like a hot feather. His scent seeped into my senses. He reached out, and his palms locked onto my waist, infusing my torso with heat. Want built in my weakening knees, then reached upward taking control of my limbs, my heart.

I slid my arms around his neck.

He leaned, and pressed his mouth to mine. Desire synchronized. Blossomed. My hands moved up his neck, savoring taut chords and muscles as his head moved, consuming my lips, continuing in exploration into the thick waves of his hair.

His body, tight as a fist against mine, pressed me back a step, two, until my spine hit the edge of the open door. With his foot, he nudged it. It nearly shut.

I broke the seal of our mouths. "Have to keep…" I gasped between kisses, "the door… open."

His hands moved, one sliding behind me, the other tracing the side of my body, lighting me with delicious fire. Need bubbled. I pulled him closer.

My eyes cracked open just enough to see if his were closed in bliss or if he was checking me out as well. My heart stopped. Albert hovered over Weston's shoulder.

I shoved Weston back and gasped. "Stop."

"Why?" Weston panted.

"We can't."

"Why not?"

"Because."

Albert's lips lifted in a glittering grin. "Yes, why stop, Zoe? This was just getting interesting."

"You are sick! Sick!"

"I'm sorry," Weston sputtered his face paling with shock.

"No, not you." I took his hand, words racing out. "I'm sorry. I just... think... things were going too fast."

"I thought you wanted to."

"I did, I do."

Albert leaned close. "She does, she does. And so do we."

We?

Albert nodded at something behind me. I glanced over my shoulder. Brady.

Brady grinned.

I forced outrage, surprise and fear aside and focused on Weston's wary, flushed face.

"No, I moved too fast." Weston scraped his hands down his cheeks. "I'm sorry."

"You didn't move fast enough, bro," Brady snickered.

"There's an art to seduction." Albert floated in a circle around Weston and I—Brady joined in, eyeing Weston like a dog eyes a steak. *Uh-oh.* "Apologizing for a natural desire. Tsk, tsk." Albert shook his head and drew in a deep breath. "Ahh. Lust. The scent is so... potent. So irresistible. So unstoppable."

Brady stopped behind Weston and his hands began a slow roving of Weston's body. Albert stopped behind me. My heart spun out of control. I kept my gaze on Weston's, but tried to keep in tune with what Brady was doing to him and what Albert was attempting to do to me.

A hot surge of desire swept through my system, taunting fingers beckoning, urging, me toward Weston's smooth skin. His lips.

"It's natural to want him," Albert whispered in my ear. Craving swam through my veins and pooled low in my body, surging through my legs, pushing me toward Weston.

No. This is Albert, not me. I took Weston's face in my hands and stared him straight in the eyes. His eyes had changed from surprise, to desire. He licked his lips.

"Look at me," I said.

"I am," he purred.

"You're not yourself right now, Weston. Trust me."

"Oh, I'm all here," he said, eyeing my mouth. "And I'm ready."

"Come on," Brady's hands moved faster. "Rip into her. Tear off her clothes."

"Sex is hot," Weston's voice slipped into slick mode.

"Yeah, when you *love* someone," I put in.

"I do love you." His mouth neared mine.

"Quit talking," Brady hissed, stimulation now frenzied. "Do it."

I flattened my palms on Weston's chest. "I say we talk about this."

"I say you strip down and let me have at," Weston whispered against my jaw. Then he froze, inched back, his face twisted and flushing red. "Did I just say that?"

I pulled Weston into a hug. "Hold me." His heart rammed against my cheek. I closed my eyes so I couldn't see Albert or Brady, and then opened my mind to as many positive, loving thoughts of Weston that I could.

At first Weston's grip was aggressive, but it didn't take long before his arms gentled.

I hugged him tighter. "Weston. The feelings I have for you are different than anything I've felt for another guy. I want it to stay that way. You've said you feel the same for me. You told me that you... love me. Is this love? To me it feels more like lust."

Weston drew in a breath. "Jeez, Zoe, talk about deflating a guy's libido."

"Just calling it what it is." I eased back. Brady had moved away, fear twisting his face. "You told me that's one of the things you love about me."

"Yeah, true." Weston touched the side of my face. "Maybe I'm caught up in the moment. But there's nothing wrong with that."

"We don't think clearly when we're caught up in the moment. We make rash decisions. I've done enough of that. I'm not allowing myself to lose control *ever* again." *How's that Albert?.* "I need to tell you something."

Confusion and panic widened Brady's eyes. In my peripheral vision, Albert appeared.

"Remember how I saw Brady at the funeral? Standing behind his mother?"

"Yeah." Weston's brows slowly drew together.

"He was there in the parking lot today… riling you."

"What?" Weston's arms fell away from my waist. His flushed face drained of color.

"No. Shut up, shut up!" Brady screamed.

A look of annoyance flashed on Albert's face. He flicked a hand and Brady vanished.

"You saw him… again?" Weston barely breathed the words out.

I nodded. Wrapped my arms around myself. "It's scary. I hate it."

"What did he want?"

How to tell someone their dead best friend from hell now wants to destroy their soul? "He… he's…" I swallowed. Weston might freak if he knew the truth.

"He'll never believe you," Albert said.

"Zoe, what?"

"He wants to bring you down."

Weston's bottomless brown eyes widened with fear. "He said that?"

I nodded. "He was here… just now." I chanced a look at Albert. His look of arrogance grated at my nerves. "He was trying to get you worked up because—"

"Stop." Weston jammed his hands into his hair. "Just stop."

Albert's lips lifted at the corners.

"You told me you didn't want me to lie to you, and I won't. Not when this means everything to me."

Hands dragging down his face, Weston didn't blink through his locked gaze, hard and stunned on mine. "What means everything?" he asked quietly.

"You. Us. The truth."

He studied me with deciphering eyes. Then his gaze fell to the floor. He shook his head, let out a helpless-sounding laugh. "You're…" He looked at me, searching gone, a trace of fear now coloring his pale expression. "You're sure?"

"Positive. Look." I stepped closer to him, but he inched back. To my right, Albert crossed his arms over his chest. "Whatever's happened to me, this ability I have to see guardians and stuff also enables me to see evil spirits."

He swallowed. Didn't respond.

"He doesn't believe you," Albert murmured.

Yes, he does, I thought, even though Albert couldn't hear me. *And then you don't have a reason to be here.*

Finally, Weston closed the space between us. "I have a girlfriend who sees guardian angels and murderers. You are—" He stroked the side of my face with the back of his fingers, "—something else, Zoe."

"Girlfriend?" My insides tingled and I smiled, approving of his endearment.

Weston slipped his arms around my waist and snuggled against me, his forehead pressed to mine. He closed his eyes. "One more reason I love you."

Albert's arms unfolded and went behind his back. I grinned inwardly to myself.

I inched back and looked Weston in the eye. "I never want to be the cause of why someone *I* care about loses control. Ever."

"I love you," he whispered, then held me close. "I'm sorry I acted like… an idiot."

"It's okay. *Making love* is not something I've ever done before," I admitted.

"Me neither."

I was relieved he understood the difference. Albert's eyes hardened. He zigzagged like a caged wildcat. The word *trapped* kept surfacing in my head. Trapped. Afraid.

And gone.

Cool relief sighed from my chest. I pressed Weston's cheeks gently with the palms of my hands, and he reached up, covered my hands with his. "You make me crazy, Zoe."

"That's cool." I grinned.

"I want to make you crazy," he murmured.

"Well, you're getting close."

"Yeah?"

"Yeah."

He tilted his head back, smiled. "Yes!"

After Weston left, I offered to babysit Abria for Mom and Dad so they could go out. I wanted to make sure they had all the time they needed to talk. I didn't like the idea that they might succumb to Albert's influence, which could tear the family apart. After everything we'd been through with Abria and Luke and even my issues, I'd do everything in my power to see that Albert had zero opportunity to hang around and spread his malicious intent.

I bathed Abria, allowing her the freedom to splash and play in the water like a seal without screaming at her to stop drenching the walls, tile and everything in the bathroom. Telling her to behave was useless, anyway. Her cherubic face, framed by damp curls, was irresistible and she smiled up at me as if to say, 'thank you!'

Abria thrived on predictability. I dried her with a towel, amazed that the smallest and often oddest things made her happy and content. Like water. The same Disney towel. Holding a toy in her hand. Jumping.

"If all I had to do was jump to be happy, that'd be pretty sweet," I told her, slipping one of my old t-shirts over her head. She wouldn't sleep in anything else and loved to run, naked, into my bedroom after her bath and 'steal' one from my collection. I kept a bunch in the bottom drawer of my dresser just for her.

"Jum! Jum!" After the t-shirt fell into place on her squirmy little body, she climbed onto her bed and started jumping.

"Yeah, yeah," I grinned. "I get it."

"Hey." Luke's bass voice came from the open door. He stood with his hands in his pockets.

"Hey. Have you been with Krissy all this time?"

He blushed, nodded and leaned in the jamb.

"So… what was that all about?"

"Just talking."

"That's a lot of talking." Abria continued to jump and I held my hands out, ready to catch her, just in case. "What did she say?"

Luke's shoulder lifted. "Stuff. Where's Mom and Dad?"

"They went out. They needed it."

"What happened?"

"They were fighting," I said.

"They've been doing that a lot lately."

"I know. I hate it."

"Yeah, well, there's not a lot you can do about it, Z. It's their choice."

He was right. Ultimately, even with Albert—or any negative influence—the choice was up to the individual. But it was hard to see this close to my heart.

"Back to you and Krissy," I said, smiling. Luke's cheeks bloomed a soft pink shade and he dipped his head. "What happened when you took her home? Was her psycho dad on a leash or did he attack?"

"She had me drop her a block away. I'm telling you, that guy's a loser. He needs to be locked up."

"What? Did Krissy tell you something?" My mind raced with the image of Krissy's dad's evil infestation along with all of the other insidious prospects my imagination had conjured since I'd met her.

"That girl can talk, I'll say that much."

"Yeah, but about what?"

"About a whole bunch of stuff. She needs somebody to listen, you know? She and her mom don't talk, and her dad's this control freak who talks *at* her. I hate people like that. Man, if Mom and Dad were like that, I would have been out of here years ago. I don't know how she takes it."

Abria jumped higher, her head coming within a foot of the ceiling. "Hey, tone it down, Abria," I warned. She swooned louder and jumped higher so I grabbed her, held her wriggling body for a minute in hopes of calming her down then put her feet on the floor. She scrambled right back up on the mattress.

"So," I fished, "she wasn't specific about anything?"

Luke yawned and scratched his belly. "No. But I get the feeling there's something bad there. I've seen it at my friends' houses, and it stinks. She kinda has that beaten down personality thing."

"Well, you were sweet to listen to her."

He cracked another yawn. "Don't mind." He lifted his arms overhead and stretched. "Wish there was something I could do." His cell phone vibrated, and he reached into the front pocket of his worn jeans and pulled it out. "Speaking of."

"She's calling you?"

"Texting. I told her she could."

"I'm surprised her dad lets her have a phone," I mumbled, grabbing Abria into my arms again. "Okay, time for bed, pretty girl."

Abria howled in protest.

"No kidding." Luke read the message then tapped out a response. "Another way for daddy-o to keep tabs on her, I guess."

I pulled back the sheets and blankets on Abria's bed. "Get in, Abria." She stiffened. The effort was like putting a stone slab under the covers. "Come on." Trying to press her statue-like body down was impossible.

The sound of the front door slamming caused the house to shudder. Luke and I exchanged glances. "Will you try to put her to bed? I need to check on Mom and Dad." I passed him in the doorway.

"Check on them? They're not kids, Z."

"Just do it," I snapped, panic seizing me. Until I was certain Albert wasn't stowing along with them, I wasn't going to do anything else.

I skipped down the stairs, ears alert for raised voices. Sure enough, the heavy tension that accompanied Albert like a putrid smell slugged me in the face once I was on the main floor.

Dad passed me in the entry hall, on his way upstairs, his face drawn, serious. He didn't say anything. My heart pounded with each step as I neared the kitchen.

Mom stood over the sink, staring out the corner window into the black night. The expression on her face was icy.

Albert hovered around her like a menacing crow. Had he gone with them or was he simply returning to the scene to do more damage?

He glanced over when I came into the room but quickly returned his intense focus to Mom. "Lovely woman, your mother."

I ground my teeth to keep from spouting off in front of Mom.

"Things went exceptionally well, Zoe. Hearts are harder now than they were before they left."

My hands fisted at my sides.

"Mom." I crossed to her, struggling to remain composed in spite of Albert's menacing presence and words. "Are you okay?"

Her stare remained fixed and cold. "Fine."

"What happened? I thought you two would be better after a night out?"

"One night can't change months of issues," she said.

I moved closer, positioning myself on her right side. Albert mirrored me on her left. His teeth flashed in a grin. "One minute can change anything, if you want it bad enough," I told her.

Her eyes met mine. She studied me for a few quiet moments. "You're right. Maybe neither of us want it bad enough."

EIGHT

My heart crashed to my feet.

"Brilliant!" Albert clasped his hands at his chest. "So, so brilliant."

I took Mom by the arm and led her a few steps away. "You can't think like this. You have to work it out. Go up there and talk to him."

Mom ripped her arm free. "Excuse me?"

Beaming, Albert came up behind her.

"Yes, now," I insisted. "He's upstairs. Go."

"Zoe," Mom's tone was baffled. "I just spent two hours talking to your dad and I don't need to spend another minute hashing out the same problems. We both need a break."

"Yes, breaks are marvelous." Albert nodded. "Left unattended, breaks widen the gulf between hearts until they separate irreparably."

"Please go talk to Dad again," I begged, gripping Mom's arms. "Please."

Shock covered her face, then her expression blanked. She pulled away. "I'm going to sleep." She started for the stairs. "Is Abria in bed yet?"

"Yes," I mumbled, devastated that my attempts to help reconcile them were brushed off.

"Good." Mom disappeared in the darkness of the unlit hall. Her footsteps thudded up the stairs. Overhead, I heard a plunk. Albert radiated black light into the room, pleasure and victory on his face.

"I thought you said she was asleep!" Mom shouted from upstairs.

"Luke's up there with her!" I shouted back then cringed at my harsh tone. I glared at Albert.

Albert's eyes closed, and his hands lifted into the air, moving like an orchestra conductor directing a symphony.

"You're pathetic," I hissed, glad we were alone so I could ream him.

Faintly, Luke and Mom's raised voices seeped out from Abria's room.

"We can end this right now." Albert stepped closer. My body went into a fit of shivers. "Give yourself to me, Zoe. Save your family."

Fear and panic loose inside of me whirled fiercely at his words. For a second, I entertained his suggestion. Then I remembered Matthias' warning: Albert was a liar.

"You don't want me, you want Matthias," I said.

"Yes, I do. You're a nice bonus."

"Sorry. I'll never be another link in your tie. And neither will Matthias."

"Oh, I wasn't going to put you or Matthias with these poor souls." He stroked the tie of bound, writhing prisoners and their screams lifted into the air, the screeching sound like ice water rushing through my veins. The taut weave of the ghastly noose recoiled beneath his touch.

"They don't like you." I nodded at the tie.

He ignored my observation. "I have somewhere special prepared for you two."

The breath in my chest sucked out. My knees wobbled; I was sure I'd crumple into a heap. "Forget it," I managed. "Matthias will never fall, not even for me."

Albert's brows arched over an amused smile. "How little you know him, my dear."

"I am not. Your. Dear."

"But you are. We're almost family. Once you and Matthias join me, it will be—"

"We'll never join you! He'd never do that. Never. You really have lost it, haven't you?" Fury pumped through my blood. "You lost your soul, your son and your wife. You're alone, Albert! Face it."

His bright eyes darkened.

"You don't even have a body," I continued, momentum fueling my words. "You think you do, but those sensations you have? They're just ghosts. Ever wonder why they're all the same, never new? Because you're a pathetic impersonator. Matthias told me, the followers of Satan can't have a body. That means whatever you *think* you're sensing is only a memory. Sucks to be you."

Albert remained eerily silent. Was he going to strike me down now? I readied for an assault. But if I was in mortal peril, Matthias would be here. Albert and I remained alone.

Upstairs, Abria's door slammed. Luke mumbled something at Mom. Then another door closed with a whack. Followed by another.

"You're done here," I said, relieved my family was in their bedrooms. *Everybody go to sleep, fast. You can't invite evil when you're asleep.* "And I'll carry my sister on my hip for the rest of my life if I have to."

"You could never keep up with me, Zoe."

"I'd die trying. Then Matthias and I would be together, living happily ever after in Paradise. That leaves you alone with your pathetic tie."

"Your family will be mine then."

A boulder formed in my throat. *No.* "Abria will keep them safe. Besides, they love each other enough that they'll work past this."

Albert inched closer. "You think this is a temporary condition? Temptation? Discord? Dishonesty? Infidelity?" His voice sliced me to the bone. "No, Zoe. These conditions have always existed and they will always exist, fertilized by those like myself who are more than willing to help spread destruction."

My body shook with the reality of his words. I was mortal. When my life ended, my efforts to help my family would go with me. No, they wouldn't. I knew for myself that guardians were there to help. That evil would never triumph over good.

"You're wrong," I said. Nothing Albert said or did could change an eternal truth. Surprise flashed over his face. He straightened. Had my conviction really been that powerful as to render him shocked?

His strong resemblance to Matthias reminded me of Matthias' undying hope that someday his father would be redeemed. I marveled that Matthias could see a thread of decency somewhere in this lost soul standing in front of me.

I sighed. "Kudos to Matthias for thinking you can still be salvaged," I mumbled. "I'd have bailed on you by now." I didn't need to spend another second in Albert's presence. This was my life. My home. I hadn't invited Albert into it.

I turned and headed to the peace and safety of sleep that awaited me.

Blinding night surrounding me. Pine needles pierced my arms, my bare thighs. Frosty air sliced my naked skin like razorblades. Shivers erupted through my body in endless, voracious shudders from the soles of my feet to my head. I was naked. Running. Alone. In the forest.

Fallen pine needles carpeted the ground, their shards poking into the tender soles of my feet as I raced on, heart pounding against my ribs

Albert's heavy presence bore down on me, into me, an invisible, suffocating cloak of evil that kept pace with my frantic feet as if to torment me. His deep laugh strangled my throat, the sound fingering through the reaching branches of the towering evergreens disappearing into the midnight sky overhead.

"You can't outrun me, Zoe."

I yearned to cover myself. Survival forced priority: run. Branches slapped my cheeks. Skin stung. Feet ached. Breath slowly evaporated. How long I darted through evergreens and spindly aspens I don't know. My body bled. Couldn't breathe fast enough. Muscles began to shut down, each pulling tight in rebellion as if to scream: I'm finished.

Albert's laugh rang around me, filling the quiet eeriness.

I pushed on, forcing my legs to keep going. Couldn't feel them anymore. Not even the sharp prickling of needles beneath my feet.

"Give yourself to me."

I jerked upright.

My lids opened. *What day is it?* Had I slept?

Sleep lured me, but the thought of returning to the awful nightmare pricked me to complete wakefulness. I scrubbed my face, relieved I'd only dreamed the horrifying scene. A bone-wracking shudder overtook me. I thought I was safe in sleep. Had Albert invaded my dream? Or was overwhelming stress clamping its jaws in my subconscious? I couldn't take it. *If only I could bail on school and catch up on sleep.* The last few days had taken a toll—more than a toll— I was exhausted.

I reached for my cell phone. Five calls from Chase. One message from him. Three texts from Krissy. Another from Weston.

luv u

Seeing Weston's message soothed my crimped nerves a little, but the eeriness of the nightmare clung to me like black spirits clung to their hosts, and I glanced over my shoulder just to make sure one of the grotesque creatures hadn't latched onto me.

I texted Weston back: *u 2* even though he'd texted me that he loved me hours ago. I didn't care. The words sent a fresh flurry of birds in my stomach. Prom was coming. Would we go together? I couldn't wait to see him, and a familiar excitement tingled in my blood thinking about being with him.

I opened Krissy's texts next:

your brother is nice

he is sweet

does he have a girlfriend?

I smiled.

Chase's message was typically enthusiastic: "Call me when you can. Or, we can meet at Starbucks." It seemed like forever since I'd enjoyed a relaxing infusion of coffee and its accompanying aroma. I could use an hour of gossiping, scouring the newspaper and watching people.

I slapped the phone shut, got out of bed and stumbled into the bathroom. My chest hurt briefly. Any lingering aches and pains I'd carried from the accident weeks ago had mostly vanished, thankfully. But some mornings I woke stiffer than usual, reminded of the accident by phantom pain.

After a shower, I threw on some blush, mascara and tied my dark hair in a knot at the back of my head. I pulled on some jeans and a purple hoodie, tossed a look out my window at grey skies, and chose my fur-lined black boots.

Standing in front of the mirror, I surveyed myself. Did Weston like me in purple? I thought the color magnified the green in my eyes. Mom had told me that a million times. Mom. Abria. How quiet the house was. Usually, Abria's running, giggling or screeching leaked underneath my bedroom door. Water streaming through pipes hummed in the background. Not this morning.

I opened the door and listened.

Nothing.

My pulse tapped through my veins. Where was everyone?

Abria's bedroom was empty. Luke's, empty. Mom and Dad's, empty.

I skipped down the stairs, panic causing my knees to shake. Luke was at the kitchen table, spooning Cheerios cereal into his mouth.

"Hey," I said, glancing around, half expecting Albert to be sitting on the countertop like a cookie jar.

"Hey."

"Where is everybody?"

"Dad's gone. Mom took Abria to the dentist or something."

"Abria at the dentist? How are they going to manage that?"

Luke shrugged. "Laughing gas?" We both chuckled in unison. As if.

I crossed to the refrigerator and opened it. I hoped Mom and Dad had made up. I wouldn't know until later, and a knot formed inside of me, lodging next to my heart. It would be there until I got home from school and saw for myself where my parents stood with each other. *I shouldn't worry about them like this. I should let them do whatever.* But that thought fit like a sweater that was too small and more than that the idea was irresponsible. A few months ago I might not have gotten involved in my family's issues. Now, I couldn't ignore them.

Luke slurped the last of his milk down, rose and carried his empty bowl to the sink. "You gonna eat?" He let out a belch.

"Not hungry. Ready?"

He nodded. We grabbed our backpacks and headed out the front door to his car.

March didn't warm the chilly air. A blinding sun rose up over the mountains behind our house, the white light beaming between towering evergreens and winter-naked aspens. The air was clean and bit through my lungs with each breath.

Neither Luke nor I spoke during the short drive to school. No matter how much I tried to distract myself with thoughts of budding spring, prom and the possibility of going with Weston, finals, graduation and anything else I could think about, my mind gravitated to the black forest. Me naked. Running. From Albert.

"Heard from Krissy again?" I asked, half-joking but eager to get my mind on something other than the unpleasant dream.

"Yeah."

"She asked me if you have a girlfriend."

His cheeks flushed magenta.

"She wants someone to talk to, that's all." Luke's tone was artificially calm, but I knew he was covering up. He pulled into the drag, the parking lot buzzing with student cars searching for empty slots.

He parked and we got out. His stride up the drag was uncharacteristically faster than mine and he kept a three-foot lead without as much as a backward glance in my direction.

I wouldn't push the Krissy issue. The subject was delicate.

I was curious to see where Luke was going—to class, or to meet up with Krissy somewhere. There was no harm in his being her friend. I just didn't want her to hurt him. And she definitely did not need an introduction to drugs.

Luke's blonde mass of hair melded into the crowd of bobbing heads and bodies flowing into the high school.

"Zoe!" Chase's voice came from behind me.

I turned and waited for him to catch up with me. He wore khakis and a blue and white oxford cloth, button-down shirt. His dark hair was neatly combed in place and his backpack hung on both of his shoulders evenly, not from one side like most teens carried them.

He smiled. "Hey."

"Hey."

We walked side-by-side. "So, Luke's in a hurry. Krissy?" he asked.

"She seems to have a crush going on."

His brows arched. I was relieved I didn't see any disappointment on his face.

"What about you?" I asked. We ushered through the glass double doors and into the stale-smelling hall. "Things okay at home?"

"My parents think I'm guilty by association, so I'm grounded until school is over. Forget that I'm a senior, will be an adult in a few months and for all intents and purposes am the most responsible child in our family. Those facts don't weigh in at all."

"I'm sorry they're being hard on ya." I patted his shoulder and he shrugged, then his brown eyes shifted to my hand for a brief second. "I should have listened to you, Zoe."

We held each other's gazes and came to a stop outside his first period classroom. Students filed around us. "I'm sorry," I said.

"Yeah. What about you and Weston?"

"We're talking again."

A flash of disappointment colored his eyes, and a twinge of guilt pulled at my heart.

"Oh. Well, that's good. That's cool," he said. "See ya in journalism."

He went into a room and I headed to my class with a knot in my heart.

I walked in, and automatically my gaze shot to Britt's empty desk. I hoped that wherever she was, she was okay and getting the help she needed.

I texted her.

u ok today?

I barely tuned into what the teacher was saying, my eyes glued to my phone screen, hidden in my lap.

No reply.

NINE

When lunchtime came, the smell of garlic and tomato sauce wafted into the halls. I shut my locker door and closed my eyes. *Please let everything be okay with Mom and Dad.*

Strong arms wrapped around my waist and my back was suddenly flush with the familiar strength of Weston's body. I relished being held, sharing a moment of human comfort that soothed my fizzing nerves.

I turned and wrapped around him.

"Hey, what's wrong?" His warm breath brushed my head.

I'm worried. Afraid. Hold me for a little while. "Nothing," I murmured. I wouldn't be a whiner and unload the moment I saw him. What kind of greeting was that?

"Want to go get something to eat?"

I nodded. His arms cradled me as we walked, and I snuggled against him, enjoying that he was there for me. He wanted me. Cared about me.

Our cuddling garnered the curious stares of the social divas and jocks who passed us. Weston ignored the whispers. In fact, he didn't even acknowledge the jocks who walked by—some of whom had been his friends and teammates.

There was, of course, the occasional chick who glared at me with the how-could-you-stab-your-best-friend-in-the-back look. I didn't care. I didn't have anything to prove to them. That crowd always believed what they wanted to, anyway.

Outside, the noon sun hid behind thick March clouds. Snow-drenched grass peeked out from beneath the heavy white blanket covering and the walkways and asphalt showed stains of draining water. Weston opened the passenger side door and I climbed into his truck. The scent of his cologne, and the sun-warmed upholstery of the seats, soothed me. I checked my cell phone, just to make sure I hadn't missed a text from Mom.

Nothing.

Weston got in, started the truck and something raucous boomed from his CD player. I stared out the window, too worried about Mom and Dad to care what was playing. The next thing I knew, the music was off.

"What's up?" he asked.

"My mom and dad have been fighting a lot."

"That sucks."

"Yeah. Do your parents fight at all?" I looked at him.

"All the time."

"What do they fight about? Sorry, maybe it's none of my business."

"No, it's okay. I don't know. Stuff. I always walk in and they're in the middle of it. Something big is going on, but I can't figure out what it is." He scrubbed his jaw with his free hand.

"Do you have ideas? You don't have to tell me. I'm sorry. I shouldn't have brought it up. It's just that my parents have always gotten along really well. We weren't raised in a house with a lot of arguing, unless it was Luke and me doing the arguing. I don't know, I think about where it might lead and I feel like a helpless kid, you know?"

He nodded. "Sometimes it's stupid stuff, Zoe. I mean, only some things are marriage breakers. That's what I think is going on with my parents."

"A marriage breaker?"

He nodded, dark eyes meeting mine. He swallowed. "I think my mom is having an affair."

"What? Oh no, how did you find out?"

"I catch pieces of things when they argue. You know, they do the typical shut-up thing when I come into the room. Or they did anyway. Now, they keep arguing."

"Like, what kind of things are they saying? Or do you want to tell me?"

He eyed me. "I haven't told anybody yet—not even Max, my brother."

I remained silent, leaving the space open for him to share his feelings.

"One day I walked in and heard Dad say, 'You and your little man-whore'." His fearful, shocked eyes met mine. "What else could that mean?"

"Yikes," I mumbled. "That's... I'm sorry." Did Brady have anything to do with Weston's parents' fights? Was his family under attack like mine, because of me? I hoped not.

Weston drove onto State Street. I was pretty sure he wasn't concentrating on where we were going to eat lunch.

"I guess I should have seen it coming. My parents go on trips and stuff, but I think it's all show. I think Dad is trying to hold onto her."

"Oh, Weston, I'm really sorry."

His shoulder lifted in feigned indifference, but I didn't miss the way his body drew tight beneath his clothes as if holding back an explosion of emotion.

He blew out a breath. "I... don't know what to do."

I reached out and laid my hand on his tense arm. "What do you think would help?"

"I'm not sure anything would help. When we're together, which isn't very often, it feels like I'm standing between two lightning rods about to get struck. I mean, there's all this angry energy, you know?"

Albert's energy felt the same way. I nodded.

"I'm afraid to interfere because they might snap—one or both of them."

"I tell my parents how I feel. Sometimes, my mouth gets me in trouble, but I say it like I see it."

"Seriously?" He laughed. "I can see you doing that."

"You should do it. What do you have to lose?"

"I don't know." We sat at a stoplight. "I wish I had your guts." He grinned, leaned and kissed me. "You're amazing," he murmured.

"You throw passes with huge guys coming at you at forty miles per hour, Weston. You can talk to your parents." His brown eyes flashed with something close to frustration. I got the impression I'd tread on his ego. "Sorry, I'll keep my mouth shut."

"You're right, I should say something." The light turned green and he drove on. "But… I'm not you, Zoe. I've never called my parents on their behavior. They'd think I was… I don't know, but I don't think they'd buy it."

"If it matters to you, and I can see that it does, you should be proactive."

He thrust his free hand back into his hair.

"Okay, I don't mean to beat the issue. They're you're parents."

"If I don't do something, will it be partly my fault if they split up? Is that what you're saying?"

"No. No. I forget not everyone is obnoxious like I am, saying everything I feel like saying. I'm getting better at keeping my mouth shut, but I'm in the habit of spouting off and I don't want to cause you or us problems, ok?"

Again he scrubbed his jaw, as if in thought, and stared out the window.

"One more thing," I piped. I could tell he was listening, but a few protective bricks had been erected since we'd started talking about this topic. "You deserve to know what's going on. You're not a kid. If something's happening, wouldn't you want to know before they dropped a huge bomb?"

He didn't respond.

"You confronting them will tell them that you're watching."

His gaze and his mind were elsewhere, in a sad place. I shouldn't press and I should definitely stop talking about it. "You still want to eat?" I asked, afraid I'd squashed his appetite.

"Sure." His tone was unenthusiastic. He pulled into the parking lot of Subway. My cell phone vibrated and I pulled it out. Dad.

"Hey."

"Zoe," his strained tone caused my heart to skip, "Abria's had a reaction to the anesthesia."

"What?"

"She's in the hospital. Get here as soon as you can."

TEN

A stinging, rough wind seemed to push us through the hospital parking lot and toward the emergency room entrance. Weston held my hand and we waited for the automatic doors to slide open. They did, and sterile air gushed at our faces. We rushed inside. I was struck by the sight of dozens of heavenly beings comforting loved ones in the waiting room, their pure luminescence filled the otherwise cold, drab space with warm light and energy. They were completely intent on providing comfort. None noticed me, even though I felt an instantaneous kinship seeing them.

I gave my name to the nurse at the desk. She eyed Weston and me. "Family only."

Weston gave my hand one last squeeze. "I'll wait out here."

The receptionist pressed a buzzer and allowed me to enter another door, to the closed off section.

A nurse led me through an open area, lined with curtained sections, some open, some closed, crowded with guardians and family of the ill. At last the nurse pulled back a curtain and Mom and Dad stood, flanking Abria's bed.

Abria lay on a stiff white-sheeted gurney. A thin, white blanket loosely covered her from the waist down. An IV bag hung at her side, its tube attached to her delicate arm. Her skin was flushed pink from the allergic reaction, and her chest had big red blotches—bruises blooming—across the fair skin where CPR had been administered. At the head of the iron bed stood Matthias, his shining countenance radiating in an orb that encircled him and Abria. His positive energy instantly relieved my fears.

His lips lifted slightly when our eyes met.

Is she going to be okay? I kept my gaze on Matthias, heart pounding in anticipation for his answer, and I moved to Mom's side. Mom's eyes met mine. I didn't see tears or redness. A good sign.

I don't know the answer to that, Zoe. Her life, like all of our lives, is in God's hands.

I bit my lip, forcing back a surge of panic, and my gaze shifted to Abria's resting form on the white sheet.

"Mom." I wrapped my arms around her. She buckled against me in a soft sob.

Dad's gentle pat on my shoulder, the scent of his cologne took my gaze to him, now standing behind Mom. His eyes glistened. Could my parents take another blow? How would they survive something as devastating as the loss of a child? They'd already had this test once—with me. I wouldn't give into fearful conclusions before reality set its foot firmly in one direction. I'd hope.

"Oh no." Luke's voice broke the fragile silence. Mom eased from my arms to turn around. Luke's stride was speedy from the ER door to the curtained area our family occupied. His face paled, his eyes locked on Abria. Though he glanced at Matthias for a moment, he was too absorbed in the sight of little Abria to pay him much notice.

"What happened?" his voice scratched.

"She had an allergic reaction. It's rare. Something like one in every three-hundred thousand people," Dad's voice tore. "She stopped breathing. They couldn't get it regulated."

"What the hell were they doing using anesthesia?" he shrieked.

"Luke." Dad placed his hands on Luke's shoulders. Luke jerked free, his face red with fury. "She'd never have let the dentist touch her unless she'd been put out."

"So they put her out for a couple of freaking cavities?"

I glanced at Matthias whose expression remained compassionate.

Luke looked ready to jump out of his skin. Dad pulled him in for a hug, but Luke didn't respond, didn't soften, just glared at Abria lying on the bed. "This is so screwed," he bit out, wrenching away from Dad.

"They're doing everything they can," Mom offered. "Every hour she's stable and breathing on her own is a good sign that she's going to be okay."

"What do they know? They're the retards who gave her the anesthesia!"

"Let's go outside for a second." I crossed to Luke and wrapped an arm around him, urging him toward the door. "Come on."

Luke tore free and stormed through the ER door. I glanced at Mom and Dad. My final sweep landed on Matthias whose eyes calmed me before I turned and took off after Luke.

Luke marched through the waiting room to the sliding glass doors. I tossed a glance at Weston who jumped to his feet. I held up my palm, indicating not to follow us. The doors groaned open and Luke went out into the frigid, windy afternoon. He paced in the load/unload area.

I wrapped my arms around myself against the bite of wind, taking in a deep breath of non-hospital air. "She's probably going to be fine," I said.

"You don't know that. No one knows that."

"Did you see Matthias? He was there."

He stopped, turned, faced me. "Yeah, I saw him." He shifted, and his gaze fell to the concrete sidewalk we stood on. "She looked so small." His voice was a frightened whisper.

I crossed to him and hugged him. His arms went around me, held tight.

"No, no, no," Albert's sarcastic tone caused my heart to leap. I broke my embrace with Luke and stood in front of him, in hopes of shielding him from Albert. Albert, in his black suit and burgundy shirt with that grotesque tie stood three feet away, his hands clasped at his lips. He shook his head, grinned. "A little hug won't appease young Luke's fury, Zoe."

"I can't believe you're here, ambulance chaser."

"Opportunist, yes."

I wanted to lunge at him and strangle him. I would have, if Luke hadn't tweaked his face at me.

"Who are you talking to?" He looked around.

Albert's gaze seemed to challenge me to admit his existence to Luke.

Whatever. I had nothing to lose. "Nothing," I savored the word, and Albert stiffened slightly as I said it.

"You seeing spirits again?" Luke queried, his tone, his demeanor shifting from agitated to curious.

"Not any worth talking about." I forced my gaze to Luke and took his hands in mine. "Let's go back in and—"

"Luke."

I turned and found Krissy hurrying across the parking lot toward us. "Is your sister okay?"

"You were with her?" I whispered to Luke.

He lifted a shoulder.

"Ah, the seductive chameleon returns." Albert clasped his hands behind his back.

"Hi Zoe. I'm so sorry to hear about Abria. Is she okay?"

"She's... we're not sure." Why had Luke brought Krissy to the hospital at a time like this?

Krissy wore her blue jumper but had her hair down around her shoulders. Instead of her usual lace up boots, her feet were clad in brown flip flops in spite of the chilly weather. Even with the fragile moment, her lips quivered, hanging in the balance of a smile she seemed unable to control.

"I hope she's okay." She lowered her head.

"Thanks for your concern," I said.

Behind Luke, Albert's grin grew. The sight burned my insides.

I opened my mouth to verbally slug him, remembered Krissy standing to my right, and snapped my lips shut.

I tugged Luke's sleeve. "We should get back inside."

"Yes, you should." Albert rocked back on his heels. "Nothing will stir the fire in Luke like seeing his little sister lying helplessly in a hospital room due to the negligence of doctors."

"You get away from us," I growled.

Krissy's eyes widened.

"Z," Luke whispered.

"I didn't mean—sorry, Krissy," I slapped my forehead. "I'm a little out of it with Abria and shock, and the smell of rubbing alcohol and everything. Brain damage." Luke's sleeve in my fist, I started for the ER doors.

Krissy followed.

So did Albert.

Inside, the spirits there to comfort loved ones snapped to attention the moment the ER doors slid closed behind us. My heart pounded. My feet came to a halt. Luke, noticing my wide-eyed stare around the waiting room, came to a stop beside me. "What?"

Weston, too, seemed to notice I was spellbound. He rose from his chair and crossed to me. "Zoe?"

At first I thought the beings gathered were staring at me. Then I realized their glowing gazes were fastened behind me. On Albert. A soft yet urgent pitch—like the hum of speechless voices—resonated through the air.

I turned for a look at Albert.

His hands hung at his sides. A look of arrogance tightened his features and his shoulders were proudly erect. Would he cause these wispy translucent beings and the guardians present to disappear with the wave of his hand?

Suddenly, the beings cocooned their charges in orbs of light. One grey-haired guardian wrapped her arms around a weeping woman for a moment. From every corner of the waiting room and down a nearby hall, they started in Albert's direction, the lemon sun color they each possessed gradually growing stronger, more heated, shooting out dynamic white rays that caused me to squint. An overpowering feeling of love pressed through my skin and filled me.

My breath stalled. Luke took Krissy's hand, and the two of them exchanged glances. Could they see what was going on? Feel it? Weston touched my elbow. "Zoe?"

As the beings' rays encompassed me, I was bathed in comfort, safety and serenity. Unease drained from my body. My pounding heart slid into a steady beat.

Albert's back was against the glass doors. The arrogance on his face had been replaced by rounded eyes and an open mouth. His stark black suit bathed in the purifying beams was bleached white. He scrambled like a sewer rat caught in a searchlight.

His arms lifted, crossed over his face in a futile effort to keep the light out, but that was impossible. The power, the piercing whiteness, the sheer love in the room was undeniable and completely inescapable.

Albert fell to his knees.

"Z?" Luke's soft whisper broke through my consciousness. I felt him at my shoulder, saw his face near mine. "Are you okay?"

"Talk to us," Weston turned me to face him, but my attention remained riveted to what was happening to Albert.

"I'm okay," the words squeaked out.

"You sure she's all right?" Krissy whispered.

I was fascinated. Awed. Spellbound. The beings gathered around Albert, closer. Closer. Some reached out to him, though there was no contact. He cowered against the door. The sight of his shame was so pathetic and horrible—so misguided—my heart ached in my chest.

Matthias stood five feet away, his blue eyes fastened on the beings surrounding his father. There was no maliciousness in the beings; rather they seemed driven to protect those they were there to comfort. No pleasure danced on their faces. Their countenances, like Matthias', radiated caring and love. A love so powerful, evil had no place anywhere near it.

Albert dissolved.

As soon as Albert was gone the beings returned to their loved ones within their protective golden orbs. The orbs opened and encompassed each party.

My gaze met Luke and Krissy's astonished faces. Weston's grip tightened on my elbow as if double checking that I was all right.

Matthias was gone.

I left Luke and Krissy and went to the buzzer-door. I pressed the button over and over. Pounded. "Let me in!" I had to find Matthias, see if he was all

91

right after seeing his father.

"Z," Luke hissed in my ear.

The nurse glared at me then allowed the door to open. I stepped through. "Only family," she barked at Krissy and Weston, who remained behind.

Luke and I wove through the busy ER. "What was that all about?" he asked.

"I'll tell you later."

We found the curtained area where we'd left Abria, Mom, Dad. And Matthias.

Mom leaned over the bed. Abria's hand, clutched in hers, was pressed against her chest. Dad stood nearly conjoined to Mom's back, his face tight in grief. Matthias stood between the wall and the headboard, his hands just above Abria's head, his head bowed, eyes closed. *Albert. I'm sorry you had to see him.*

Matthias' sharp pain of loss, regret and sadness for his father jabbed once through my soul, then was gone. His gaze lifted. *She's coming around.*

Tears of gratitude sprung from my eyes. I moved to Mom, touched her shoulder. Mom's free hand reached up and covered mine. Squeezed. Hands grabbed me. Dad. He pulled me into his side. My tears spilled onto his shoulder. "Pray she's going to make it," he said.

I nodded. "She will."

Hours dragged by. The thick scent of antiseptic stripped my senses, leaving me numb. Without sounding overzealous about Abria's recovery, I tried to comfort my parents and Luke with positive comments and plenty of hugs.

At one point during one of the many long hours, I caught Mom watching me. Curiosity filled her eyes. "Is he here?"

The question seemed to perk Dad and Luke. Luke glanced at Matthias. Mom and Dad followed his gaze.

"Yes," I said.

Mom's mouth opened a little.

"He's there." Luke nodded toward the head of the bed, where Matthias had been since the ordeal began.

Both Mom and Dad looked in Matthias' direction. Mom wiped her eyes. "Thank you," she whispered.

The compassion Matthias shed into the area was strong, and filled me. I was certain Mom and Dad felt it, too.

I let out a silent sigh and prayer, grateful that, even though Abria remained motionless, I knew she was going to be fine. That didn't change the fact that she looked delicate. So mortal. Mom didn't let go of Abria's hand, keeping it sandwiched between hers. Dad sat on a chair next to the bed. Luke sat on the tile floor with his back against one of the walls, his head in his hands. He hadn't left once.

I'd texted Weston an hour into our waiting and told him to go home. He said he'd wait, and I hadn't heard from him since. I didn't check to see if he was still out there in the lobby, the chance of missing Abria coming to consciousness too great to risk.

Doctors and nurses came and went.

Weariness crept over each of us, leaving its tiring effects in dark shadows under our eyes.

Matthias' piercing blue gaze never dulled, his body never slumped, his comfort never waned. He was an energy force I drew from as the hours crawled by.

I envied his state of existence.

Frailty is part of being mortal, Zoe. How else can we learn to appreciate good health and vitality unless we have sickness and death?

I'm too tired to argue that point with you now. Back against the wall, I slid down next to Luke who didn't stir when I plopped shoulder-to-shoulder next to him.

Matthias wrapped Abria in an orb of light, then he came to me and reached out his hand. Magnetic as a brilliant sunset, I couldn't take my eyes from his, and I accepted his outstretched support.

He drew me to my feet and his comforting touch filled me to the core, settling me.

Thank you.

He nodded. His fingers skimmed my cheek. I closed my eyes, sighed, relieved and comforted beyond expression.

Luke cleared his throat and I opened my eyes. Mom, Dad and Luke all watched me with piqued curiosity.

Abria's waking, Zoe.

Abria's right foot twitched. Then she stirred. Mom leaned close to her, gazing at my little sister's face in earnest. "Joe," Mom whispered.

Dad rose, and so did Luke. We gathered around the bed.

Abria's eyes opened, but remained heavy-lidded.

"Hello, sweet girl." Mom stroked Abria's face and Abria turned her head away from the sensation. "She's back." Mom smiled at Abria's dislike of being touched. The gray clouds in Mom's countenance shifted, replaced by a brightness that filled the room. She wrapped around Abria for a short embrace and when she sat upright, wiped tears from her eyes.

I looked at Matthias. *This could traumatize Abria.*

Don't worry. Matthias leaned over and placed a kiss on her forehead. *She won't remember.*

Some ten hours later after Abria was stable and the staff and doctors had kept a watchful eye on her, she was discharged. Dad carried her subdued little body in his arms, her head resting against his shoulder in atypical lethargy. I could hardly believe we'd spent nearly twenty-four hours in the hospital.

I went to the ER lobby, Luke dragging behind me, and was shocked to find Weston in one of the chairs, his legs stretched out, head back, eyes closed, mouth open in sleep. Two seats away Krissy was curled up like a kitten, her eyes closed, head tucked into her arms. The room was empty except for an older man sitting with his wife. I didn't see any guardians or spirits.

"Oh, man," Luke said. "I totally forgot about her."

"I can't believe she stayed," I said. "Her dad's probably got the whole PG police department out looking for her."

Luke let out a snort and started toward Krissy. "Not likely."

Curiosity piqued, I wanted him to elaborate, but I headed to Weston. I lightly nudged his rock-hard shoulder. He blinked twice then sharpened as he arched his back in a stretch, forcing his tight sweater to pull taut against his lean, chiseled chest and abs. Something in my stomach fluttered.

"Hey." His voice was low and rough. He stood. "Is she okay?"

"She's going to be, yeah. I can't believe you stayed." I touched his arm. His focus tightened on me and he stepped closer.

"And you?"

"I'm good."

His lips lifted slightly. He glanced around the room. "Was Matthias here?"

"Yeah."

"Is he still here?"

"No."

"So, that means she's okay, right?"

"Abria is fine."

Weston scrubbed his face with his hands and let out a sigh. His gaze shot over my shoulder to Luke and Krissy. "That chick's a trip."

Luke and Krissy stood—close—talking. "Not sure what's going on there," I murmured.

"She's into him, that's what's going on. Besides your sister, he's all she talked about."

"You talked to her?"

"We sat out here for, like, twelve hours. You're not jealous are you?" he teased.

"Hardly."

"She kind of reminds me of a kid. In a lot of ways she's really young, you know?"

"With her dad, I'm not surprised. Did I tell you about how he banged on our front door the other night, threatening us?"

"Seriously?"

"He's got some bolts loose upstairs. Something's weird about him. The guy's infested with black spirits."

Weston's face paled.

"Whatever's going on, I'm sure it's going on with Krissy, the way he controls her every move. It's creepy."

Weston looked at Krissy again, and his shock sharpened. "What do you think is going on?"

"Imagine the worst."

Color drained from Weston's cheeks. His gaze locked on Krissy, horror and disbelief widening his eyes. He swallowed. "It's cool Luke's her friend."

"As long as she doesn't use and dump him."

"I don't think she's a player. She's kind of backwards. Luke's smart, anyway."

I studied the two of them from across the room. Luke definitely was attentive to her. And she was to him.

I was ready to go home. I yawned. "I'm beat. I didn't sleep at all in there." I started toward Luke and Krissy and Weston followed.

"You don't look tired," Weston observed. "You look hot."

I snorted. "I guess that's something."

Luke and Krissy looked over as we neared, but neither stepped back from the other. "We're taking off," I said. "Krissy, does your dad know where you are?"

Krissy lowered her eyes. "No."

"Last time he was at our house, he threatened us," I said, trying to keep my agitation under control. If her dad knew she'd been with our family for the last twenty-four hours, he'd shoot all of us dead with a sawed-off shotgun.

Luke tilted his head at me, his blue eyes sharp. "I'm going to take her home now, so it's under control, Z."

You can't see the loathsome creeps her dad harbors. "Just be sure you drop her off a block away so her dad doesn't see your car," I suggested.

I felt Weston's hand wrap around my elbow. He tugged me toward the door.

"Luke's taking care of it," he said.

Frustration simmered in my blood, but I accompanied Weston out the glass double doors of the ER. Luke could take care of himself.

Weston kept walking in the direction of his silver truck and I remained in step with him. He studied me as though he was deciphering whether or not to say anything.

"Krissy's not out to hurt anybody, not purposefully, anyway." He unlocked the passenger side door and opened it for me.

I paused in the opening. I admired Weston for calling me on my behavior towards Krissy. No guy had ever done that.

A grin spread my lips wide and a tingle shot down my body. His gaze slipped to my mouth. He inched closer, and wrapped around me. He pressed a gentle kiss against my lips, and my arms wove around his neck. Weston's hands explored my back, trailing my waist, dipping further and lower—

Suddenly, he jerked away and the morning air cooled my lips. His wide eyes darted around and he inched back. "You sure Matthias isn't here?"

"Positive."

My answer didn't seem to ease his jitters. His gaze still swept the parking lot as if he didn't believe me. "We'd better go."

"I told you he was gone."

"Yeah, but what if he shows up? You know, because we're kissing?"

"He's not going to do that."

Weston eyed me but he didn't make a move to return to kissing. I climbed up into the cab, sighed and inwardly smirked. *Is this how it's going to be from now on? Weston afraid to touch me for fear Matthias will poof and appear?*

Something had to change.

ELEVEN

We drove home in silence, the air between us sticky, a familiar thickness that crowded me and Weston whenever Matthias was around or was the subject of conversation. How could I assure Weston that Matthias was not going to interfere with my life unless under the calling of guardian? I could hardly blame him for being jumpy. Matthias had indeed stepped in once and stopped what had promised to be a seriously hot make out session between us. That was when I'd admitted to Weston I saw spirits.

The news had taken some time for him to digest, but he believed. And I loved that about him. His faith in me bound us together more deeply than I'd been bound to any other person besides my family. And Matthias.

"This can't come between us." I wanted to clear the murky air.

He scrubbed his jaw. "It's hard."

I laid my hand on his thigh. His sharp gaze shot there, then to my face before returning to the road.

"Careful," he said, voice gravelly.

Butterflies swarmed in my belly. "Just making myself clear."

"Making me hot is more like it," he said.

"That too."

He took a deep breath and sighed. He turned onto my street and parked the truck at the curb. No sign of Luke's Samurai. After shutting off the engine, he faced me. My pulse skittered, anticipating a continuation from where we left off in the hospital parking lot.

A minute ticked by.

He opened his door and got out, and my anticipation deflated. He rounded the hood of the truck, his dark gaze pinning me through the front windshield. I followed him until he reached my door and swung it open.

Seconds passed. He shifted. "I better get home."

I climbed down, my ego a little bruised.

He shut the door and slowly walked with me up the pathway to the house. When we reached the porch he stopped a good five feet from the door, his hands stuffed into the front pocket of his jeans.

He leaned forward and placed a kiss on my cheek, pausing, his warm breath heated my skin. "Bye, Zoe."

His tone was so cryptic. What did he mean?

I watched him return to his truck, get inside and drive off, my heart fumbling in my chest.

The front door shut behind me and I whipped out my cell phone. Texted Weston: *r u ok?*

yeah

u sure?

yeah just tired

k

Hadn't we all just spent the last twenty-four hours in the hospital? I felt a little better believing he was simply tired.

Mom and Dad's voices drifted down the stairs in low murmurs. I headed up.

The door to Abria's bedroom was open, and I rounded the corner and peered in. Abria lay tucked in her bed. Mom sat on one side, Dad on the other. Mom hovered over my sister. Behind Mom stood Aunt Janis, her radiant glow spilling onto Mom's body. Aunt Janis stroked Mom's head as she would a child.

Aunt Janis smiled at me. "Zippy, how are ya, honey?"

I opened my mouth to reply, and stopped, stepping into the room. "How is she?"

"Your mother's a wreck but I'm workin' on her."

"She's so docile," Mom answered quietly, petting Abria's hands. It was strange seeing Abria so passive. She never *let* anyone comfort her. I imagined the moment was bittersweet for my parents, wanting to savor the ironic experience.

Dad glanced at me. "Is Weston with you?"

I crossed to the foot of the bed, trying not to glance at Aunt Janis and not wanting to ignore her at the same time. "No. He dropped me off and went home."

Dad nodded. "He seems like a nice young man."

"He stayed at the hospital the whole time?" Mom looked up at me and I caught the red rimming her eyes.

"Um, yeah."

"Was that Krissy I saw in the waiting room?" Dad asked.

"Yeah."

Dad's brows drew together. The late night and Abria's hospital stay had already taken a toll on him, leaving him pale and shadowed beneath his green eyes. I hated that he looked concerned now—for Luke.

"I take it her dad knew where she was?" he asked.

"He probably did," I said, though Krissy had said no. I glanced at Aunt Janis, gauging whether or not she knew anything about Krissy's situation.

Aunt Janis didn't react, only remained intent and focused on comforting Mom. "You have got to loosen up, Deb. Have some faith. Your little girl is gonna be just fine," she cooed.

Mom let out a sigh, then leaned over and kissed Abria's head. Abria didn't resist, or push her away; she lay quietly and closed her eyes.

"Maybe I should rest in here with her," Mom said, her voice weary.

"That's my job," Aunt Janis piped, placing her hands just over the top of Mom's head. Aunt Janis closed her eyes and the light illuminating her intensified for a moment, seeming to rush into Mom, cocooning her like I'd seen the beings at the hospital administer to their charges.

"You need to rest," Dad said.

"Yeah," I added. "Abria's out. Let her sleep."

"What if she needs me?" Mom asked.

"I'll be here for her." Aunt Janis' soothing voice seemed to transcend barriers. Mom's countenance lightened and she took in a deep breath as she stared at her sleeping child.

Dad rose and came around the foot of the bed, then gently urged Mom to her feet. "She's going to be fine. Time for you to take a nap."

Aunt Janis smiled, nodded.

"Maybe I will lie down for a little bit," Mom conceded, glancing at the window. The late morning sun creeped up the eastern sky, its orange rays spilling over the mountain peaks.

Dad wrapped his arm around her and ushered her to the door. "We all need to take naps," he said with a glance at me.

"You're right." But I wanted to talk to Aunt Janis. "I'm gonna kiss Abria then take one of my own."

Mom leaned her head on Dad's shoulder as they walked down the hall toward their bedroom. Once they were behind their closed bedroom door, I returned to Abria's room. Aunt Janis smiled.

"You wanted to talk, Zippy?"

"It's Zoe," I teased.

"I know." She waved a hand at me. "Listen, your Mom needs a break. I know you help her, and that's wonderful. Encourage her to have more faith, Zoe. Like you."

"I'll do what I can," I said. "Where's Matthias?"

Her bright countenance softened to a marshmallowy glow and her eyes twinkled. "He really is special, isn't he?"

"I didn't see him after his... father showed up at the hospital. Is he all right?"

"You don't have to worry about Matthias, honey." Aunt Janis crossed to me, her nearness warming. "He's one of the strongest souls I've ever met."

Of course Matthias was all right. But had seeing his father hurt him? "I just—Albert is so awful… I didn't want Matthias to be sad or hurt."

"Don't you trouble yourself over this."

"But I care about him. His father's such a loser, I can't—"

"Tsk-tsk." Aunt Janis shook her head. "How can the bad ever be good if we don't have faith in them?"

I snickered. "Have you ever seen or been near Albert?"

"I haven't, but every soul deserves hope, Zoe."

"But he's so far gone it's…" *Sad.* No wonder Matthias didn't want to give up on him—his family. His blood. "Do you know anything about Matthias' mother?"

"Not a thing." Aunt Janis glanced at Abria. "Your mother and Abria are resting now, so I'll be on my way." She brightened. "Good to see you again. Take that nap, you've got circles under your eyes." She pointed with a teasing gleam and then, in a flash of white, was gone.

Abria remained asleep in her bed. I sunk to the mattress and sighed. Kissed Abria's cheek. She didn't stir. I lay down next to her and focused on the soft rise and fall of her chest, allowing the movement to gradually drain the adrenaline from my body. The smell of her, the very fact that she was alive and well and breathing next to me cradled my weary soul.

The far-off slam of the front door jolted me. It had to be Luke. I didn't want him to awaken Mom, Dad or Abria. I stood and tip-toed out of Abria's bedroom, shutting the door behind me.

I went down the stairs, any welcome relaxation I'd invited watching Abria sleep vanished with each step closer to the kitchen. Luke had his head in the freezer side of the refrigerator.

"Hey," I said. "Everybody's napping so if you could be super quiet it'd be—"

He pulled out a bag of peas, shut the door, and my breath caught. His eye was blotched red and purple.

TWELVE

I crossed to him. "What happened?"

"Damned psycho," he mumbled, placing the bag of peas over his blackening eye.

"Krissy's dad?" Anger rushed through my veins. "Did he do that?"

Luke's hands shook. Either he was fuming or whatever had happened between him and Krissy's dad had scared him.

"I took Krissy home and was going to drop her off a block away, like I usually do. The goon appeared out of nowhere. He must have been hiding in some neighbor's bushes or something because he stormed up to the car and pounded on my hood. Scared the hell out of us. Then he ripped open the door and yanked Krissy out of the car by her hair. By her hair! Like some effing caveman! Who does that?" He shifted, and readjusted the bag of peas over his eye.

"I got out of the car and told him off, the freak, which of course he didn't stand for. But I don't care, I had to. The guy is so effed up it's ridiculous. He freaking dragged Krissy down the street by her hair. I told him to stop and he shoved me back. I jumped him and—"

"You jumped him?"

"I wasn't going to let that moron treat her like that. I had to do something," Luke hissed. "He's...he's..."

"What?" I demanded.

Luke avoided my gaze, left me and crossed to the family room couch where he plopped into the cushions.

"He assaulted you. I'm calling the police."

"No!" Luke bolted to his feet.

"Why?" Every nasty and grotesque image I'd imagined about Krissy's dad flashed through my head. "Did he threaten you too? You know better than to listen to someone like that. People like him live off threats, Luke. That's how they control their victims. Are you going to let him control you now?"

"I certainly hope so," Albert's smooth voice came at me from my right. He leaned against a wall, hands in the pockets of his suit. I took a deep breath to calm myself, but the underlying violation I felt on behalf of Luke remained—a low current I hoped to squelch before it revved out of hand.

"It's not me I'm worried about, it's her," Luke said. "What he'll do to her."

I faced Luke, keeping Albert's image behind me. "Did she tell you what's going on?"

Luke's pale-faced discomfort told me that he probably knew exactly what was going on, but was afraid—or too shocked and disgusted to say. Did I even want to know the truth?

"He's sexually abusing her, isn't he?" My heart stopped, waiting for him to confirm what I had long believed was going on between Krissy and her Dad. Albert moved into my line of vision, his eerie presence pressing into my side with ominous foreboding.

Luke froze. "She told you?"

My gut twisted knowing the truth. "No. I figured as much. I told you, the man has black spirits crawling all over him."

"Yeah, well, he should be in jail."

I whipped out my cell phone. "And he will be, now that he hit you."

Luke lunged for my phone and I darted back. Albert applauded and moved closer to us. "You're not calling the police," Luke snapped. He wrenched my phone out of my hand.

"Give that to me!"

"Can't. You don't know what this will do to her."

"You mean save her from more abuse? I can't see how calling the police

104

won't help." I thrust my open palm at him. "Give me my phone."

"Ah, sibling arguments." Albert rocked back on his heels. "There's nothing more destructive to the delicate weave of the family unit."

"Shut. Up!"

"Screw you!" Luke turned, shoved my phone into his pocket and headed for the freezer.

"Zoe, you never disappoint," Albert commented, like a sportscaster commentating a UFC. "You're a master at—"

Ignore him, ignore him. "I wasn't talking to—look, if I promise not to call the cops will you give me my phone?"

Luke eyed me. "You have to promise, Z. I promised her I wouldn't and I can't go back on it."

He looked so determined and fiercely protective, my heart softened. "Only if you tell me everything."

He shook his head. "Forget it."

I headed for the house phone. "Then I report the assault."

"Crap, Zoe, you're such an idiot sometimes." He threw my phone across the room and I grabbed it.

"He hit you!" I squeezed the cell phone in my fists. "And you're going to let him get away with it? You're going to let him continue to rape her?"

Luke shuddered. "Don't say it like that."

"That's what it is, isn't it?"

"She just told me about it," his voice rose. "What kind of ass would I be if I turned around and snitched on her?"

"You're not snitching on her Luke, you're saving her. He's going to continue to molest her until he's locked up."

He averted his eyes. Luke headed for the couch and fell onto it with a moan, turning the bag of frozen peas over on his blackening eye.

I joined him at the couch but remained standing, too angry to relax. Albert slowly moved closer. I shot him a warning glare to keep his distance which he, of course, disregarded. "Call the cops," Albert hissed. "Call them."

"She's so sweet…" Luke's voice softened. "She doesn't deserve this."

Luke rested his head on the cushion and closed his eyes. "You know those people you connect with right away? You feel it, inside. She's one of those people."

I bit my lower lip. Luke's feelings for Krissy were deeper than I thought. I tried not to be alarmed. I didn't know how much time Luke had spent with Krissy, but whatever the time had been, their association had made an impact on him. Of the two of us, it was Luke who'd brought home the occasional stray animal, tried to save dying baby birds and couldn't bear killing a grasshopper. His caring heart was big and tender, a characteristic he'd tried to cover up with drug abuse, unable to deal with his natural gift of compassion.

Albert stood to the side of the couch as if waiting for Luke or me to explode again so he could jump on the rocket of fireworks.

"For all the crap she's lived with," Luke went on, his voice drained of anger now, "she's amazingly innocent."

"How did she get around to telling you about… everything?" I sat down next to him.

"I don't want to talk about it. I'll just get angry again."

"Oh, do ask him for more details," Albert piped with enthusiasm. "He doesn't need much to be pushed over the edge."

"As if you'd know."

Luke stared at me, then bolted to his feet, started for the stairs. "I'm sick of your talking."

"I'm sorry," I blurted. "I need to tell you something. Luke?" He ignored me. "Luke, stop for a second and listen to me."

"I'm done here."

I clenched my teeth. "What are you going to tell Mom and Dad when they ask you about your eye?"

He was halfway up the stairs. "That you slugged me."

I ground my teeth. Luke's bedroom door slammed and I turned my fury on Albert. "Get out!"

"I'm growing rather fond of your family."

"Why? Because you lost your own?" I marched closer to him, ignoring flashes of warning in my head to keep distance between us.

Albert's shoulders lifted. "Family is overrated. Female companionship… now that's something else altogether. Ask Matthias."

"Liar." What I didn't know about Matthias' life and loves stung, a pinch I felt afresh any time I thought about it. So I fought thinking about it. I should have known Albert would bring up Matthias. "I think you hang around here because you want what you can't have. It's sick, yes, but that's you. A sick, voyeuristic opportunist who leeches what he will never get. By the way, what happened to you at the hospital?" I cocked a brow at him.

Albert's gaze hardened.

A sudden shock of energy sucked every last ounce of oxygen from the air. I couldn't breathe. Mouth gaping, heart pounding, my gaze connected with Albert's. Fear paralyzed my limbs. My heart raced like a butterfly caught in a jar. Panic took hold of my soul until warm heat pressed into my back.

Rays of light bathed me from behind, and every muscle in my body loosened. Albert's gaze shifted to something behind me. Matthias. I felt him, and knew he was there without needing to confirm with a look.

"Leave." His serene voice filled the room.

Albert's nostrils flared. His sharp gaze remained fixed over my shoulder. A second passed, then he dissolved before my eyes.

I turned and flung myself into Matthias' arms.

"Zoe."

"I know, I know. I got carried away. I—I'm sorry."

His hand stroked my hair. "Please don't entertain him again."

"Entertain?" I choked out. "I was hardly entertaining him."

He stepped back, cupping my face. "You know what I am talking about. You enable him by confronting him."

I nodded, grasping his wrists and closing my eyes. I savored his nearness. "I couldn't talk." My throat felt like Albert's hands were wrapped around the tender flesh. "I've never been so scared."

"Remember, he can't touch you. He uses fear because it paralyzes. It's much easier to capture a frozen soul than a moving one."

"So I just need to not be afraid of him." I swallowed. "He can't make me do anything. He can't."

Matthias nodded. "Now you're on the trolley."

"It sounds easy but it's so hard." Staring hell in the face was the most terrifying thing I'd ever done, and I was doing it over and over again, facing Albert. I should be getting better at it.

Matthias' thumb grazed my chin. "You're..." His soothing tone softened, he swallowed. "Amazing."

"He keeps bringing up you...and women." My voice faltered. *Please don't think I'm weak, wondering about your past. Please.*

Matthias closed his eyes for a moment. I searched his expression, my heart trembling. "What happened?"

My mind flashed with pretty painted faces, women laughing.

"That's your imagination, not my memory," Matthias spoke in earnest. "Zoe, my life, those choices I made, the people I knew...they're part of a past I don't care to dwell on."

Faint images ghosted through my mind. One in particular—a woman with dark hair cropped to her chin—chestnut eyes, huge and beguiling, appeared for only a flash and then vanished. I wanted to see more of her. Who was she?

Matthias' strong palms gripped my shoulders. "Have you done things you're not proud of?"

"Of course."

"Once you've put them behind you, you want them behind you."

"I know, but if there was something about me you really wanted to know, I'd tell you."

His blue eyes dove deeper into mine, so deep, so questioning I almost turned my face away, ashamed. How could I demand something of him he clearly wanted to keep private and protect me from?

His grip on my shoulders lightened. "Contrary to my father's insistence, I was not the man about town he claims. After my mother left us, he was hard boiled, finding solace with any Jane who came along. Whereas my taste was more… dangerous."

"Dangerous?"

Again, the face flashed across my mind: innocent doe-eyes, short dark hair, red pouty lips.

"Who was she?"

Matthias' steady gaze held mine in unblinking dissection of my soul.

Why are you doing this to him? "Forget it," I said. "I'm sorry. You're right. I shouldn't make you share something that obviously brings you pain."

"It's not pain. I don't want you hurt over a phantom."

I stepped away, a sliver of cold unworthiness cutting into me. "I'll try not to think about you and your… past."

But even as I said the words, I waited for more memories. The face… such captivating eyes. Whoever she was, she was beautiful. Jealousy sprang into my system like a wildcat on the hunt. *Stop this.*

"She's someone who doesn't matter anymore." His hands once again rested on my shoulders.

"Where is she?"

Any suspicion still prowling through me was momentarily satiated by the look of grim finality pulling his features taut. Still, curiosity scratched away at every catty female part of me that, in spite of his angelic nature, continued nipping at me.

"Well," I tried smiling, hoping to lighten the mood I'd hefted like a log between us, "as long as she's not up in heaven tempting you."

"The only sheba tempting me is you."

Images of women crawling all over Matthias lodged in my brain. Like a celebrity mobbed by adoring fans, the women in my fantasy clawed at his clothes, kissed his face and ripped into him with lusty desire. Worse was the image that he smiled, had that lulled, aroused expression as if he enjoyed the adulation. The images shamed me. I couldn't meet Matthias' gaze. Surely, he saw the scene.

I moved away, turned, giving him my back. I closed my eyes and willed the images not to grow more sordid. But Albert's suggestion that Matthias had savored women in his life planted wretched seeds that now sprung wild pictures of tangled bodies lusting after one another.

No, no, no. Supercalifragilisticexpialidocious. I repeated the phrase over and over. But the pictures remained, winding on an endless loop of sweaty nakedness. I kept my back to him.

"Zoe." His soft voice penetrated the licentious show in my head.

I swallowed. "I'm sorry. I'm human."

"He's doing this to you."

How could I be sure the images in my head weren't Matthias'? We could read each other's thoughts, after all. They had to be his. Had to be. A shot of anger bolted through me that he'd recalled the memories, let alone lived them. I turned. Stared. Tried to decipher.

After all this time, don't you think I have more control than that? And I'd never lie to you.

Another slug of shame hit me in the stomach but was replaced by an overwhelming cloud of distrust. "Sure, you have control but that doesn't mean it didn't happen—and the fact that you won't talk about it means you have something to hide."

Matthias' crystal blue eyes narrowed. "That's Albert, Zoe."

Fear scurried through my veins. I didn't want Albert here, and I most definitely did not want him slipping inside and taking me over because I was turning into some crazy female. What was happening to me?

I grabbed my head, sunk to the mattress and let out a groan. Matthias was right. I knew he was right. But I wanted to satisfy the craving I had inside to know his past. I wanted to see that woman. Know about their relationship. Teenage girls thrived off gossip like hard candy, slowly sucking each morsel for detail.

I took a deep breath. *I can think about you and other women without Albert influencing me. I can get beyond this.*

Silence.

I turned, looked up at him. A slice of trepidation cut across his face. What did it mean?

I can, can't I?

Silence. Emptiness. His beautiful eyes that had given me comfort with just a look so many times before, now stared into mine. Fear and doubt cut me wide open.

This can't be happening. I can't doubt you. Tears filled my eyes. Matthias knelt before me, his blue eyes deepening to midnight. He took my hands in his. "Look at me."

Don't take your eyes from mine.

I won't. Please. Don't let Albert do this to me.

Matthias' grip tightened around my hands. *I can be here for you, but you have to choose, Zoe, whether or not to believe me.*

I do believe you. At least I had. Why was I questioning now? My mind seemed possessed. *He's hiding this from you because it's the truth and no matter how ugly it is, the truth is that he was with other women. What you saw in your head is truth. No it's not. Don't be stupid. He's an angel.* Anger started like a fire racing from my toes up my legs, filling my body.

Disgusted, I pushed to my feet. Walked away. Breath heaved in. Out. Nerves wound tight. Tighter. I wanted to scream. I closed my eyes. *I can't be around you right now.*

His power radiated behind me like an inferno. If I turned around, I could touch it. I could try again to look into his eyes and glean some of his soothing comfort.

He's not telling you the truth because the truth is exactly what you thought it would be, Zoe. Women. Lots of women. Sex. Intimacy. Nausea filled my throat. I swallowed.

Zoe, your heart—

My head was at war with itself. *He loves you. You know he does. Why are you doing this to yourself? It's not like you haven't had your share of guys, you can hardly judge him.*

"Zoe." Matthias' touch on my shoulders caused me to start. His comfort wafted through my body. "See this for what it is—Albert's efforts to hurt you."

Of course that was what it was. Knowing that didn't remove the resentment lingering in my blood, or wipe the graphic images of my own creation from my mind.

"Maybe you should leave." The words left my tongue with the bitterness of profanity.

Matthias turned me to face him, his palms anchored to my shoulders. "I'll stay until you're convinced that you're all that matters to me."

"I hate being human," I mumbled, grasping his hands. Our fingers linked at my shoulders.

Matthias took in a deep breath. "I'm sorry."

Afraid he might think I didn't want him in my life anymore, I pulled his hands from my shoulders so our hands gripped tight, and brought us chest-to-chest. "I don't really mean that." I wanted him in my life no matter the cost. I'd spend the rest of my life fighting Albert's influence if it drove me to death.

The sober look on his face told me the unending nature of Albert's assault might do just that. "I don't care what Albert tries to do," I said. "You're not leaving me."

His fingers left my hands to trace my face. "He'll tear you apart, and that will…" *tear me apart.*

"I won't let him. I won't. I'm sorry I thought those stupid thoughts. I shouldn't have."

He took me to the edge of my bed, set his hands again on my shoulders and gently eased me down so that we both sat facing each other. "This is where he's going to dig. Here. With this. He's going to continue bringing up my past because he knows it will hurt you the most."

The very idea tired me, and it had only begun.

Matthias cradled my hands in his. "Her name was Violet."

His clear gaze was as true as it had always been. Why hadn't I siphoned it moments ago? How could I have let Albert's influence linger even a moment in my soul, creating frustration, feeding weakness?

My heart thrummed in my chest. *Violet.* The woman's face came into my mind. Pale, flawless skin. Enormous brown eyes. Parted ruby lips. Matthias' expression stiffened a little, like even speaking her name caused him discomfort.

"Stop," I blurted. "I don't have to know anything else."

"Her father was Pop's rival." His voice remained controlled. Factual. I searched his eyes for emotion—old love, pain, regret—anything. But the discomfort I'd just seen was gone and nothing else surfaced. "I thought I loved her. I thought she loved me, but I found out later that she…did not."

Gravity thickened the air. Did he know that his grip had closed tighter around my fingers? Matthias glanced at our joined hands and his hold loosened.

"She was a bad seed, Zoe," he said. "A mistake for me."

"I'm sorry." *Did she hurt you? How long did you love her? Did you sleep with her?*

"I don't want Albert using her to get to you in any way, so… I'll answer your questions." *Prepare yourself for the answers.*

My palms began to sweat on the brink of having my curiosity satiated.

"Yes, she hurt me. But only because we were young and not smart. We both knew better than to fall for the enemy. I suppose she craved Jack's attention as much as I craved Pop's."

Images shifted through my mind spottily then: Violet holding my hand, leading me through the dark smoky makeshift bar in the church basement I'd seen before when I'd ventured into Matthias' memory.

Music fills my head. Someone's playing Scott Joplin from a ratty old piano in the corner. Couples dance. The stuffy air is thick with alcohol and perfume.

I feel Violet's small, warm, hand in mine, leading me to a tiny space in the raucous crowd. I'm wearing the same suit I wear the night of my death. The same shiny shoes. In fact, one look around this bawdy place and I know I've been in this memory before.

Hours later.

Someone bumps into my left shoulder. "'Scuse me, Matty." The robust voice belongs to Junior Cracciola—the man who will kill me. But this moment, I only know him as a friend.

And brother to Violet.

Violet's gaze lingers on Junior and the brown color in her eyes flashes with something. Her head tilts slightly in that way that sends a tremor of excitement racing through my gut. Does she want me to leave with her? Take her home?

We remain in the smoke-filled room and any questions I have about Violet and the secret look she shares with her brother I dismiss the moment she slips her arms up around my neck and pulls me close. The softness of her body against mine, the way she sways with me—slow like rich molasses—even though the music taps in my ears at a cheery pace, causes my mind to empty of all thoughts but her.

Violet's gaze holds me captive. Her mesmerizing brown eyes seem depthless, and I see something in them as Zoe, something that Matthias didn't see in them that fateful night all those years ago. Betrayal.

I looked at Matthias, staring off, his face stark with realization.

"She set you up," I murmured.

No anger or hurt passed over his countenance. Only realization. Understanding. Then his blue eyes widened and as my words hit home, his face shifted to horror. His gaze met mine.

Albert hadn't been the one to send him to his death. Violet and Junior had arranged it. Albert had been an unwitting accomplice.

Matthias closed his eyes a moment, his hands, holding mine, stilled. He swallowed. The silence in the air was dense, heavy with lament. My heart plummeted to my feet. Sorrow wound through my limbs, nearly causing me to crumple in grief.

You pushed him to tell you. You and your curiosity couldn't leave things alone. You had to ask, had to know.

Anguish scored Matthias' face. *Zoe.*

"I'm sorry I asked. I'm sorry I wanted to know."

"I wouldn't have understood what had really happened if I hadn't seen it through your eyes. You saw something I didn't. I'm…grateful."

But you hurt. I'm sorry. I don't want you to hurt. What have I done?

You've shown me the truth. He rose to his feet and crossed to the window, looking out. *How could I have ever thought he would do that?* He shook his head and bowed it.

Pressed to comfort him, I joined him at the window and laid my hand on his shoulder. His reassurance swelled through me, and I took in a tremulous breath, infused with joy and peace and everything wonderful he provided me as my guardian.

What can I do for you?

He laid his hand over mine and squeezed. *This revelation has brought me unspeakable comfort, Zoe.*

He turned, looked into my eyes and all traces of the sorrow I'd seen moments ago at the news, was gone. I admired his ability to quickly come to terms with such things.

"Part of my refinement," he murmured, smiling.

"Lucky." I felt stronger knowing the truth, layering yet another coat of armor over me so I was better prepared to face Albert.

"Regardless of what actually happened that night, Albert lies, and he'll continue to. There weren't multiple women. I was too… oh, I don't know… lame, as you say."

A small laugh escaped my tight chest. He smiled, lifting the mood instantly. "I think Pop was ashamed I wasn't more like him. A ladies man. But that wasn't me."

"She was the only girl you liked? In your whole life?"

"Well, no." He chuckled. "When I was six I had a mad crush on this girl I met in one of the boarding houses we frequented. Her mother ran the place. Her name was Ginny Birk."

"I want to get in your head and see everything about your life."

He touched my cheek. "Someday you can know those things. If you want to, you can see it all."

"Why do I have to wait? And what about our connection? I want to know more about that."

"I've told you what I know. You and I will be together someday."

"How do you know that, anyway?"

He lowered his head a moment, closed his eyes. Was he praying? Angry at me?

Not angry, Zoe. I love you, remember that. His eyes lifted to mine. My heart fluttered. "When I first saw you, I felt something deep down awaken. Like a memory."

His conviction spoke to my soul like it had so many times before. A conviction that wiped away my need for immediate understanding, replacing that need with total acceptance that at some point, my questions would have answers.

I wrapped around him, and his arms surrounded me. "Albert should leave me alone now," I said, vowing to not let Albert's smear campaign get to me. I wanted to protect Matthias from Albert's intent to destroy him. "You don't deserve this." I let out a sigh against his shoulder, then eased back and gazed into his eyes. How could anyone want to hurt him? Albert's hate didn't compute in my head.

"You're years ahead in your ability to love and forgive." Matthias' warm hands cupped my cheeks. "Apply that to each soul you come into contact with and you'll have everyone you meet eating out of the palm of your hand."

Every soul? But that thought, though automatic because we were discussing Albert, was outrageous.

Matthias took a deep breath and gazed away.

Even Albert.

Had I heard his wish or was that my own mind giving me the suggestion? Matthias' gaze remained off somewhere, and suddenly my head filled with images.

I'm lying in a bed. The room is dark, but a window at the end of the space lets in a slice of white moonlight that illuminates the room in a knife of light. The ceiling is pitched, slatted. The room is lined with beds, filled with people, sleeping. In spite of bitter cold air a strong, pungent odor fills my nose: sweat, body odor, dust.

Someone shares the bed with me. I recognize the body instantly: Pop. He lies beside me, his warmth; his strong frame nestled against mine.

"Matty," his voice is a low whisper.

"Yes, sir?" My voice—Matthias'—is small, light, youthful.

"You sleepy?"

It's hard to sleep, even though I'm bone tired. I itch from head to toe, am dirty and have nearly forgotten the smell of my own bed. My stomach growls. "No sir."

Pop shifts and the bed waves beneath us, squeaking. I wish he'd put his arm around me like Mama used to, but he doesn't. He does pull the stinky blanket up around me though, like Mama did when she tucked me in. A memory I can barely conjure.

"There." He secures the blanket around my shoulders.

"Do you have some?" *Won't he be cold?*

"I don't need any. I've got you."

I feel better hearing this, and a smile fills my lips for a moment. He needs me after all.

"Matty," his voice is soft.

"Yes, sir?"

"This is the last time we sleep in one of these places, I promise."

I am relieved but wonder where we will sleep tomorrow night if not in a boarding house? I hate sleeping in the train station; the conductors always discover us and kick us out. The alleys are worse: cold, wet and the rats like to chew on our shoes and gloves.

I don't say anything.

"I promise," he says again.

"Yes, sir."

His hand strokes my head and my heart jumps. A hunger—one I am well familiar with, but not a hunger for food—ignites in my soul at his touch. One stroke is all he gives me.

He shifts behind me, shivering, while I lay under the smelly blanket.

My eyes met Matthias'. He looked at me like a little boy, with questions—old questions—haunting his gaze.

I should have figured Albert hadn't been all bad. He was Matthias' father after all. But I'd seen so few memories of him through Matthias, less than sterling moments in Albert's life; I hadn't stopped to consider that, like all mortals, Albert had both good and bad qualities.

"You really do think he's redeemable, don't you?" Awe lined my tone. The disbelief I'd carried inside about Albert being a savable soul was slowly being replaced by the faintest hope that Matthias' faith in the power of love and forgiveness was applicable even to someone like Albert.

"It's my fault the poor memories popped into my head." Matthias' voice was soft. "And you saw them."

"So?" I tightened my arms around him. "I love you. I want to know everything about you, good and bad."

"Bad isn't worth spending even a second on, Zoe."

"Yes, but you know all about me. The good, the bad and the ugly." I smiled.

His finger tapped my nose. "Ugly? Not hardly. My mortal life is over. Your vision is only via the memories that come into my head. That's that."

"That sucks."

"Nevertheless," he grinned, "that's the way it is."

"Yeah, yeah, yeah, pfooey."

His gaze dropped to my mouth. "Say that again."

"Pfooey?"

"Slower," he said, voice low and gentle.

"Pfo-oey."

"I like the way your lips move when you say that," he whispered against my mouth, then kissed me.

My head spun, and my body felt like it levitated from the floor.

What am I going to do with you, Zoe?

Love me. Like I love you.

That's already done.

Are you sure it's okay for me to kiss you?

He eased back, breaking the kiss with a laugh. My cell phone vibrated in my pocket. I ignored it, content to remain in Matthias' embrace, staring into the horizon of his blue eyes.

"Isn't that your Alexander Graham Bell contraption?" he asked.

I laughed. "Um, yes."

"May I?"

I pulled it out of my pocket and handed it to him, forgiving him for his electronic distraction during a romantic moment. He examined it, blinked when it vibrated, and opened it, staring at the screen.

"I believe Luke is ringing you."

I took the phone and clicked it on. "Hey."

"Zoe... something happened."

THIRTEEN

I drove the minivan to Kiwanis Park where Luke told me to meet him, ironically, the same park where I'd lost Abria and first seen Matthias. Early evening was settling into Utah County, and the towering mountains surrounding the valley cast imposing, dark purple shadows across the valley floor in jagged, devouring shapes.

Matthias sat silently in the front seat next to me. Was he thinking about Albert? I wondered if he knew about Krissy's dad. Did his refined powers, his station as a guardian, allow him to know about everything and everyone in my life? How deep did his knowledge go?

"I sense things," he said. We shared a look across the darkening inside of the van. "Being refined doesn't make one omniscient. But, yes, I do understand things that pertain to you or Abria. I receive enlightenment."

"So, do you know what the deal is with Krissy's dad?"

"The deal?"

"That he's a sicko perv loser who molests his daughter."

Matthias stared straight ahead out the window. Seconds passed in dense silence. The corner of his jaw twitched. "She's lucky to have found Luke."

"I don't want Luke to get hurt, though," I said, wondering what Matthias' 'enlightenment' was on the subject.

"Zoe." He tilted his head at me, kindness in his eyes. "Luke's going to be all right."

But her dad's a psycho. I sighed, drove on. *Trust. Have trust.* Luke hadn't said anything more to me on the phone except that something had happened and I needed to meet him at the park.

"Why do some people do stuff like that?" I asked. Matthias had been vehemently infuriated by Brady and Weston's attempt to assault me, and he'd as much as said that anyone who harmed a child was culpable.

"Even in my current state of being," he began, "it's difficult for me to comprehend why one human seeks to hurt another. The only absolute I take comfort in is that, one day, justice will be served."

"I agree, but how does that help someone like Krissy now? How do you help someone with scars that deep?"

"You begin with good friends like Luke. And you. Whatever Krissy faces in the future, you and Luke can offer her the support she will need to make it through."

"No pressure or anything."

Matthias' strength reached out, wrapped around me and infused me with palpable hope. The wave of strength poured into me, like water in a vase, filling me completely. "You can do it, and so can Luke."

I pulled into the parking lot skirting the fringe of the park. Luke's blue Samurai sat between two spots, the driver's door left open as if he'd been in a hurry. My stomach dropped to my feet. I parked the minivan.

I opened the door and, by the time my feet hit the pavement, Matthias was already by my side. "How do you do that?" I chided him, my pace picking up speed as we crossed the grass.

"All it takes is a thought."

"Some of us have to work to get where we want to go," I quipped.

"A true statement for us all, sassy bearcat." His gaze left mine and focused on something in the park. Luke.

He stood about thirty feet away, his skin pale, his purple and black eye like spilled ink on snow. A sober expression tightened his face— the same way he'd looked at Brady's funeral. My heart began a slow, fearful pound. I started in his direction and Matthias stayed with me.

"What's going on?" I asked Luke as we approached.

He jittered like he was choking on snakes. "Krissy…" He dragged his hands down his face. He looked at Matthias. "You're here."

Matthias nodded.

"That's... good," Luke observed.

"Battle scar?" Matthias pointed to his own eye, nodding in reference to Luke's injury.

"Yeah." Luke's blue eyes dipped for a moment.

"What happened? Is Krissy all right?" I asked.

"She's... man... this is bad, Z. She was with her dad, you know? And... she got home and she... hit him. She thinks he's dead."

"What?"

Luke nodded. "It just happened. Just now."

"Where is she?"

Luke jerked his head in the direction of the pavilion. "Over there."

Luke led us to where Krissy sat behind a red brick wall, crouched, trembling, sobbing. Next to her, with his arms around her, was her guardian. He looked up at us and his eyes sparkled when he saw Matthias.

The putrid scent of vomit filled the air. The mess covered her jumper and shirt.

I knelt next to her and Luke joined me. He lightly touched her shoulder. "Krissy..."

"I... I... I..." Words tumbled out of her mouth, mushy incoherent sentences. Her guardian continued embracing her, his face kind and compassionate. Did Luke see him?

Luke's attention was completely riveted on Krissy; I doubted he could see the other guardian. "Krissy, Zoe's here," Luke's tone was gentle. "We're going to help you."

What should I say? I have no idea what to tell her. I couldn't imagine what she was feeling: terror, fear and relief at the same time?

Krissy's sobs began to subside. Finally, she let out a tremulous breath and lifted her emotionally bludgeoned face to mine. A long, belt-wide welt rose from the skin on her cheek and down the side of her neck. Blood oozed from her nose, mixing with the snot and vomit dribbling down her chin.

"I... I couldn't take it anymore," she hiccupped, her hands wringing each other over and over and over.

I nodded, stroking her arm. "I know." I couldn't say 'it's okay.' How could I know if it was okay?

"I think I killed him," she whispered.

Luke and I exchanged glances. "You don't know for sure?" I asked.

She shook her head, wiped beneath her nose with the blood and vomit coating the cuff of her long-sleeved tee shirt.

"Maybe we should go see," I suggested to Luke.

"Hell no," Luke said. "I'm not going anywhere near that place."

"What happened?" I asked Krissy.

She wiped her face with her sleeve. Her tear-ravaged eyes shifted from me, to Luke.

"It's okay," he said. "You can trust Zoe."

Krissy's fragility was laid bare: a girl who could not think or do without the permission of someone else—even in the face of disaster—was as naked and vulnerable as a soul can get.

"Tell me," I urged.

"He was..." she muttered. "He was mad. He..."

"Hit you?" I suggested. If it was too hard for her to say the words, I wouldn't make it any harder.

She nodded. "I picked up these glass grapes we have and when he started to... when he wasn't looking... I... hit him." Her eyes searched mine as if I might be able to forgive her.

"You defended yourself."

"What if I killed him?" She wept again, burying her face in her hands. Her guardian's efforts to comfort remained steady. Often, he looked at Matthias. At me. Were they communicating?

"We should call 911," I suggested.

Luke pulled out his phone but Krissy grabbed his wrist. "No, you can't."

"We have to." Luke's response was gentle but insistent.

"You were defending yourself, Krissy," I said. "The police will see that.

When they take a look at that welt on your face they'll get what was going on."
Still, did she have the strength to admit the uglier part of the truth?

Zoe, the wheels of justice can't carry her to safety until she steps forward.

I swallowed the knot in my throat and took a deep breath. "Krissy, Luke
needs to call."

She shook her head. Tears poured down her cheeks in rivulets. Her grip
on Luke's wrist remained unbroken. Luke's gaze met mine, then shifted to
Matthias. Krissy's guardian wrapped her in an orb of comfort so bright it stole
my breath. A low buzz filled the air, a powerful yet soft pitch that soothed as
the light illuminated.

Slowly, Krissy's weeping stopped. The tension stringing her limbs taut
smoothed and she finally let go of Luke's wrist. "Okay," she whispered.

Luke walked out of earshot and made the call. No one spoke as he
explained what happened, gave names and addresses and took instruction.
After the call was completed, he slipped his cell phone into his pocket.
"They're sending someone here. We're supposed to wait."

Krissy's face lifted her red, swollen eyes bulging in fear. "What's going to
happen?"

"It's gonna be okay." Luke's strength and conviction took control of the
moment. He took her hand and held it.

She latched onto him, sobbing against his shirt. I admired Luke's sense
of decency and compassion and I was proud of him.

You're on the trolley now.

Nothing about this feels trolleyish.

The quiet stillness in the air filled with more of Krissy's weeping.

I bit my lip, fighting tears.

When Matthias didn't respond, I turned to him. His face was rigid,
grave. I waited for his thoughts but none came.

FOURTEEN

Not three minutes passed and sirens filled the air. Two navy and white police cars sped to a stop, their lights flashing yellow and white and red into the quiet stillness of the public park.

Krissy jerked upright, panic causing her to move like a caged cat next to Luke. Luke tried to stroke her arms, but she took off, heading deeper into the shrubs and trees of the park. Her guardian remained with her.

Luke trailed after her. So did the three police officers who had just jumped from their cars.

One officer remained, and he jogged my way. "Can I ask you a few questions?"

I told him everything I knew.

Within minutes, the other officers were in sight, emerging from behind a smattering of evergreens two of them holding Krissy's arms, the other walking with Luke.

"Her dad…" Should I tell the police what I suspected? What if Krissy chickened out and didn't tell them her father was molesting her? "He came to my house threatening our family the other night. He didn't want Krissy out of his sight. Ever."

The officer listened but didn't respond. His gaze was fixed on his fellow officers escorting Krissy our direction.

Krissy collapsed. The officers surrounded her. Another siren pierced the air and a Fire and Rescue truck barreled down the street, followed by an ambulance. Cars passing the park, slowed. Some stopped, and their occupants craned their necks for a look. A few slowed for a better view.

"I need you to wait here, miss," the officer I was talking to said.

I swallowed and nodded.

He took off across the crispy iced grass where his fellow officers huddled around Krissy. A lonely howl arose from the center of the circle. Luke's blonde head of hair finally emerged from the cluster. He stepped back, face pale, hands plastered to his cheeks as he looked on in shock.

"Poor Krissy," I whispered.

Matthias' comfort engulfed me. Though he didn't say anything, I took hope in the steps she'd taken to free herself from the nightmare.

Krissy's guardian's glow pulsed from within the circle as he administered to her.

Suddenly, Krissy screeched and, from between the hunched blue uniforms I glimpsed her legs and arms flailing. The officers scrambled to hold her in place. More cries filled the air.

The EMTs rushed across the park, their portable emergency supplies dangling from their shoulders and arms. Between the two of them, they balanced a stretcher. The officer's huddle opened for them. More screams.

"Let me go!" Krissy screamed. "Stop! Stop!"

Luke stepped away from the people surrounding Krissy.

I crossed to him, catching slivers of Krissy between the sandwiched officers and EMTs. Her guardian's glow intensified and her sobs turned to whimpers.

Luke's eyes, latched on the scene, rimmed with tears. I slipped my arm around his shoulder and hugged him.

Seconds later the officers and emergency medical technicians separated. Krissy lay still on the grass. A blanket covered her, leaving only her face exposed. My heart tore. The low murmur of their voices filled the air.

Krissy was lifted and gingerly placed on top of the stretcher then carried to the ambulance, her guardian moving with her, the two of them encompassed in a soft golden hue.

Two policemen headed toward Luke and me.

"They're taking her to American Fork Hospital. You can call the hospital later to check on your friend. She'll be there for the next few hours."

"It's not her fault," Luke blurted. "Her dad was hurting her." He scrubbed his face with his hands, smearing tears across his cheeks.

"That black eye is from her dad." I nodded at Luke's bruise.

"I'll make sure that gets in the report. Do you two need a ride?"

"No, we're good," I said, bringing Luke to my side in a hug. His body shook.

The officer left and joined his fellow officers at the back of the open ambulance and within moments, the door to the vehicle was shut and the red and white ambulance sped away.

The police returned to their cars, got in and drove off. The silence left in the aftermath was cold. Empty. Curious on-lookers lingering at the fringe of the park now watched Luke and me. *Show's over, people.* A shudder scraped my spine.

My cell phone vibrated in my pocket and I dug it out. Chase. I kept my arm around Luke still pale, speechless and dazed, and led him to Matthias. Luke was in shock, no doubt about it. "You okay if I get this?" I asked him.

He blinked dazedly. "Sure."

Matthias stood before Luke and ticked his head left. "Let's you and I walk a bit."

Luke followed Matthias' lead and the two of them started at a slow pace toward the trees.

I clicked on my phone. "Chase, you won't believe what happened."

"What?"

"Krissy attacked her dad."

"What?"

"First the guy hits Luke, then Krissy slams him over the head and now—"

"Are you serious? Why did he hit Luke?"

127

"Because she's been hanging out with him and the guy's a possessed psycho. I don't know." I explained to Chase what had happened at the park, complete with police, Krissy carted away and the uncertainty of whether her dad was alive or dead."

"Wow-oh-wow."

"I feel like I live smack in the center of a frying pan. I'm sick of the heat."

"Was Matthias there? Was your life in danger?"

"He's here, but my life wasn't in danger. He's with Luke right now."

"Where was Krissy's guardian during all of this?"

"With her. I wouldn't want his job. I just hope she makes it through all of this. Her dad shouldn't take one more breath if he's just going to get out and hurt her some more. Luke and I are going to the hospital. Wanna meet us?"

"Yeah… sure."

I told Chase which hospital Krissy was going to and said goodbye. Luke and Matthias were now a good distance away from me.

I stuck my cell phone in back my pocket. I hoped Matthias was helping Luke. But of course he was helping him, what else would they be doing? Having a guy talk?

Luke wouldn't tell me what he and Matthias had talked about, but for a guy who'd been tied in emotional knots just a little while ago, Luke's countenance had taken a complete turnaround. Color pinked his cheeks and his blue eyes were bright.

Matthias bid us goodbye—a moment I never looked forward to—and Luke and I dropped the minivan off at home. I jumped in his car so we could head over to American Fork Hospital. I called Mom and told her what had happened and it wasn't two minutes before my phone vibrated.

I flipped it open. "Hey, Dad."

"Krissy's in the hospital?"

"Yeah."

Dad sighed heavily into the phone. "Be careful, Zoe. Her father's not someone to fool around with."

"Her dad is… well, were not sure where he is, but he's not on the streets. She hit him in self defense."

"I can't say I'm surprised. The man was out of control. Is she okay?"

The extent of Krissy's injuries was undeniably deep and scarring, even if they weren't visible on the surface. "She's hurt, yeah. She tried to run away. It was awful. I think she's going to need some support."

"Does she have other family?" he asked.

"Her mom. And an aunt. But Luke says her mom is clueless."

"Well," Dad's voice was stiff. "She won't be clueless after today." A moment ticked by in silence. "I'll keep Krissy in my thoughts."

"Thanks, Dad." I hung up.

Neither Luke nor I spoke for a few minutes. Was he thinking what I was thinking? That he and I were lucky to have the parents we had? That, in spite of our family problems we weren't mistreated, neglected, unloved or any other myriad of anomalies that can damage people?

Luke's countenance lightened a shade. "Everything's going to be okay," he finally said.

Luke, Chase and I sat in the hospital waiting room. The place was empty except for a youngish couple. Both looked pregnant, but only the female was. They sat in their over sized t-shirts and hoodies staring at a plasma screen hoisted on one of the walls.

"So, you see anything?" Chase swept the room with a curious gaze. "No guardians, no black spirits?"

"Nope." What a relief.

Luke's face was buried in his hands. I wrapped an arm around his shoulder. "By the way, I'm sorry about earlier, yelling at you. I wasn't really yelling at *you*."

His white-streaked, finger-scraped face lifted to mine. "Doesn't matter any more."

"Yeah, it does. I tried to tell you, but…" I looked to Chase for support. His brown eyes brimmed with excitement behind his glasses. "I was talking to Matthias' father."

Luke's tired expression sharpened. I nodded. "His name is Albert—"

"And he's trying to destroy your family," Chase piped.

"Chase." I tilted my head at him, my tone heavy with *cut the drama.*

Luke bristled. "Are you serious?"

"Unfortunately," I said.

"W—wait." Luke shifted like he sat on hot coals. "How long has this been going on?"

"A while." I withdrew my arm from his shoulder, clutching my hands in my lap. "When Matthias and I… connected… Albert showed up. He's trying to destroy Matthias, and he's using every way he can to do it."

"Including your family," Chase added.

"Yes, thank you, Chase," I deadpanned. "Albert shows up whenever somebody's arguing or whatever. He's got an open invitation, intentional or not."

"Serious?" Luke gulped. "Man."

"Yeah."

"And the dude's not your average bad guy, either," Chase interjected. "He's, like, the quintessential bad guy."

"That's trippy," Luke mumbled. He eyed me. "I don't envy you, Z."

"When Abria was in the hospital, you asked me what was going on? I wanted to tell you, so you'd know I wasn't talking to air or was crazy."

"Z, nothing would surprise me about you any more," Luke said with a light smirk. "Why you, you think? I mean, you're deep and all, I told you that before. But, maybe you need to be exorcized or something."

I snorted. "I'm about ready." In truth, though my ability to see spirits both good and evil was at times overwhelming, I knew to my core that seeing spirits was precious gift. I wouldn't give it up for anything.

Not when I could help people, like Krissy.

"Wonder how she's doing." I looked around, hoping we'd get a chance to talk to her. See her. Show her we were there for her.

There was no guarantee we would see Krissy. We weren't family. "So, you've never seen her mom?" I asked Luke, my eyes trained on the arched opening that led to another wing of the hospital.

He shook his head. "Never been inside her house. She said boys aren't allowed." He let out a sneer. "What alternate universe are her parents living in, anyway?"

"Seriously," Chase said. "And I thought my parents were weird."

"Like they can keep their kid caged up forever." Luke shook his head. "She's lucky to be free of them."

"Let's hope her aunt is normal," I said.

"You think she'll go live with her?" Chase asked.

I shrugged. "Then again, if her mom just needs a wake-up call, maybe being at home is the best thing."

"Yeah," Luke murmured.

Heels clacked on the tile floor to our left, the sound echoing from the hall that led to the other wings of the hospital. A woman appeared, dressed in a black suit. I'd seen her at Brady's funeral—in Krissy's parents' van. Two police officers accompanied her. Her hands were behind her back.

Krissy's mom. Her dark hair was slicked in a tight knot. Her empty eyes latched on us. Nerves fluttered in my stomach. Her face sharpened like a knife glinting under light. The officers glanced at us, but continued escorting her to the exit. What was going on? The answer was on the woman's back in the form of a horde of inlaid black spirits, just like her husband's.

The sight caused me to gasp. Chase and Luke both looked at me.

Chase's gaze followed mine to Krissy's mother, now disappearing with the officers through the double-door exit.

"Krissy's mom?" he asked.

I nodded.

"She was cuffed." Luke shook his head, disbelief whitening his face.

"I've got to talk to Krissy, see if she's okay."

"I know, I know." I wrapped an arm around his tense shoulders.

Luke's blue eyes turned to mine, struggling hope in them. "You said she has a guardian?"

I nodded. "He's with her, I saw him."

Luke's gaze turned down the empty hall.

We didn't get to see Krissy. When we asked about her, the hospital staffer only said she wasn't privileged to give out any information. I asked the nurse to let her know we'd been there. We left not knowing anything more than what we'd known when we'd arrived.

During the drive home, Luke asked me about Albert. I told him everything I knew, watching his blue eyes brighten with fascination. His gaze lingered on mine, his expression ponderous. The two of us were getting closer through these experiences, and nothing felt better. Stronger. If Albert was trying to tear apart our family weave, he'd have a harder time now that Luke was aware.

"I want you to tell me next time this douche-bag shows up, k?" Luke pulled his car to the curb in front our house and parked. Overhead, the skies darkened with troubled clouds.

"Yeah, okay."

He extinguished the engine. Didn't move. I waited. Outside, the sounds of an impending storm brewed: rustling naked branches of nearby aspens.

After long moments of quiet, Luke's gaze shifted to me. In those wordless moments, unspoken feelings passed between us and I thought, oddly, about Albert. How wrong he was.

Family wasn't overrated.

There's no rest for the wicked, or so the saying goes. I think the saying should be: There's no peace for the victims of the wicked. Luke and I barely walked inside the house to find another mêlée. At least I wasn't completely alone in this battle any more.

Sure Chase and Weston knew some things, Chase more than Weston. Mom and Dad knowing about Matthias also helped. But Luke knowing about Albert lightened my load, spread the armor and the battle strategy to the both of us rather than me hefting the heavy responsibility alone.

Luke and I paused in the entry, Luke tentatively closing the front door at our backs. We exchanged glances, our gazes then shifting to the closed French doors to our right, where the unmistakable, gut-wrenching tempest of our parents' voices gusted from Dad's office.

"Okay, fine," Dad hissed out a sigh. He stood on one side of his desk, Mom on the other. "You win."

"I win?" Mom sneered. "This is about all of us *winning* as you so democratically put it."

"Not when we can't afford it, Deborah. A conference will cost us a couple thousand dollars between the flight, hotel and the conference itself. We can't spare that right now."

"When will we ever be able to spare it, Joe? In five years when Abria's lost developmental ground? She's still young. She can still make headway if we do something now. I've heard the conferences are life-changing. They have experts in the field of autism and they talk about everything from diet to supplements to—"

"I said fine, didn't I?" Dad boomed.

Luke swallowed, his eyes blinking fast. I laid my hand on his stiff arm.

"You said it but you don't want to do it." Mom's sharp tone sliced the fight in two: his and hers.

Albert was here.

The thought, so close to his last encounter, drained me.

Torrential silence followed, drowning the air with implication, censure and blame.

"He's here," I whispered. "Albert."

Luke's head jerked my direction, though I couldn't see Albert in the office, I was certain that's where he was—smack in the thick of the fight.

"Keep your cool," I whispered to Luke. "He hates peace."

Mom and Dad hadn't noticed our entrance, and Luke swung open the glass door. "Mom, Dad—" After entering the office, Luke looked around, but of course saw nothing.

The tension bouncing between them notched up a level with Luke and me there. Albert sat like a king in the leather wing chair tucked in the corner, legs crossed in his sleek onyx suit. He looked ready to proclaim *you're fired*.

"Now's not a good time," Dad barked.

"It's never a good time," I mumbled.

"Maybe if you two respected our privacy, we could get some time alone," Dad snapped.

"Well, maybe if you two listened to each other instead of screaming at each other all the time, you'd want to talk," Luke's voice rose with agitation.

"Bravo," Albert laughed. "Bravo, young Luke."

I stepped close to Luke and took his sleeve. "Dad's right. Let's leave them alone."

Luke looked at me as if trying to read some quiet message I might be trying to share. Gradually, the frustration taut across his face, softened. His blue eyes swept the room. "Yeah, okay." I was relieved he seemed to be letting go of his anger.

Then Luke hemmed a moment longer. "I've got some money from unloading my stuff. You can have it. Maybe it'll help with this conference thing."

No one spoke for a few minutes. I blocked any frustration and anger trying to surface, and kept a wary eye on Albert whose delighted face gradually drew into hard angles and planes. The air slowly began to shift from heavy and suffocating to clear and cleansing. Dad bowed his head.

"That's a nice gesture," Mom's voice broke. Her eyes glistened.

"A hundred bucks," Luke put in, hope in his tone. "I had a ton of stuff." He looked at Dad. "The conference sounds important."

Dad nodded, his gaze on Luke's, gratitude for the offer deepened his green eyes.

The mood around us softened, gentle fingers of appreciation working each heart. Albert stiffened. He uncrossed his legs. His shoulders pressed against the tall back of the chair, his cocky demeanor gone. Annoyance brewed in its place.

I wanted to smile at him. *See what just happened here, Al?* But his image started to break into zillions of microscopic specks, diffused by the eternal law that good can override evil.

I awakened the following morning to my cell phone vibrating on the table next to my bed, the vibration disturbing as it rumbled through me. Grey streams of light peered through my shutters and the air in my bedroom was chilly. I reached for the phone. 6 a.m. Weston.

u up?

yeah

i need u

I sat up, pushed the hair out of my face with my left hand, texting with my right.

what's wrong?

The phone rang and I clicked it on. "Hey."

A short silence caused my heart to trip, wondering what had happened. "My dad walked out last night." His voice sounded hollow.

"Oh, no. Weston, I'm sorry."

"They were screaming at each other all night. I tried to talk to them but it was like jumping into a bonfire. Then I got mad and we screamed at each other. This is my mom's fault."

"I'm sorry."

"She screwed that loser. She screwed my dad. She screwed Max." His voice hitched. "I'm so—I've never wanted to kill anybody before, but I really think I could do it."

135

My heart skittered. Was Brady there, making things worse? "Calm down, Weston."

"I can't. I'm going to find her."

"Weston, don't—"

Click. The phone was dead. My hands shook. I ripped back my covers and stood, my fingers pressing the redial button over and over, but Weston didn't pick up.

In a flash, I yanked on a white hoodie, green sweatpants, and tugged on some thick, fur-lined boots. I grabbed my bag and went out the door, passing Mom—still in her robe and on her way to Abria's room—as I ran down the stairs. "Can I please borrow the van for a second? Please?"

I tore through the family room and to the kitchen, making a grab for her keys, sitting on the counter.

"Where are you going?" she called from upstairs.

"Weston's."

"This time of the morning?"

"Mom, yes. Please?"

"Be back soon." Her words were eaten up by the door closing behind my back.

"Hold on, Weston. Hold on."

FIFTEEN

I started the engine and backed out, careful not to screech this close to the house. Right hand on the wheel, left hand on the keyboard, I tried Weston over and over. His masculine voice greeted me in his recorded message: "This is Wes. Say what you want."

After I was half a block away from home, I pressed on the gas pedal, flooring it. I cursed and threw my phone onto the passenger seat. "Don't do anything stupid."

I sailed through the handful of residential streets it took for me to get to Weston's sprawling brick estate. I parked in the circular drive, turned off the engine and threw open the door, flying across the yard to the porch. Snow dotted my face, lancing my eyes with thin flakes of ice.

I pounded on the front door. "Weston!"

Images of him being dragged to jail assaulted my mind and I continued to pound, until the door finally swung open and a woman with Weston's dark hair and eyes glared at me. Her red-blotched face appeared swollen. She wore a blue satin robe with a furry collar.

"Is Weston here?"

"Who are you?" she demanded.

"I'm Zoe. I need to talk to Weston." I swallowed. "Is he here?" I searched the darkened entry over her shoulder. She crossed her arms over her chest, tightening the silky robe.

"Zoe?" Weston's agitated voice came from the darkness behind his mother.

Mrs. Larsen eyed me with renewed interest.

Weston sneered at his mother and shouldered her aside.

Mrs. Larsen pinned him in the doorway with a look meant to kill. "Watch it," she growled.

Weston advanced, and his mother jerked back. The two glared at each other for a long, sweaty moment before Mrs. Larsen swiveled around and took off down the hall. A black spirit rode her back.

Weston's fury filled the area like a raging fire. "I hate her," he hissed.

At least he hadn't killed her. "Can I come in?"

He let me pass and slammed the door. When he turned, I saw Brady inlaid inside of him, his grinning face peering at me from the back of Weston's head.

I sucked in a gasp, covered my mouth with my hand to keep a roll of nausea from coming up my throat.

"He's where I want him, Zoe," Brady laughed. "Soon, we'll be even."

Weston paced in rigid silence. "Weston." My voice shook. "Brady's here."

He stopped. Shock flashed in his eyes. I hoped he would see this for what it was and let go of his anger. But the alarm slowly faded. "So what? I hate her."

"I know she hurt you, and you have every right to be angry. Just control your anger so Brady—"

"I don't care if Brady's here. Bring it on."

I made a grab for Weston's arms, hoping my touch would calm him, but he jerked away, eyes wild and ferocious. "Where is he?" he demanded.

"Right here, buddy." Brady's image wafted in and out of Weston then began circling him fluidly, like black spirits did.

Weston followed my eyes and began grabbing at the air. "As if that will do anything, loser," Brady snickered, dancing in and out of him.

Weston let out a growl.

"Don't you feel him?" I asked, goosebumps all over my body. I tried to reach for Weston again, but he was too caught up in chasing an invisible ghost

138

to notice.

"You're letting him get to you, you have to stop," I pled.

"Is that the best you can do?" he shouted.

Brady fumed. He slid inside of Weston and Weston swung around and faced me. My heart banged against my ribs. "You want me to be rough, like Britt did."

"That's disgusting."

Weston lurched forward and shoved me against the wall, pinning me. His hot breath seethed out between his clenched teeth. Brady's ghosted image lifted through Weston's, his face sneering.

Weston's hips ground into mine and he reached up, grabbed a handful of my hair and yanked my head against the wall, then dove for my lips. "Baby make it hurt so good, huh? You like it like this, don't you? Britt did, too."

My lungs nearly collapsed from the pressure of his body against mine. "No. I. Don't."

"Uh-huh. Now we're talking."

"No. You're. Not." I grunted, jerking my right knee upward. Weston bowled over, clutching his balls. Brady jumped out of him, laughing. Weston crumpled to the floor, paralyzed in the fetal position.

"Man-oh-man. That sucks, buddy."

A burst of white light filled the entry, causing Brady to whirl around. Matthias extended his hand. Brady's arms shot up to shield himself and then he dissolved. Blinding light slowly softened, and Matthias' concerned gaze met mine.

Back still against the wall, I let out a tight breath, muscles beginning to relax at the sight of him. Matthias didn't say anything. His blue eyes held mine for what seemed like endless seconds, concern emanating into the white purity of his aura, causing the colors to shift to white gold.

He looked at Weston on the floor. *This is serious business.* The power in Weston's body just moments ago reminded me of how helpless my mortal efforts could be.

Thank you.

Weston let out a moan and started to uncoil.

I closed my eyes. *Am I destined to lose the people I love because Albert and whoever else he recruits will forever be out to get me?* The thought deluged me with grief. *If this keeps up, I'm not going to make it.*

Matthias came toward me and his light surrounded me in an embrace. *Weston is susceptible, just like any other mortal. He has to make his own choices.*

I nodded, tears gushing up my throat. *What should I do?* It seemed every life I touched, I bruised.

Not so. Matthias' gentle fingers traced my jaw bone.

Weston lay on his back, his hands coming away from his crotch, dragging up to his face. He scraped his fingers over his skin as if waking from a dream, looked around and his gaze found me.

"Zoe." He stood. His shoulders slumped as if a sack of guilt was lodged on his back. His dark brown eyes remained averted. "I'm sorry." Weston covered his face with his hands again. "I can't believe what happened."

I crossed to him. "I'm sorry I had to hurt you. Brady was inside of you, I couldn't let him do that."

Weston's face twisted in disgust. His skin blanched. "What?" He swallowed. "I—don't know—that was—I'm sorry, Zoe. That's disgusting. I can't believe I did that. I felt different. Pushed. Driven. You know? Out of control."

I laid my hand on his arm. Weston's fearful eyes glanced around the entry. "Is he still here?"

"No."

"How did you get rid of him?"

"Matthias."

Weston's eyes widened. He inched back, breaking our contact as his gaze searched the room. "I didn't mean it. I didn't. I'm sorry, I would never hurt Zoe."

Matthias' silence sliced my nerves into shreds of distrust and confusion. *Should I be worried?*

I told you Weston was a safe companion for you. The right corner of his jaw steeled, his hands dove into the front pockets of his ivory slacks and fisted.

"Zoe?" Weston queried, noticing my gaze was locked to his right.

"Give me a second, please," I said, holding up my hand. *What's wrong?*

Matthias lowered his head momentarily. When his gaze lifted, penetrating and unblinking, the sight caused something inside of me to tear. *I wish I was mortal.*

His longing ripped through my body, melding with my own ache for him, the two twining, reminding me that our connection was real and undeniable, in spite of the seemingly impossible breach of Heaven and Earth. He loved me, and wanted me to be happy. I loved him and wanted him to be happy, too. Why did it seem like we were both unhappy?

Matthias cleared his throat and his expression lightened some, but it was only in an effort to make me feel better. His anguish remained an open wound inside of me.

I'll go.

I never wanted Matthias to go. Ever. But time, life, was teaching me that I, too, had to let him go if I was to live my life. My heart, still weighed down by a portion of grief, slugged painfully in my chest as Matthias' light blinded me with his departure.

I forced myself to put longing for him aside and focus on the moment.

"Zoe? Is he gone?"

I nodded, and took the two steps that brought me close Weston. His scent filled my head. Calmness settled over him, soothing away traces of fear and confusion. He studied me, and I wished the two of us could read each other's minds like Matthias and I could—then he'd know how much I wanted him to control his anger, that vengefulness wasn't worth the damage words caused or the evil it invited.

Weston's penetrating gaze remained steadily with mine, as if just looking at me strengthened him. Maybe it did. I reached out and laid my hands on his arms, let my hands slide to his and link.

Weston's fingers tightened around mine. "I'm so sorry."

"I know. It's over, don't think about it."

"How can I not when I acted like some possessed freak?" He embraced me, and stroked my hair.

"Brady's seriously out to destroy you. Be careful, your anger invites him in."

Weston nodded.

I sighed, relieved. "I'm a mess. I better get home and get ready for school."

Weston stepped back and glanced down the hall where his mother had disappeared.

"Will you be okay? With her?"

He nodded. "I'm gonna shower and leave." With a gentle tug on my hands, he pulled me against him and kissed me. Then he led me to the front door and opened it. I stepped through the threshold, but his hand kept hold of mine. He drew in a breath and leaned close, and pressed another kiss on my cheek.

I stripped and showered, enjoying the hot water flowing over my skin. I toweled off in front of the mirror, pleased that no dark circles shadowed my eyes. My gaze drifted to my breast and the soft red lines—the scar I'd have the rest of my life—from the accident. I'd had perfect breasts before that truck had slammed into me, sending glass and metal flying. What would Weston think? Would he be repulsed? Turned off?

Shame heated me that I would spend any time worrying about something so insignificant. I was alive.

The accident could have been much worse. I'd almost died.

Paradise, and the precious, unique moments I'd spent there with Matthias flashed briefly into my mind, but the memory had faded. Shocked, I stood staring at my reflection in the mirror. How could that happen? *The single most extraordinary experience of your life and you're forgetting it?*

Momentary panic threatened me to the point where I closed my eyes and tried visualizing what Matthias and I had shared in Paradise. The vivid colors of the trees, the softness of the grass we walked upon, the ultra clear blue sky stretched endlessly overhead and the sun—warm and soothing in its glory—all played before my closed eyelids in three dimensional brilliance.

Matthias' face, the color of his eyes staring into mine… here is where the memory stepped back enough that he appeared vague. Ghostlike.

Angry at myself, I opened my eyes, meeting my reflection in the mirror again. *This is temporary, that's all. A stupid brain loss brought on by stress or something. It doesn't mean anything.*

I wouldn't fall prey to over analyzing. I dressed in jeans, a brown shirt with black angel wings on the back—just what I needed—and smiled at the false security such an artistic endeavor provided, though I was sure the design wasn't meant to actually provide comfort.

After brushing blush on my cheeks and applying shadow and mascara, I tied my hair up in a haphazard knot at the back of my head and grabbed my backpack. School seemed so mundane and trivial compared to the life I led keeping my family and friends from Albert. I almost laughed at how insignificant learning in the classroom was in comparison to what I'd learned over the past few months.

You're not saving souls. That's not your job. Thank heavens. I laughed. I passed Abria's room and found Mom dressing her in pink sweats with colorful little ponies dancing across the chest.

"So what was that all about this morning?" Mom asked.

"Just helping Weston with a crisis." I nodded at my sister. "How is she today?"

"What kind of crisis?"

"His dad walked out this morning."

Mom's hands went still. "Oh no."

"Yeah. He was pretty upset."

"I can imagine. That's too bad." She resumed pulling Abria's hair back into clips at the side of her face.

"Is Abria okay today?" With a kiss, Matthias had wiped away any unpleasant memory of Abria's frightening experience. Still, I was curious.

"She's fine. I mentioned being at the hospital to her and she looked at me for a second. But that was it. Stand still, Abria. Please." Abria flapped her arms.

"So, are you guys going to go to the conference?"

Mom smiled. "I think we are, yes." Her eyes shared a joy she knew I understood.

"Exciting. Where it is?"

"Boston."

"Nice."

"We're taking Abria. They'll have experts there. I want to make an appointment with some of them, have them observe her and get their ideas. You know?"

I nodded. Not a vacation, by any stretch.

"Z!" Luke called from down the hall. "Let's hit it."

I stood erect, hands in the pockets of my jeans. "Coming. Bye Abria. Bye Mom."

I turned, and Mom's voice stopped me.

"Zoe?"

"Yeah?"

"Be careful."

I crossed to her, wrapped her in a hug and then patted Abria on the head. I followed Luke down the stairs. He wore baggy jeans, a black and blue checked hoodie over a sky blue t-shirt that reflected in his eyes. Black checkerboard Vans donned his feet.

"Where's the party?" I asked, wondering why he was in such a rush.

He pulled open the front door and a gust of cold air wafted in my face.

"Did you hear from Krissy?" I kept in step with him until we reached the Samurai and he swung open the driver's door. I skipped around to the other side.

He started the engine, then blew in his cupped hands, sending white mist into the cab of the little car. "Man, when's spring gonna come?"

I shut the door, shivering. "Soon, I hope. You trying to change the subject?"

He pulled onto the street, the car sputtering to life. "No. Krissy's gonna meet me at school. "

"She called?" Her mother's back, crawling with evil spirits, came to mind. I suppressed a rumble of disgust.

"Yeah, well, the control Nazis are out of her life now, thank God. She called me this morning."

"Her mom is gone, too?"

Luke thrust his free hand into his shaggy blond hair. "Yup. She wouldn't go into details, Z. She was crying. Said she was coming down to clean out her locker and get checked out of school."

"Oh, no. I'm sorry."

"I guess she's going to live with her aunt after all."

"She's better off away from her parents."

After a long pause, he nodded. "Yeah. Still, Ogden's two hours from here."

Separation wasn't easy. "Maybe it won't be for that long."

Luke pulled his car into far end of the school parking lot—the area closest to the park—and turned off the engine. His gaze swept the area for Krissy. Mine did too.

Krissy, dressed in her camel coat and jeans, was walking out of the school with a woman wrapped in a gray coat and red scarf. Krissy's aunt? A social worker? Krissy carried a brown box in her arms. She seemed to see us, as her slow gait quickened when her head turned our direction.

"There she is," Luke said. He got out of the car, stood in the open driver's side door, his hand tapping on the roof of the car.

Krissy and the woman walked over. I glanced at the clock on my phone. Five minutes until school started. I wanted to talk to Krissy myself, but the urgent yearning Luke tried to mask with typical coolness was as potent as love. I remained in the car—a selfless act Luke didn't notice, too focused on Krissy.

The three of them met a dozen or so feet away from Luke's car. Luke shoved his hands in the front pocket of his hoodie. Krissy's pale face beamed, though her smile faltered with expected weariness.

It was the first time (outside of the party, when she'd been dressed by Britt in some of Britt's skanky clothes) I'd seen Krissy wearing jeans beneath her camel coat instead of her denim jumper. Her hair hung down around her shoulders.

I cracked my window an inch, hoping to catch their conversation but only heard Luke's bass tone muted by Krissy and the woman's voices as the three of them talked. Soon, the woman took the box from Krissy's hands and returned to a sedan parked a few slots away, leaving Krissy and Luke alone.

Krissy stepped closer to Luke, her smile trembling. Luke reached out and laid a hand on her shoulder, his gaze flicking behind Krissy to the woman sitting in the car.

It wasn't long before the pitch of Krissy's voice rose like a siren getting closer and closer. Her shoulders buckled and she wept. Luke hugged her.

Krissy's arms wrapped tight around Luke, her hands fisting around the baggy gold fabric of his hoodie, drawing the garment tight across his back. Talking ceased. Luke slowly stroked Krissy's hair and her weeping finally subsided.

From the car, the woman watched, at one point dabbing at her eyes with a white tissue. I sighed, looked away from her, from Luke and Krissy.

When I looked up again, Krissy was backing to the sedan, her red-eyed, puffy face fastened on Luke with the need of a prisoner wanting food. He didn't move. Krissy got into the sedan, keeping her stare on Luke, and the woman drove away.

I got out of the car, retrieved our backpacks and shut the passenger side door. The empty parking lot held Luke's gaze for a few long moments, then he turned to me.

We started up the drag. The tardy bell shrilled in the distance.

Inside, halls were lined with tacky posters urging students to choose a date and attend prom—scheduled to be held at a hotel in one of the ballrooms in a few weeks. The Paradise theme still caused me to shake my head. *The irony.* Would Weston ask me? My life had been barraged with life *and* soul-threatening matters. I'd barely had time to do homework, much less contemplate going to a dance. I'd have to do some serious cramming.

The halls were empty. Luke's head remained bowed. I hoped he could make it through this episode with Krissy without relapsing. After quick goodbyes, we went our separate ways. I searched for Weston's dark mass of hair and straight, erect shoulders but didn't see him. I hoped he and his mom hadn't gotten into another argument, that he had come to school. Maybe he was already in class. I pulled out my phone and sent him a text: **u here?** Then I opened my locker and exchanged books.

"Right here." Weston's voice slid into my ear. His strong arms wrapped around me and his chest pressed into my back. "Mmm, you smell good." His teeth nipped my earlobe and I giggled.

He turned me, keeping his palms at my waist, and kissed me. "You smell good yourself," I whispered, breathing in his spicy pine cologne.

He closed my locker door and kept his arm around me as we strolled through the empty hall toward my first period class.

"Thanks for coming over this morning. I was angry as hell at her. When I think about it, I want to smash something." His fierce gaze met mine. "So… Brady was really there? You weren't just saying that to wake me up?"

"I'd never do that. He was there, and he was going in and out of you."

Weston's eyes left mine. He stared straight ahead, face and neck whitening. His body shuddered. "Why were you late?"

"Luke was saying goodbye to Krissy."

"Goodbye?"

"She was checked out of PG this morning. I didn't tell you about what happened after you dropped me off." I relayed the Krissy drama from Luke walking in with a black eye, to the park, to visiting the hospital for Krissy and seeing her mother walk out in handcuffs.

Weston whistled. "Wow."

"Apparently she's going to live with her aunt."

"At least she has some place to go."

"Yeah."

Weston's gaze left mine and for a long moment, he stared off into nowhere. "How do I make sure Brady leaves me alone for good?" Fear flashed in the depths of his eyes.

The same way I keep Albert away from my family. With every ounce of energy I could muster, every single day. I didn't want to overwhelm him. Scare him. "Stay as far away from me as you can."

He eyed me, as if deciding whether or not I was joking. I shrugged. "It's true. Brady seems to be attached to Albert's hip. Albert's set on ruining Matthias, through me, and he's using practically everyone I know."

"Well, forget that." Weston's jaw knotted. "I don't care what the freak does, he's not getting to me. Period."

I smiled, pleased with his determination. But did he have any idea how hard it might get? How ruthless the tactics? How stealthy? "I'm serious, Weston. This will get ugly."

"I don't care."

"It'll be hard."

"Don't care."

"Harder than anything you've ever been through."

"I said I don't care. I'm not going anywhere."

He drew closer. Was he going to kiss me?

We stopped outside the door of my first class. "I want to ask you something." His fingers skimmed my cheek and the taut skin over his face relaxed some. My head spun with possibilities.

I nodded. "Sure."

He glanced around at the vacant hall. "This isn't the right place. Lunch?"

SIXTEEN

Anticipation soared through my blood. I couldn't sit still through morning classes. I wanted to share the excitement with Britt, like I had so many times. To laugh and gossip, scheme and plan. Now, that was impossible.

Thinking of her fizzled some of the thrill coursing through me. *Oh well.* She was where she was, and I was here. It had been days since I'd taken her home. How was she? Was she in rehab now? Did she still have her phone?

I bit my lower lip, made sure the teacher had her back turned and slid out my cell phone, debating texting her. What would communicating accomplish? She probably still wanted me dead. She'd see my efforts at contacting her as rubbing her nose in my relationship with Weston, celebrating her confined existence.

I slipped my phone back into my pocket.

The lunch hour finally came, and my phone vibrated in the depths of my pocket. I pulled it out.

go 2 ur locker

I grinned, and practically skipped through the halls to my locker. After turning the knob and unlocking it, I opened the metal door and inside was a bouquet of white orchids.

I glanced around, caught admiring eyes watching but didn't see Weston.

"Nice, Zoe," someone said.

"Oooh, sweet," a girl commented.

Heat flushed my cheeks. I reached for the black envelope hanging on the tail of colorful ribbons wrapped around the vase and opened it, tugging out the petite card.

I'm no angel, but I want you for prom.

Once again I swept the hall for Weston, my gaze connecting with his when I looked right. He was dressed in a tight black t-shirt and ash black jeans—had he looked that good this morning before class? The smile on his face tempted with mischief.

A crowd slowed and gathered, watching, and I heated from head to toe. Weston slid through the bodies like a panther, students parting for him, eyes following his smooth movement until his body was flush with mine. He took my face in his hands and kissed me.

Swoons erupted. Whistles. Laughter. Cat calls. Shock and thrill launched my system into hunger.

"Way to go, Larsen!" somebody shouted.

Weston drew back, but kept his strong palms cradling my cheeks, his dark eyes pinned on mine. The crowds began to break up around us and move on. "Say yes," he whispered.

"Yes."

"I've been wanting to do this, but there's been so much going on."

"Yeah," I nodded.

"I didn't want you to think I was a slouch asking you this close to prom. It's not that I haven't wanted to, you know?"

"Don't worry about it." Prom hadn't been front and center in my thoughts until recently, either.

His mouth covered mine again in a possessive kiss. I slipped my arms around his neck. More whispers filled the air around us, mixing with a few snickers and whistles, but I was lost in the oblivion of him.

His lips grew more urgent, and soon my back was against the locker in a clattering bang. *Stop. You hate PDAs. You hated watching Britt and Weston. Stop now.*

Reason forced me to pull back, leaving his lips parted, eyes closed, head extended for more. I blushed at the students walking past who eyed us, and something inside of me—maybe my past with Britt—caused embarrassment to trickle through me.

"What?" Weston asked eyes hooded.

"Not in public, k?"

His tight gaze didn't leave mine even for a glance around the hall. "Whatever you say. Your wish is my command."

Matthias had said those same words to me. Coming from Weston's love-struck lips, I should have been flattered. Why then, did an eerie feeling blanket me?

Albert?

I jerked left. Right.

"What's wrong?" Weston asked.

A lump of fear lodged in my throat. Why? Albert wasn't here. Neither of us was inviting him. My head was a jumble of guilt. Was I being disloyal to Matthias?

"Is something wrong?" Weston drew me against him, and the solidness of his body comforted me a little.

I shook my head and returned his tight embrace. Something white flashed in my peripheral vision. I had to stop psyching myself out. I was safe with Weston. Matthias had told me I had my life to live. That's what I was doing.

The autism conference in Boston fell on the same weekend as prom. As the weekend drew near, Mom grew anxious. I caught her packing Abria's suitcase, talking to herself as she folded each piece of Abria's wardrobe and set it neatly inside the small, ladybug travel case. Abria then proceeded to yank each article of clothing out, trying to dress herself.

Mom was too lost in her thoughts to notice or stop my sister. I stifled a chuckle watching the two of them: pants in, pants out. Shirt in, shirt out.

"Um, Mom?" I came to her aid by scooping Abria into my arms and handing Mom the sweatshirt Abria had tried to heist.

Mom smiled absently, took the shirt and refolded it, mumbling something under her breath as she placed the clothing into the suitcase.

"You okay?" I asked.

"Hm? Oh, fine. Just making sure I don't forget anything."

"Looks like you've got Abria taken care of." I squeezed Abria and kissed her cheek. She squirmed for freedom, arching away from my embrace but I held firm.

"All packed." Dad popped his head in the door. He'd warmed up to the idea of attending the conference, I heard the two of them discussing it over breakfast more than once since they'd decided to go.

"Oh, good." Mom nodded. "Good."

"You okay?" Dad stepped into the door, his questioning gaze shifting from Mom to me, as if I had the answer to Mom's distraction.

I shrugged.

"Let me take Abria and get her some lunch." Dad held out his arms for my sister, and I passed her to him.

Mom stood staring at the contents of Abria's suitcase, dazed. I nodded at Dad in approval.

"You want something to eat, Deb?" he asked from the doorway.

"Hmm? No. Thanks."

Dad left.

"You sure everything is cool?" I touched Mom's arm and she looked at me.

"It's hard…" Her eyes filled with tears.

"Mom? What?" I hugged her.

"Leaving." She sniffed against my shoulder. "I'll miss you. And, I can't believe I'm going to miss your prom."

"Don't worry about it," I said, easing back. "Don't."

She blinked away the remaining tears and sighed. "It's your last prom, Zoe. I wanted to be here for you. Help you get ready, see you walk down the front stairs. All that."

"I'll be fine. Everything is going to be fine. Of course I want you here, too. But this conference is important."

She nodded, eyeing Abria's open suitcase filled with clothes. "It is, I know. I just don't want you thinking it's more important than you and Luke."

"We don't. It's an issue of timing, that's all." I patted her shoulder. "You need to do this. I know you're excited about meeting with the specialists and stuff. That's going to be exciting. I can't wait to see what they say."

"Me too." She smiled at me, and gave me another hug. "How about I treat you to the dress?"

"Really? I'd love that."

When the three of them finally left, and the door closed behind them, silence echoed through the rooms of the house. A few months ago, I would have seen the opportunity to be alone as an open invite to host a party or three. But the events of the last few months had bound my family in a deep connection of trust and respect. Not five minutes passed and I missed hearing Abria run through the halls, Mom inquiring about my day at school, seeing the back of Dad's head as he sat on the couch unwinding in front of the TV.

I half expected Luke to rejoice at Mom and Dad's absence, but he hadn't skipped school in weeks, was regularly talking to Krissy on the phone and had actually said he wanted to hang with me while they were gone.

I wondered when we'd actually hang out, because whenever I saw Luke, he was either on his cell talking to or texting Krissy. I tried asking him what was going on with her, how she was doing and what the status was with her parents and he told me she was happy at her aunt's house but missed her life here. She also had conflicting feelings about her parents—missing her mother one day and resenting her the next.

There was a brief news report in the paper that Chase had read and shared with me: Krissy's parents were both in jail for child abuse—her father for sexual abuse, her mother as an accomplice—and Krissy was living with a 'family member' who had been given temporary custody by the court. It didn't look like Krissy's dad was going to be free any time in this century.

I was relieved to hear that—for Krissy's sake.

"Hey, Z," Luke called from upstairs. "Can Krissy spend the night here tomorrow night? That way her aunt doesn't have to stick around down here in Utah County waiting for prom to end and stuff."

"Fine with me," I said, searching the refrigerator for what Luke and I would eat for dinner.

"Cool." Luke appeared. His black eye had finally faded. "Her aunt wants to talk to you."

"Me?"

He nodded, held out his cell phone. His thumb covered the mouthpiece. "Be cool about it, k?"

I took the phone. Connie, Krissy's aunt, was very anxious for her niece to participate in as many 'normal' activities as possible. She also acknowledged Krissy's admiration for me and our family, and her budding feelings for Luke. She wanted to know the prom day itinerary and make sure Krissy would be sleeping in my room with me. I reassured her that I'd make sure Krissy was in her sleeping bag, next to my bed.

I plopped Luke's cell phone back in the palm of his hand. "Done."

Luke's eyes brightened. "Cool. We're going to prom. Who'd have thought, right?"

I mirrored his easy grin. "You might even like it, bud."

"Oh, I'm gonna like it."

The smile on Luke's face reminded me that, for most guys, prom equaled sex. "You and Krissy?" I asked carefully, hoping he'd get my implication.

His face twisted. "No way. She's... no way, Z. I wouldn't expect that from her. She's way too... I dunno... fragile at this point."

I patted his shoulder, admiring his maturity. "Can't wait to see you in a tux," I teased.

Luke's brows waggled. "Neither can Krissy, apparently."

Krissy's part in Luke's venturing down the drugless path was undeniable. He'd connected with her and his interest in her helped take his mind off using.

His face lit when he talked about her—which wasn't often—but when he did, his tone softened and his countenance was as cheery as a kid building sand castles.

I'm not sure when I realized that, as a family, we'd actually had a few weeks of peace, but at that moment, seeing the joy on Luke's face, it hit me that Albert hadn't been around. I wasn't going to spend even a millisecond wondering where he was and why he'd left me alone. Maybe his forces really had moved camp to Weston's and were working that angle now.

Weston's relationship with his mother remained tenuous. He gave me regular updates on the fights—all of which ended with him regretting participating. But he stayed in control, determined not to let Brady influence him into losing it. The result was that he forced his mom to talk through stuff. I swear he told me just to get a kiss out of me.

I hadn't seen much of Matthias. Had he heard me silently grumbling about things having to change between Weston and me? I reminded myself that he'd assured me that I had my life to live. Maybe his absence was due to the fact that Abria's dangerous behaviors had lessened over time and we, as a family, were more adept at circumventing danger.

A pang of sadness echoed through my heart. Was my love for Matthias destined to drift off in memory like a cloud evaporating in the sky? As life went on, where was his place in it?

The reality was that we lived in different spheres and, as he'd told me so many times before: I had to live.

As he had to live. Without me.

"You okay?" Luke asked, interrupting my train of thought.

"Yeah." I couldn't allow myself to get carried away with impossible thoughts of Matthias. He loved me. I loved him. We were going to be together someday. Mine was the challenge of keeping perspective in the interim. "So, prom. Has Krissy said anything about a dress?"

"Just that the color is blue."

"Like your eyes," I grinned. His cheeks flushed.

"That's what she said." His tone carried amazement that I would know such things.

"You want me to go look at tuxes with you?"

He dipped his head. "I got one."

"Yeah? Cool. I'm proud of you. You're gonna look awesome."

He shifted, and with a flick of his head, his shaggy hair swung out of his blue eyes. "What about you?"

"I need to go find something fast. I bet there's nothing left anywhere. You want to come with me?"

Luke's brows arched. "Me? Uh, I'm not very good at picking out girl's clothes."

I hooked my arm in his. "Come on, it'll be fun. Besides, I need your car."

All I needed was my iPod, a dock and some speakers booming cool tunes and my adventure trying on prom dresses could have felt ripped right out of a movie, complete with Luke shaking his head at most of my choices.

He finally nodded at a pale lavender dress in a flowing chiffon fabric. The dress was long, with poofy capped sleeves and a wide, velvet black tie just under the breast that tied in a huge bow in the back.

"That be the one," he said with a nod.

The soft petunia shade accentuated my green eyes and dark hair. "You have taste, I'll give you that," I said, turning in front of the three-way mirror. I loved the way the fabric floated with my every move. The style was kind of retro, and the design flattered my small build. I figured my black heels would finish the look nicely.

"Can't wait to see Weston in a purple tux," Luke joked after I'd paid for the dress. We walked out of the formal dress shop and into the cold afternoon. Patches of blue sky tried to peek out from behind a broken wall of thick clouds.

"He'd look hot in purple," I played back, "but I want him in black. I love a guy in a black tuxedo."

Luke jangled his car keys in his hand as we approached the blue Samurai. "That's what Krissy said."

"So, yours is black?" I opened the passenger-side door.

Luke nodded. We both slid inside the car and shut the doors. Luke inserted the key and revved the engine, bringing the car to life with a rattling growl. His eyes met mine. "What about Matthias?"

Was I imagining the heaviness suddenly in the air? Luke's expression was childlike curiosity. "He won't be there," I joked.

Luke didn't laugh. He cared about Matthias; the soberness that flashed on his face was clear as a baby's conscience.

"I don't know what to say except that he wants me to live my life."

We sat in the idling car outside the formal dress shop. "That must be hard," he said. "At the same time, you should listen to him. Be realistic, Z."

When had Luke gotten so wise? I smiled, patted his shoulder. I cared for Weston. My feelings were definitely gravitating toward love. But the love residing inside my deep reservoir, the love I held for that one special soul was for Matthias. I had to come to terms with loving both of them.

Luke drove. Silence accompanied us. For the first time, I wished he'd put on one of his loud, crass bands.

My cell phone vibrated and I retrieved it. Weston.

"Hey."

"Hey. So, the day date. Are we doing this with Luke and Krissy or going solo?"

Krissy's aunt had given her permission to attend the prom if she and Luke doubled with Weston and me. "We're doubling." I gave Weston Luke's phone number so they could plan together.

"You okay?" Weston asked.

"Yeah, of course." I didn't like that he might feel insecure about how I felt about him. He deserved my full attention, heart and soul. "I found a dress."

"Cool. Can't wait to see you in it."

"Aw, that's sweet. And I have a feeling you're going to look hot in that black tux."

"Anything to get you worked up."

"A black tux is a good place to start," I said.

"Start, finish and everything in between," Weston's voice took a warm plunge. "I better call Luke."

"You better," I laughed. "See ya."

"I love you," he said.

I swallowed. "Love you."

Weston held the line for an extra long second before hanging up. A swift tranquility filled my conscience for having admitted my feelings to him, and a smile lingered on my lips.

Luke's cell phone blared hard rock. He dug for it in the front pocket of his jeans and flipped it open, pressing it to his ear.

"Hey." He glanced at me, mouthed *Weston*. "Uh-huh. Sure. Yeah. That sounds good. Fine with me. Uh-huh. Okay. See ya." He closed his phone and slipped it back into the front pocket of his jeans. "Well that was easy," he said.

"So, you two agreed on something to do?"

Luke lifted a shoulder. "He suggested, I agreed. I dunno. He's a senior, I'm a junior, plus, I figure he's gone to a lot more of these things than I have."

That was for sure. I'd seen him at a handful of proms—each date clinging to him like he was their lifeline. I suppressed a cringe. I would never look like that.

I didn't ask Luke what Weston had planned. It was supposed to remain a surprise until that day, and that was exactly what I wanted.

Mom and Dad texted both Luke and I, telling us that they'd arrived in Boston just fine and Abria had actually enjoyed the airplane ride. The flight had gone without a hitch. Except when Abria stood in her seat and jumped— twelve different times—during the flight, bringing the aggravated stewardess over. And Abria's attempted escape: crawling down the aisle. Abria cried when the plane descended, grabbing her ears. Mom tried to give her chewing gum, but she swallowed four pieces and nearly choked on the fifth.

I could easily envision the looks of pity Mom and Dad endured, and I wished I could have been there to glare back. Glare? *What's gotten into you, you haven't glared at politically incorrect, clueless eyeballers since Matthias came into your life.*

My reflection in my bathroom mirror brought a lonely sigh from my chest. The house was entirely too quiet without Mom, Dad and Abria and as darkness filmed each window in nighttime, emptiness crept into my heart. I wished I had gone to Boston. I'd be so busy chasing Abria; I wouldn't have time to think about Matthias. Or Weston.

"Z!" Luke's voice drolled up from the family room.

I surveyed myself in my flannel pj bottoms and white tee shirt—ready for bed—and headed downstairs, passing Abria's quiet, dark bedroom with a pause.

"Yeah?"

"How about we watch something adventurous. Bond or something?"

I blinked back the flush of tears filling my eyes and moved on past Abria's room, taking the stairs down at a skip. Luke stood staring at our large selection of DVDs, stored in an antique armoire.

"No chick flicks," I said, the last thing I needed was a dose of romance.

"No argument here," he said.

The doorbell rang and we looked at each other.

"Are you expecting anybody?" I asked, heart pattering a little. We hadn't turned on a lot of lights, too ingrained by our parents to be conservative with resources. That left otherwise cheery halls and balconies dim and eerie. Luke shook his head.

"I'll check it out." He strolled toward the entry, on the way swiping the rolling pin from the kitchen. I tip-toed behind him.

He peered out the sidelight window and snickered. He tossed me the rolling pin and I caught it in both hands. "Who is it?"

Luke grinned and swung the door open.

"Hey." Weston's deep, smooth voice filled the room and calmed my

≥✢≤

159

anxious heart.

Luke invited Weston in and shut the door. Luke strolled back to the family room, a smile still on his face. "Bond it will be," he whispered as he passed knowing full well I probably was ditching him for the night now.

Weston's gaze swept me from head to slippers. "Hey."

"Hey."

He eyed the rolling pin in my hands. "Are you... baking?"

I laughed. "Uh, no." I set the wooden utensil on the entryway table.

"Is it okay that I came by?" Weston stepped closer, his voice just above a whisper. His intense eyes looked bottomless in the low-light of the entry. He was balancing my earlier admittance of love with apprehension.

"I'm glad you're here." I reached out and touched his hand. "Luke and I are just hanging out."

Weston glanced over my shoulder toward the family room where the James Bond theme song was in full swing. "It's cool you two can hang and get along." Weston stuffed his hands deep in the front pockets of his jeans. "I don't want to intrude."

"You're not. How is it at home?"

"I don't want to be there."

I took his hand and his gaze seemed to shift from uncertainty to relief. I turned and led him by the hand to the family room.

Daniel Craig—Bond, James Bond—got his body beaten so badly, I cringed watching. Luke and Weston sat forward on the couches, like they were ringside at a live fight, laughing at Bond's snappy comebacks, even as he endured torture.

Guys were weird.

When the movie was over, Luke stretched, eyed Weston and me sitting close on the couch, and stood. "Guess I'm going to bed."

"Night," I said.

"Yup." Luke strolled past Weston who lifted his fist in typical testosterone greeting and Luke slugged knuckles with him.

Luke's heavy footfalls trudged up the stairs, and Weston and I were alone. He slipped an arm around me. "This was cool. Thanks."

"You're welcome. Yeah, it was nice."

The burn of desire moved swiftly into the air between us, pressing us together. He watched me, waiting for even the slightest hint on my part that I was ready for a kiss. Or more. He leaned closer, slowly, tuned into my face like his next heartbeat depended on what unspoken expression he might find there.

I slipped my arms around his neck and kissed him, enjoying that my body sparked with desire. His lips hesitated beneath the pressure of mine, but only for a second. Then his arms wrapped me in a breathtaking embrace. Hungry. Neglected. Weston kissed me as though we hadn't kissed in weeks. His whole body covered mine, as if each muscle and sinew had to absorb me. I relished the strength in him, the scent of desire, ripening with each move of his mouth over mine. His chest pressed into mine. Our breaths became one in a frenzied rhythm, like rain against the roof, drowning me with him.

His lips coursed my neck, my collar bone, and up the other side of my jaw until he'd come full circle back to my waiting mouth. Beneath my exploring fingers, his tight body filled with urgency. The pound of his heart slammed against my chest.

His hands explored: my ribs, waist, stomach. His fingers fluttered at the elastic edge of my flannel pjs. Then slipped beneath.

"Luke's here." I jerked my head left, gasping. "No."

Weston's lips skimmed my face. His hands continued exploring. I tingled, heart flying out of control, want building in my bloodstream.

I tried to bring my hands between our chests, but his body had adhered to mine. "Weston, no."

"I want you," he whispered between kisses.

"I want you too." Indeed, my body was in a luscious frenzy. "But not here."

Weston's hot mouth slid to my ear. "Then your bedroom." He slipped his arms beneath me and effortlessly pulled me against him, and stood. My arms instinctively latched around his neck, my gaze locked with his.

He walked slowly, easily, as if I was no more than a delicate bundle in his arms. But the heat in his gaze spoke of serious desire and I knew what he wanted. Even though my feelings for him were clearer, stronger, I wasn't ready to make love with him.

His muscles shifted and worked as he took the stairs up.

The bedroom was just feet away, the bed, the moment drawing closer. Pulse skipping, I squirmed to release myself, but his arms tightened.

He crossed the threshold into my bedroom and kicked the door shut and again I tried to wriggle out of his arms but he didn't let me go. Pitch blackness surrounded us, save for the slanted moonlight which came in soft, white slices from the nearly-closed shutters at the window.

Weston's breath started to pick up speed. Face shadowed with concentration, he focused on my mouth. His warm lips slipped over mine. His kiss, the urgent sound of his hungry breathing intoxicated me, and for a second I forgot that I meant to keep this under control.

I barely felt him moving until he finally laid me on the softness of my bedspread. One of his strong arms remained around my back as he lifted and positioned me on the mattress. His other arm supported his body, crouched over mine.

I should have stopped him downstairs. I shouldn't have let him carry me up here. The door is shut. Luke will never see us now. Not that I wanted him to, I wanted the possibility as a reason not to do this.

"Weston," I managed between kisses. "I can't make love to you."

Weston's fervent kisses slowed. Still poised over me, he eased back, the slatted light from the moon casting white and black cuts over his face and body. "I thought you wanted this too."

"I thought I did. You wanted honesty, so I'm being honest. I can't do this with you."

He eyed me a long moment. "For now or forever?"

I swallowed the knot in my throat. "Now."

Weston let out a sigh and collapsed to my side. Around us, black tension swirled in the silence.

I reached over to turn on the lamp at my bedside, but his body suddenly rolled over mine, his hand cuffing my wrist. "No."

Panic fluttered in my chest. "Why not?"

"I don't want—I can't look at you right now." He fell back, staring up at the ceiling. His hands gripped his head, as if a skull-wracking ache tormented him. Beneath the snug black t-shirt, his chest lifted and fell in rapid motion, like a wounded animal at the side of the road—fear, fury and frustration submerging him.

I remained quiet, hoping time would ease his complicated feelings but his breathing continued to accelerate, the sound stirring me into a bundle of anxiety.

"You realize what this means," he finally ground out.

"What do you think it means?"

He jerked his head my direction, the depths of his eyes frightened me. Beyond him, in the murky corner of my bedroom, shadows moved. I bolted up, straining to see. Flashes of onyx eyes, gnashing teeth in a huddled mass started filling the room. My heart leapt to my throat.

Weston sprang up beside me, blocking my intense study of the growing mass. He grabbed my cheeks, forcing my face in front of his. "It means that you can't *live* without Matthias."

SEVENTEEN

"That's not it," my voice scratched out. My gaze flicking from his twisted face to the hordes of evil spirits inching toward us.

His fingers gripped my head like he might crush my skull. I grasped his wrists, tried to break his grip but his hands remained fixed like iron. "Why can't you let go of him?" The question tore from his lips.

"I am letting go of him." Weston's grip on my skull intensified. My heart screamed with fear. Behind him, the black eyes and hissing teeth of the crowd of spirits flashed and shifted like smoky vapor, spreading in choking clouds around us. I dug my nails into his flesh, tried to break free. The anguish on his face shifted to anger.

The shadows behind him moved closer. And not just evil spirits; Brady. Albert. My mouth fell open. Weston, seeing my horror, loosened his hold and shot a look over his shoulder.

"Brady's here," I gasped.

He saw nothing, of course, which brought fury into his outraged eyes. "You told me you loved me. You've been lying all this time, Zoe. All of it's been lies. The whole story about Brady. Everything." He squeezed my head. I tried to pry his fingers from my skull, but he tossed me back to the mattress.

"I haven't lied," the words burst from my lips. "I promised you the truth."

Albert and Brady slid around the sides of the bed. The spirits with them filled in, so that Weston and I were surrounded by a thick wall of malevolence.

I silently screamed for Matthias.

"He's not coming," Albert hissed, leaning over Weston's shoulder. "Little minx. You've gotten him in trouble." He nodded. Brady grinned, licked his lips.

Trouble? *No.*

"He's in hell, Zoe. Your involvement got him in trouble, and the only way he could make it right was to give himself to me."

"You're lying!" Adrenaline infused me, and like wildfire I twisted, bucked and freed myself of Weston who fell back on his haunches, his eyes huge. I shot upright, tears springing from my eyes. "He's with my parents. With Abria."

Weston jerked back, looked around. Seeing nothing, he stared at me.

Brady was behind Weston, as if waiting for the ripe moment to possess. Weston's face drained of color. Did he feel what I felt? The pressure of hell was so great, I could barely remain conscious—deluged with thoughts of Matthias in hell—let alone worry about what Weston was thinking. I shook my head. "Matthias is protecting them."

"No, Zoe." Albert shook his head. "Matthias is being punished." Albert floated behind Weston and stood nearer to me, looking down into my eyes with a blinkless control that threatened to steal my soul with my next heartbeat.

"Punished," Brady echoed.

No. No. No. Tears slid down my cheeks.

"You're crying for him?" Weston shrieked in disbelief. He squatted on the bed poised to attack and my heart hammered. Brady jumped on the mattress next to him.

"Weston." Fear closed my throat, threatening my voice, "Brady's—"

"More lies," Weston spat.

"Zoe?" Luke's voice from came from somewhere behind the closed door.

The room and its occupants closed in on me. *Matthias—punished. Gone. Suffering. Because of me.* The thought submerged me in hopeless desperation. Matthias wasn't here to protect me. Could Albert be right? But then, I'd chosen to put myself in harm's way. I couldn't deal with Albert's ruthless attack one minute longer. I wanted to disappear. Cease existing.

I leapt from the bed, bursting through the crowd of black spirits, causing them to shrivel back. Heart pounding, I lunged for the door, flung it open. A scream rang out. Mine? My consciousness floated in a place out of my reach—that place we escape to for survival.

I flew down the stairs, passing a saucer-eyed Luke in the entry.

"Z?"

I opened the front door and fled around the corner of the house, the icy night air nipping through my sheer pjs. Faint light from the moon cast ghostly shadows on trees and shrubs. I dove through them. Streaming tears froze on my cheeks. Dodging bushes and pines, I kept running, deeper and deeper into the shadowy forest.

My lungs burned with the frigid air. My mind raced with images of Matthias suffering. Paying for being with me. Punished for loving me. I couldn't bear the unfairness. Heaven was cruel. God was unjust.

Anger drove me on. I kept running. Harder. Faster. The trees grew thicker. More dense, becoming sinister spindles towering over me. Spines tore the fabric of my t- shirt. Through the padding of my booted slippers, the soles of my feet hit rocks, sending jagged pain up my calves.

Unable to suck in air fast enough, I slowed. Gasping. I stopped, fell to the forest floor, and wept uncontrollably.

My sobs filled the silent air. I rolled onto my stomach, fallen pine needles sticking to my tear-ravaged face.

I'm so sorry, so sorry Matthias.

"You can't outrun me, Zoe." Albert. I opened my eyes. Could barely catch my breath. I sat up and futilely backed away on my hands, needles slivering into my cold palms but the distance between Albert and me was closing in.

"Give yourself to me."

I shook my head. Closed my eyes.

"You can be with him. Show him you love him, and give yourself to me."

"No."

"He's there, waiting for you."

"No." Even if Heaven was cruel and God wasn't just, I couldn't give my soul to Albert.

"Then his sacrifice was for nothing," Albert said. I opened my eyes. Trembled. He stood over me, his hands behind his back.

I couldn't believe Matthias wanted me to give up my soul to Albert to be with him. As if he read my thoughts, Albert said, "Give yourself to me and you can be with him."

I desperately wanted to believe him. Being with Matthias—even in hell, sounded better than spending the rest of my life and forever without him. Albert's steel blue eyes reminded me of the pure truth in Matthias.' I closed my eyes, but tears of hopelessness fell anyway.

Leave me alone. I collapsed to the earth, burying my face in the rough bed of fallen pine needles beneath me. My fingers clawed. Dug. Maybe I could bury myself, and die.

My mind conjured up a dark abyss, a place where I stood poised to abandon myself to, not caring where I ended up.

"Do it." Albert's voice slithered into my consciousness.

No. No. No. I ground my face into the needles scratching my cheeks, chin and forehead. I had to get away from him.

Mustering every muscle, I lifted myself up and forced my legs to run. Through my sobs, I heard my name, the call faint, distant as a dead leaf falling to the ground. Luke and Weston. Both were shouting for me, over and over.

Part of me wanted them to find me; another part wanted them safe— far away from Albert and the gaping jaws of hell.

Albert stood in the middle of the darkened path in front of me. I tore left. He was there, waiting. Each direction I turned to flee I found Albert.

I stopped in a clearing, my breath heaving, blowing white plumes into the air.

Albert strolled closer, his hands clasped behind his back. Hordes of black spirits materialized from the night, surrounding the clearing. "You're content to leave him? With Violet?"

More lies? My breath stopped. I swallowed, and drunk in more air. Albert drew closer, so close, if he'd been mortal—had a body, I would have smelled him. Felt his breath. Around us, the circle of evil closed in.

I blew a large plume of breath in his face. He squinted. The corners of his lips lifted. "Bet you can't do that," I gasped out.

In the distance, my name grew louder. Weston and Luke were getting closer.

Albert laughed, but when no sign of breath came from his mouth he stopped, shock flashing briefly in his eyes. "You can't," I began, fueled by truth, "because you don't have a body. You're nobody."

Albert's eyes narrowed. His jaw twitched. The evil hosts he'd brought with him continued to inch closer, pressing me from the outside in, an overpowering fear that squeezed breath from my lungs and caused every fiber in my body to paralyze. Brady was nowhere in sight.

"Zoe?" Weston's voice was closest. My heart leapt with hope.

"Here!"

"Zoe?" Luke shouted after hearing my response to Weston.

The forest air grew thick and so cold, I grabbed myself, shivering uncontrollably. My teeth rattled. Ice instantly erupted from Albert's black shoes, jagging out along the forest floor like frozen claws. White death formed on every surface, dripping from tree branches, coating trunks, traveling across the forest floor, upward shrouding the woods in suffocating frost.

Albert stepped closer. "They'll freeze to death before they can save you."

No! I tried to shake my head, but my body was consumed in violent shudders. My knees locked. My eyes burned from the plunging temperature.

"Zoe? Where are you?" Weston's call echoed. All of this suffering. Because of me.

"Now, Zoe," Albert hissed in my face. "Now."

It seemed I was destined to die at that moment. If I died, at least Luke and Weston would be safe. Matthias would be free of his father's efforts to destroy him. We'd be together in Paradise. Pressure became so great I crumpled over, my soul buckling. I opened my mouth to acquiesce, but my voice froze in my throat.

A light formed to my left. It grew larger and larger, until its radiance spread out, illuminating the area around me and Albert. The black spirits disintegrated instantly.

Matthias. His presence caused the ice to crack, the sound filling the forest like fallen trees as each branch, tree and surface was freed from Albert's arctic grasp. Instantly, I warmed from head to toe. The thunder of feet running my direction snatched my attention to my right.

"I'm here!" I shouted.

Weston appeared in the clearing first, panting and wide-eyed, but he came to an abrupt halt when he saw the light. Luke came seconds later and ran right for me, wrapping around me in a relieved embrace. Weston remained statue still, staring Matthias' direction.

Did he see him?

Matthias' gaze locked on his father. "This has to end."

Albert shielded his eyes from Matthias' aura. "You know very well that's not going to happen," he said.

He said you were being punished, that I'd gotten you in trouble.

Lies, Zoe. I heard Matthias' thoughts, but his gaze remained fixed on Albert as if, with his eyes, he held the devil in place.

Luke and I clung to each other, for safety, for support. Weston hadn't moved since he'd come upon the scene, mouth open, his arms hanging at his sides.

"Take me." Matthias reached out a hand to Albert. "And this will end."

"No!" I lunged toward Matthias but Luke held me back. "No! Don't!" I struggled, unable to break free of Luke's hold.

Albert's arms slowly lowered from his face. How he was able to endure Matthias' presence, I didn't know, except that the menacing on his face had shifted to utter shock at Matthias' offer. Father and son stared at each other for tenuous moments until another light illuminated through the black sky above. Bright as sunlight, the power bathed the forest in purifying white so blinding, everyone except Matthias had to shield their eyes.

A faint hum filled the air. The sound accompanied the light, and soothed and comforted instantly.

I squinted, trying to see details. A silhouette was centered in the light.

Albert dropped to his knees and buried his head in his hands, his shoulders shaking. *Was he crying?* I couldn't hear over the hum filling the forest air.

Matthias's gaze stayed on his father for a moment, then his blue eyes met mine.

I drew in a breath. Something was going to happen, gravity nearly sucked me into the powerful center where Matthias and the silhouette stood. Then, Matthias was gathered into the light and the beam burst.

The forest was dark, save for the moon breaking overhead through the clouds, radiating. I tingled from head to toe. Warm. Comforted. Safe. Luke, who hadn't moved since the second being appeared, stepped back, his arms lowering to his sides, his stare fixed on the place where Matthias just stood.

Weston's face lit with a soft glow. His open mouth formed a gentle smile as his eyes met mine across the clearing.

The only sound was Albert's wretched sobs. He'd fallen to his knees when the light had appeared and there he remained. Only his suit wasn't black anymore. The color was lighter now—a shade of gray.

I ran across the clearing to Weston who met me halfway. His arms gripped me, lifting me from my feet in an embrace. Words seemed irreverent. I didn't want to speak. I didn't know what to say, feeling inadequate to follow the experience with anything that might tarnish what had happened.

I felt Luke's familiar hand on my back and lifted my head from Weston's chest and smiled at him. Weston and Luke's eyes filled with questions and they studied me as if I had all the answers.

EIGHTEEN

At home, Weston, Luke and I sat in the family room, the three of us on the floor in front of a mild fire burning in the fireplace. We hadn't exchanged words as we'd hiked out of the forest. Weston had taken my hand and led me, and Luke had stayed at my back. I hadn't felt vulnerable or unsafe. Albert hadn't followed us.

We left him on his knees, weeping.

Now, hours after seeing Matthias taken up in a stream of light, we were still speechless. I supposed each of us was pondering the experience and none of us wanted to go to bed, though the hour was way past midnight.

Most of the lights were off in the house except for the flickering flame, and the fire cast each of us in a warm, amber glow.

Weston kept staring at me, breaking out in a smile of admiration whenever I caught him. Luke's gaze rarely left the dancing flames.

"Thank you for finding me." I finally broke the ponderous silence.

Both Luke and Weston looked at me. Luke's mind was filled with thoughts, I'd seen that distracted look on his face before—but usually he was distracted by how to score the next bowl. This distraction actually had the wheels in his mind churning with pure purpose.

Weston brought his knees to his chest. "When you ran out of here, I knew something serious was up. Zoe, I felt that same feeling I felt that time in the hotel room. You weren't lying to me. I knew you weren't. I only said that because—I was angry. I didn't mean it."

Angry and taunted by Brady. "How did you get rid of Brady?"

Luke's shocked, curious gaze shifted from me to Weston.

"So he *was* here." Weston swallowed.

I nodded. "I told you he was."

"I—I felt him. Like the other day with my mom. Rage like I've never felt pushing me. I remembered what you told me about him not being able to make me do anything. Once I wasn't angry anymore, I didn't feel his presence. He must have left." He glanced around, a thread of panic in his voice. "Right?"

"He's not here now."

A tremor shook Weston's body. "I hope he never comes back."

"Brady? As in the Brady whose mom tried to shoot you?" Luke asked.

Weston gave a sober nod. "Yeah."

"Holy." Luke's blue eyes remained huge. "Z, what happened out there? I was searching for you and suddenly the whole forest became arctic. Man, I couldn't believe how freezing it was."

"Yeah." Weston nodded. "Thought we were going to die." He looked at me with rounded eyes. "And never find you."

"Albert."

Luke swallowed. "He turned the forest to ice?"

I nodded. "He was there, in the bedroom with Brady and... dozens of other black spirits." My blood chilled recalling the evil that had surrounded Weston and me on the bed. "They followed me."

Weston touched my hand. "Don't talk about it."

"Bedroom?" Luke's brows arched.

"It was my fault," Weston piped.

Luke's eyes flashed at Weston testily. "How the hell did the spirits get there?"

Weston's mouth opened, but I spoke before he had a chance. "It doesn't matter. They were there to stir trouble and when I ran out of here, they followed me. Weston got rid of Brady on his own."

"And the big bad wolf followed you out into the forest," Luke observed, his tone still feisty. "You put her in danger, man. Not cool."

172

"I put myself in danger," I corrected, sharply. I wanted all of this to be over.

"Sorry," Weston put in. "You're right. It wasn't the place to—"

"No details, dude." Luke held up a hand. "She's my sister." A brittle silence followed, but quickly dissipated. "Z, what else happened?"

"What do you mean?"

"With Matthias."

Both Weston and Luke waited for my answer. "What did you guys see?" I asked.

"Matthias," Luke said. Weston nodded.

"So you saw him too?" I asked Weston.

"Yes," Weston said around a thick swallow. "I—I'm still—I don't know if I can describe what it felt like to be there. It was... amazing."

Luke bobbed his head in agreement. "The coolest."

"Matthias' father was there. Albert. Did you see him?"

Weston and Luke shook their heads. Luke gestured to my face. "Did he do that to you?"

I touched the scratches on my face and winced. "No. I fell, and my face hit the ground. Albert told me Matthias was being punished because of me. That I'd gotten him in trouble. He told me I had to give myself to him to make it right."

The fire crackled and a log split, falling to the hearth floor. Gold parks escaped up the flue.

"I thought I was going to die, that somehow Albert would kill me and take me with him. I was willing to go to free Matthias. But I was terrified. Then, Matthias came. He said Albert was lying. And you guys showed up." I took a deep breath. I still couldn't believe Matthias had been willing to give up his soul for me.

Weston's eyes grew larger. "Wow."

"Yeah." I nodded, shivering in spite of the fire. "But then, the other being—I don't know who—came down." The gravity of wondering who had come to save Matthias linked us together in a bond of awe.

Luke nodded. "We saw him."

"You think... it was... God?" Weston whispered.

The idea sent a flush of warmth through my spirit. "I don't know," I said.

"Maybe Matthias has a guardian of his own," Luke suggested. "Blows me away," he murmured.

"Seemed to blow Albert away, too, because he fell to his knees, crying."

"Seriously?" Luke asked.

"I expected him to disintegrate, like he usually does," I said. "The other black spirits did. The second the being showed up, they were gone." Weston's mouth dropped open. I realized he didn't know about how Albert came and left. "Albert can't be around purity—it causes him to disappear."

Weston's Adam's apple rolled up his throat. "Oh."

"So I expected that to happen, but it didn't." I was perplexed that Albert's suit had lightened with the event. "When we left, Albert was still there."

Luke shuddered. "Yeah, I heard him."

"I did, too," Weston added.

A tingling of thrill raced along my skin. How fascinating that both of them had *heard* Albert, but not seen him. Albert's cries of hopelessness and realization would haunt me for a long time.

Weston's open mouth, wide-eyed expression was that of a child discovering the secret of Santa Claus. "Will Albert be back?" he asked.

"Matthias told me he'd fight me for my soul—to get to him." But where was Matthias now? Was Albert still after his soul? "I don't know who that was that came and took Matthias, but someone is watching out for him."

The silence between us prickled with unanswered questions. "This is huger than anything I've ever seen," Luke mumbled. He rubbed his face. "You're something else, Z. I'm glad you're okay." He patted my shoulder.

I leaned over and hugged him. "Thanks bud." He held me a moment, and I enjoyed the connection. The evening, dangerous as it had been, had also brought us together in a way I knew none of us would ever forget.

"Don't know if I'll sleep, but I'm gonna hit the hay." Luke stood, stretched, eyed me, then Weston. "You staying over?"

Weston's cheeks flushed. His gaze met mine and fire danced in the reflection of his eyes. "Maybe I can take the couch?"

Somehow, I was able to sleep. A shower helped. Fresh pjs. Restlessness wasn't as much about Weston sleeping downstairs on the couch as it was the lingering vision of Matthias ready to give himself up to his father. For me. And I couldn't stop replaying the moment he'd been surrounded by that light and taken up.

I jerked upright in bed, heart pounding as the night before played out in my head: flashes of the moment in bold scenes, over and over and over. Was Albert here? Heart leaping in my chest, I searched the room with my gaze, every corner, even leaning over the side of my bed for a look beneath.

No Albert—thankfully.

My pulse started to slow and so did my rapid breathing. What had happened to Matthias?

Would I ever see him again?

The thought of never seeing him hit me like a tidal wave. I refused to let the morbid idea drown me. Until I knew for sure, I wouldn't fixate on something I didn't understand.

Then there was Weston, who'd remembered what I'd told him about how to dismiss evil and had gotten rid of Brady. Pride, and respect, both flowed through my heart at that moment for Weston.

I grabbed my phone to check the time: almost noon. Thank heavens it was Saturday.

I got out of bed, curious to sneak a peek at Weston, asleep downstairs. Passing my reflection in the bathroom mirror, my scraggly hair screamed that I needed to freshen up first. I brushed my teeth and washed my face, careful not to scrape the red scratches on my cheeks and forehead. *Ugh.* I looked like I'd been smacked in the face by a pine tree.

Hair finger-combed, pjs adjusted so I was completely covered and somewhat presentable, I crept down the stairs and into the family room, alert for any sign of Albert. I felt nothing. Saw nothing.

Weston lay on his back, one arm hung off the side of the couch, the other across his chest. His eyes were closed, and his lips were parted a little. His thick, dark hair barely looked mussed. Unfair.

Suddenly, his eyes popped open, and I jumped.

He looked around, rubbed his face with his hands, then noticed me standing, gaping at him. "Hey." His voice was rough.

"Hey." I inched closer, tingling with pleasure at seeing him. The need to kiss him sprung through my body like a cat after warm milk.

He sat up at little, pressing himself into the back of the couch, making room for me. He patted the empty spot next to him.

I sat down, and he eyed my mouth. "Man, what I'd give for some mouthwash right now."

I laughed. Leaning closer to him, I closed my eyes, and pressed a light kiss on his lips. His hands cupped my face and held me in place.

When the kiss was over, I asked, "Did you sleep okay?"

He nodded, eyes hooded for a moment, his mind appearing to race. Then his eager expression disappeared and he sat upright and stretched. "Couch is comfortable, as couches go."

"Sleep on a lot of them?" I teased, standing.

He grinned. "No." His cell phone vibrated over and over from the depths of his pocket. He pulled it out. "Probably my mom wondering where I am."

"I'd want you home every night if you were mine," I said, then wanted to slap myself. Who says stuff like that? Even if it's true.

He blinked slowly, his lips curving up. When he read the text, his jaw twitched. He shoved the phone into the depths of his front pocket, as if ignoring whatever his mother had written.

"Um," I spoke up, "breakfast?"

"Sure." He followed me into the kitchen and I showed him his options:

cold cereals or pancakes.

"You cook?" he teased. "And see angels?"

I laughed. "Ab-so-lute-ly." Matthias' smile flashed into my mind momentarily, and wonder squeezed my heart. Where was he? Was he okay? I hoped he wasn't in any trouble for saving my soul. He should be heralded a hero.

"Zoe?"

I looked up from the mix I was stirring in a bowl. "Sorry, did you say something?"

Weston's lips quirked. "Yeah. So, tonight's prom." He leaned my direction on the counter top, and bit his lower lip. "I'm excited."

"Me too." I smiled and finished whisking pancake batter. I retrieved a pan from the cabinet, flicked on the gas and waited for the skillet to heat. The domesticity of what I was doing sent a giddy tingle through my body.

"You want me to tell you what Luke and I planned? Or surprise you? Or did Luke already spill it?"

I poured flat, baseball-sized pancakes on the sizzling surface of the pan. "Luke hasn't said anything, except that he got a tux and Krissy's dress is blue—crap. I forgot Krissy's coming."

"She'll be here in a few minutes." Luke's voice came from my left. He entered the kitchen fully dressed in jeans, button-up striped shirt and freshly washed hair.

"I totally spaced." I snatched a spatula and flipped the cakes.

"It's cool." Luke pulled out a bar stool and joined Weston at the cook-top island where I flipped the finished cakes onto a plate and handed them to Weston.

"Thanks, they look great."

I handed Luke the spatula. "You finish up, I'm gonna go get ready." I jogged around the cooking island and back upstairs.

I pulled on jeans, a red thermal and topped it with a green short sleeved tee shirt. As I pulled my hair into a pony tail, the doorbell rang.

Krissy's timid voice trickled upstairs. Another female voice—her aunt's—spoke in conjunction with Luke's.

Krissy and her aunt stood in the entry. A gust of tepid air followed them in. I was surprised the air wasn't colder after last night, but the sun was out, and white-gold rays poured through every window in cheery beams. A carpet of light fell in through the open front door where Krissy and her aunt stood.

A purple garment bag hung over Krissy's arm. She wore jeans beneath her coat, and a pair of black flats with little bows. Her hair flowed in soft waves to her shoulders. She radiated. Krissy's smile gleamed at Luke, who spoke—quite confidently—to the woman. I didn't see Weston and figured he was in the kitchen, finishing his pancakes.

After introductions and hugs shared between Krissy and Luke and me, Krissy's aunt Connie turned to me. "I appreciate you having her for the night. It's a long drive for me."

I nodded. "No worries. She'll hang with me after prom is over."

"She's talked about nothing else." Connie's fond gaze followed Krissy's every move, protectively.

I could imagine the difficulty of when to rein in and when to set free where Krissy was concerned. Connie carried the burden of Krissy's welfare now, and the deep line between her brows and the concentrated way she watched her niece was an undeniable expression of guardianship and family love.

I wished, at that moment, I could tell her Krissy had a guardian angel who also watched over her and offered comfort.

"What have you got planned?" Connie inquired. "If you don't mind me asking."

"Um." Luke shrugged. "We're going to go ice skating down at the Olympic rink, then we'll come back and get ready. After that, we're taking the girls to dinner and to the dance."

"That sounds like lots of fun." Connie's gaze swept the entry hall, as if she was studying the house in which her niece would be staying for the next twenty-four hours, then her gaze fell on me. "Thank you again, Zoe."

"You're welcome."

Connie faced Krissy and they hugged. "Have fun, sweetheart. Call me when you get in tonight. It doesn't matter how late it is."

Krissy nodded. "Okay. Thanks."

Connie touched Krissy's cheek. "You're welcome."

After her aunt left, and Krissy and Luke wrapped in a long hug the moment the front door closed behind the woman. I smiled. Krissy cuddled deep into Luke's arms. Her soft sniffles pinched my heart. The tender way Luke stroked her hair touched me.

I headed to the kitchen for a hug of my own.

⚜ ⚜ ⚜

I shut and locked my bedroom door, then turned and faced Krissy who stood in the middle of my room. "We have to lock them out," I grinned, "or we'll never be left alone."

Krissy nodded, hands wringing. "Okay."

"See, guys don't get the whole it's-time-to-get-ready for prom thing." I crossed to her, feeling a bit like a mother readying her child for her first day of school. "It's a girl thing."

Krissy nodded again.

I glanced at the purple garment bag lying on the foot of my bed. "Let me see your dress."

She gingerly unzipped the bag and carefully brought out a sky blue dress—I gasped— with a black sash around the waist. My dress. In blue.

Krissy, seeing my shock, asked, "Don't you like it? Is it ugly?"

"No," I laughed. "I have the same dress. In lavender."

"Oh no." Her hands flew to her lips. "What will we do?"

I set my hands on my hips, eyeing the soft blue dress that looked just as good in blue as it did in lavender. Britt and I had spent weeks shopping for the right dress back in the day, thinking even if the guy was lame, when the dress was perfect the evening had some merit.

That attitude was stupid, I realized. Going to prom just to be going

179

or to be seen, well, that wasn't my m.o. anymore. It was the relationship that mattered now, the guy was important. At least to me, and I knew Krissy wasn't going to show off a dress.

"We have great taste, right?" I shrugged.

"Yeah." Her laugh fluttered out. "We do."

"First things first." I placed her dress on the back of my closet door so the wrinkles could fall out. Next, I grabbed my iPod and set it in the dock on top of my dresser. I chose a playlist and cranked the music up. Krissy squeezed her hands together at her chest, a grin spilling from her lips.

I guided her into my bathroom where my palettes of makeup were spread out on the counter along with curling irons, flat irons, various hairbrushes and other beauty necessities girls needed to glamorize.

She let out a gasp. "Wow. Cool."

"Do you wear makeup much?" I asked, hoping not to overwhelm her. She stared at the display like a little girl in front of a room full of dolls she wanted.

"No. Dad doesn't—never allowed it."

I picked up a foundation powder that matched her skin color, then plucked up a fluffy brush and stood inches from her. Krissy's gaze swept my face.

"What happened?" She pointed to the scratches on my cheeks, forehead and chin.

"I had a run in with some trees."

"It looks terrible."

You've gotta love innocent honesty. "Yeah, that's what concealer's for, right?" I joked. "So." I started brushing the skin-colored powder on her forehead. She pinched her eyes closed. "How are things going, anyway? You like living with your aunt? She seems really cool." I finished applying the powder and set the brush aside. "That looks awesome."

She eyed herself in the mirror. "Aunt Connie's great. We weren't really close before, but she's really nice."

I applied some faded cherry blush to her cheeks and she smiled. "Every

180

girl needs to be in a perpetual blush," I grinned. "Especially on a date." I wouldn't push Krissy, but wanted to know more. I especially wondered what was happening to her dad. I had to resign myself to the fact that it might be a long time before she wanted to talk to me about it.

"All I have to do is be around Luke and I'm blushing," Krissy said, the color in her cheeks deepening.

"Well." I patted her shoulder. "Trust me when I say he feels the same about you."

Krissy's shoulders lifted demurely. "Really?"

I nodded. "Yup." I applied foundation to my face, realizing I wasn't going to be able to cover the myriad of scratches without some serious work with the concealer.

"He says I helped him quit using." Her tone was quiet and self-deprecating. "I don't know…"

"That's great Krissy." I set the foundation on the sink and met her eyes in the reflection of the mirror. "Our family has tried everything to help him. I, for one, am glad you came into his life."

"He helped me, too."

"I'm glad you two found each other."

"Yeah." Her hand shook as she reached for eyeliner.

"Want me to do it?" I offered.

She handed me the tube and faced me. Her lashes fluttered against an onslaught of tears. I bit my lower lip. Were those tears of joy for having found Luke? Or was her life haunting her at that moment? I wanted to hug her and tell her things would get better.

After the tears subsided, I drew on a line of liner curving it up on the outer edge of her eyes. She blinked at her reflection. "Oh, thanks."

"The sparkle brings out the color in your eyes. Mascara?" I held up the purple tube.

"I can never put this stuff on," she said, leaning close enough to the mirror she was nearly nose-to-nose with her reflection.

"One layer at a time," I said, and the words brought Matthias to mind.

That's how understanding comes.

Where are you? Are you okay? I looked upward, the white ceiling of my bathroom greeting me. I wished I could see beyond and into the heavens.

"How's that?" Krissy faced me, her now-black lashes fluttering.

"Perfect."

Krissy smiled.

"Okay," I said. "Time to get dressed."

NINETEEN

The doorbell rang at eight o'clock. I waited outside of my bathroom door for Krissy to come into the bedroom. "That's Weston," I called. "You ready?"

I flattened the fabric of my dress and checked for ribbons hanging perfectly and no undone zippers.

The bathroom door swung open. Krissy stepped out, her glow almost as lovely as the spirits I'd seen. Her gleeful expression dropped when she saw me. "Your dress."

I looked down at the black garment I wore. I'd worn it to another prom, but I was sure no one would care or remember. I'd shined plenty of times. It was Krissy's turn.

"Think it'll work?"

"Why don't you wear the lavender one? I don't mind, really."

"It's cool. I'll match Weston better, don't you think?" I turned.

She nodded. Then she turned. "Okay?"

"You look ab-so-lute-ly gorgeous," I said. I'd curled her hair in big loops and piled them on top of her head like a princess.

She grabbed my hands and jumped up and down, laughing. The moment reminded me of countless ones just like it I'd had with Britt and a brief sadness flashed into me, but I didn't dwell on it.

There was a light tap on the door. "Z?"

"Coming. Go wait downstairs."

I heard Luke's footfalls take the stairs, then I extended my arm to Krissy and we made our entrance. The crystal chandelier overhead lit the room to a heavenly sparkle. At the bottom, Weston stood in all black, a periwinkle shirt and a black tie. He held a lavender corsage. His smile gleamed. Next to him, Luke's grin grew with each step Krissy took closer to him. His blue eyes shined against his black tuxedo and baby blue shirt. "Man, this prom thing is top shelf."

Krissy giggled.

Weston slipped his arms around me. "You're beautiful." He pressed his lips to mine in a quick kiss. Then he brushed his fingers over the scratches I'd tried to hide on my cheeks and chin. His brows knit over troubled eyes, and he lightly kissed each spot.

After our corsages were pinned in place, we were out the door and off to dinner. Prom was traditionally the night of nights, and I wasn't sure what to expect from Weston. We could have eaten at Taco Bell and I'd have been giddy.

The night air wasn't as cold as it had been. Maybe spring was finally on its way. Overhead, the sky was clear and sprinkled with a handful of stars that appeared tossed into the black heavens like glittering confetti.

I had a fleeting thought wondering where Matthias was and I closed my eyes, drawing in a breath of night air. *Wherever you are, I hope everything is ok. I love you.*

It was getting easier for me to think about loving both Weston and Matthias simultaneously. I'd doubted I could share my heart with two souls, but Matthias, as always, was right when he'd said the heart had room for many loves.

Weston held my hand and we walked to his truck, Krissy and Luke following us.

✦ ✦ ✦

Weston and Luke took us to The Bungalow, a quaint twenties-style reception house in Pleasant Grove. The cottage was nestled deep in a bed of bushes and hundred-year-old trees, decorated in millions of sparkling twinkle lights.

The parking lot was empty when we pulled in. "I thought this was a reception place?"

Weston smiled across the darkness of his truck. "Tonight, it's just for us. My mom knows the lady who owns it." He wagged his brows. "She helped me set it up."

A grin spread on my lips. "Nice."

Luke and Weston opened our doors for us and Krissy and I got out of the truck. Weston held my hand and we walked beneath an awning of green twinkle lit ivy to the wide arched wooden front door. The bungalow looked like something Snow White's seven dwarfs might live in with its dark greenish brown exterior and curved roofline. The diamond paned, crank style windows revealed charming lace curtains and delicate lamps centered on cozy tables inside.

Weston opened the door and the scent of cinnamon and baked bread filled the air. My stomach grumbled. I hadn't eaten since we'd ice skated.

I tried not to think about what had happened last night, and instead focused on what was happening. Weston looked so radiant and happy, I wouldn't mar one second of the night with my worrying about whether or not I was going to see Albert again.

A tall, slim woman with dark hair pulled back in a sleek knot met us in the entry. Her flattering black slacks and turtleneck sweater reminded me of something Audrey Hepburn might have worn. The woman floated with grace over the hardwood floors as we followed her to two tables, dressed and ready for our dining luxury.

Luke and Krissy sat at one, Weston and I at the other.

White lacy table cloths, linen napkins, a spring bouquet in the center surrounded by crystal goblets and pink china—the table was too beautiful to eat on. "Wow," I whispered after being seated.

"Like you, I thought it was only a reception center. Mom told me they do special stuff like this, so I thought, why not?" Weston placed his cloth napkin on his lap.

"So, you and your mom… things are better?" He hadn't said much and I didn't want to pry or bring up something painful, so I avoided the topic.

He snorted, shrugged. "We're being civil. I have to say, since that whole blow up, things haven't been as intense."

Maybe Brady was gone for good. I hoped so. "You've taken control. That's cool."

"Damned right."

I laughed, and glanced out the window into the vine-covered patio lit with pink and white lights. My heart stuttered. Albert stood watching me from against the farthest wall. How long had he been there? Why hadn't I sensed him—felt him? My stomach churned. Weston continued talking, but I didn't hear what he said, fixated as I was now on Albert's presence and worrying about what he was going to do.

"You okay?" Weston's gaze searched my face.

I tore my attention away from Albert momentarily. "I—I'm fine. I could use some water."

Our water glasses were empty, and our waitress had yet to visit our table. Weston vanished in search of help.

When I glanced back out the window, my heart jumped. Albert stood next to the table. Oddly, the submerging evil I usually felt whenever I was in his presence wasn't in the air. I wasn't accustomed to seeing him in anything but black. Last night, his suit had appeared lighter bathed in the brilliant light surrounding the being. His suit was even lighter now, a soft shade of dove gray. His shirt was the same color and—that hideous rope tie had been replaced by a simple, slim gray tie.

His eyes had changed. I tried to figure out what was different. They were that Matthias blue, and still mesmerizing in their own way but I couldn't put my finger on what was different.

His attention lifted from me to something behind me, and I whirled around. Weston was heading my direction with a goblet of water. When I turned back, Albert was gone.

I swung left. Right. But he wasn't anywhere. Had I imagined seeing him?

How bizarre.

Weston sat next to me. "Drink this. You look kinda...pale."

"Thanks" I said, sneaking in long glances around the room just to make sure I wasn't hallucinating after last night's events in the forest. "I'm fine." I sipped the icy water. I hoped Albert wasn't gearing up for more. I was tired. I was beat. I wasn't sure where Matthias was, but I wanted my prom.

The Governor's Hotel was in downtown Salt Lake City. The Victorian gothic architecture made for a stately building, surrounded by modern skyscrapers, making the historic hotel stand out. From the thirty-seventh floor there was an unobstructed view spreading out in every direction in colorful, twinkling lights.

The Roof Ballroom was where prom was being held and after the valet parked Weston's truck, Krissy, Luke, Weston and I joined the throngs of students in flowing gowns and sleek tuxedos parading into the four-story lobby on their way upstairs.

Marble pillars held up an ornate, open balcony—the second floor— above the main lobby. A monstrous crystal chandelier hung with thousands of dangling, carved crystals.

The place was stunning. I felt like a princess. How different it was to be at an event like this with someone special.

I stole a glance at Weston, admiring the strength in his chin and the way his chestnut hair feathered at the back of his collar. We strolled arm-in-arm through the elegant, busy lobby to the elevators.

On tip-toes, I kissed his cheek.

His skin flushed when he looked at me, and his arm tightened around mine.

In the cramped elevator, girls eyed my dress. I kept my gaze on the floor numbers whirling past as the car sped upward.

Once on the thirty-seventh floor the throngs of prom-goers threaded into the giant, mirrored ballroom where a DJ worked dance music from a small black stage. On one side of the room tables were set up with chairs and a refreshment bar was located near the door.

Luke and Krissy, who had for the most part remained close by during our trek from the truck to the elevator, now stood staring at the room and its occupants.

Music blasted from dozens of well-placed speakers, so I leaned close to Luke's ear. "Having fun?"

He nodded. He hadn't let go of Krissy's hand all night. "Good," I said, and gave him a quick hug. I loved seeing him happy. I felt like the pieces of our family that had floated out into oblivion were finally gravitating back home.

Weston tugged me away from Luke, shooting my brother a nod, which was returned. Then Weston led me onto the dance floor. A slow, haunting song played, and when Weston wrapped around me and his body moved in that easy rock next to mine, I started to float.

"This is the best." His warm breath in my ear sent feathers of warmth through my body. "Being here with you. This is the best, Zoe."

"I agree." I rested my head against his chest, then thought better of it, not wanting to get my makeup on his black tuxedo. Besides, I never tired of looking at him.

He studied me so intensely, I shivered. "What?"

"There'll never be anyone like you, that's all," he said. "The things you see, the way you are… you're irreplaceable."

I knew how he felt. I felt that way about Matthias. "That's nice of you to say, but—"

"Don't." His brows knitted together. "I'm serious. I don't think… I can't…" He looked away for a moment, as if struggling with words. "I'm not sure I will ever be able to love anyone the way I love you."

Weston held his heart out to me at that moment, the most vulnerable part of a human soul. The responsibility was daunting, but I wasn't frightened.

"Don't think about that right now. Be here now. That's all."

His vulnerable expression remained exposed. He held me tighter, dipping his head against mine so his lips coursed my neck, but not in a kiss, he just kept them pressed against the pulse beating alongside my throat.

I closed my eyes for a while, enjoying the way our bodies moved together. I hoped he understood how the heart was capable of holding many loves, though I, too, knew that when deep love penetrated a spot, there it remained. Forever.

When the song changed, we eased apart and jumped around with the rest of the student body celebrating. I caught Chase standing by the refreshment bar, and grinned.

I pointed him out to Weston. "Let's go say hi," I yelled over the music.

Weston nodded and we wove through bouncing dancers toward Chase. He wore a baby blue tuxedo that looked like it might have been from the 80s, complete with ruffled shirt, black cummerbund and black shoes. He looked eclectically in style, though I was pretty sure he hadn't planned to look that way. He sipped a drink and waved as we approached.

"Hey, guys." He was adorably happy. Chase and I hugged. "Wow, Zoe, you look gorgeous." Chase turned to Weston. "You're a lucky guy, dude."

"Yeah, I am. Dig the tux, man."

"Where did you find it?" I asked. Weston grabbed two pre-filled drinks in clear cups and handed me one.

"Mom insisted I wear Dad's wedding tux."

"Looks good," I said, sipping something lemon lime. Chase pulled off the look in a Clark Kent kind of way.

"It works." Weston shrugged.

"Who'd you come with?" I glanced around.

"Myself. I took your suggestion and am covering the event for the paper." Chase eyed Weston from head to toe, as if deciphering what Weston had that he didn't.

I whispered in Weston's ear, "Mind if I ask him to dance?"

Weston smiled, shook his head and took my drink. I extended my hand to Chase. "Let's dance."

Chase whirled around, searching for a place to put his drink. Weston's hands were full with our drinks, so Chase set his nearly-empty cup on the nearest banquet table.

We went out on the dance floor. The song was slow, and Chase shot glances Weston's direction, not sure what to do. I held out my hands and he eagerly wrapped around me. "So," his voice warbled nervously in my ear, "you guys having fun?"

"It's been a great day, yeah."

"Weston's a nice guy."

I leaned back and smiled at him. "So are you."

His cheeks bloomed in a bright pink shade. His eyes sparkled, but he appeared speechless.

"I've got stuff to tell you," I said. "Something happened last night you're going to want to know."

"Yeah?" His brows arched. "What?"

"Tonight's not the night, but we can meet next week"

He seemed pleased with that idea, relieved even—like, just because I was with Weston didn't mean he would never see me again. "Okay. Starbucks?"

"Starbucks."

When the song ended, he escorted me back to a waiting Weston.

An awkward tension suddenly zapped the air between us. "I'm going to go to the ladies room." I kissed Weston's cheek and started on a search for a breath of fresh air.

Outside the ballroom on the floor were windows lining one side of the wall. The view was incredible, so I stepped out on the balcony and enjoyed watching cars zoom through traffic below. The scent of city air, both dirty and with a bite evergreen carried on the light breeze coming from the canyon, tasted gritty in my mouth and nose.

"It's beautiful, isn't it?" That voice.

Albert stood next to me.

TWENTY

I reached for the balcony ledge and held tight, waiting for dense evil to submerge me. But the air surrounding us remained untainted.

"Don't be afraid." His voice had changed. Softer. Not for the sake of seduction, but the delicate tone of respect. Shocked, my mouth opened but I wasn't sure what to say.

He wore the same gray suit I'd seen him in at The Bungalow. Up close, I noted that the gray threads were actually twined with white. Where was his noose tie? What had happened to him?

"Thank you." His Matthias-blue gaze held mine in unblinking sincerity. As shocking as this moment was, the air around us was clear, crisp—like an open conduit to heaven. "I hope someday you can forgive me, Zoe."

I didn't know how to respond. Mercy shed a peculiar light on Albert. *Maybe I could forgive him someday.*

A layer lifted from his countenance, lightening him yet even more: his skin, his eyes, his suit—from head to toe.

His lips turned up slightly, and a faint aura emanated from him. He turned, facing the city and the noose tie suddenly appeared in his hands. The rope tie of souls writhed, their screams like distant screeching, filling the night air. Albert's face twisted in grief. He lowered his head for a moment, as if touching the tie brought him unspeakable agony.

I stood spellbound, my hand over my pounding heart. Tears streamed from his closed eyes, down his taut cheeks. He held the noose tie in the palms of his hands as if he held delicate tissue paper, then he lifted the tie heavenward and the white bundle of souls broke free, swirling into the black night, each sinewy thread spinning upward toward the stars until I could see no more.

Slowly, Albert's hands returned to his sides. His face remained heavenward. Long moments passed. How we were able to remain alone on the balcony was one of God's gifts to him, I supposed. Enabling him to complete what he needed to.

"Thank you," he whispered. To me? To God? I wasn't sure. He remained facing outward, and all I could see was his profile. But relief spread through his back and shoulders.

Laughter startled me. I glanced right. Four couples burst through the glass doors and joined us on the balcony. They looked at me, and I noticed one of the boys pulled a bag of white powder out from the inside of his jacket. He didn't bother trying to disguise the coke; in fact, he held the bag out to me and jerked his head in invitation to join them.

My stomach twisted with revulsion. Nothing would compare with what I'd just witnessed—most definitely not some fleeting high.

I shook my head and turned back to face Albert.

He was gone.

Weston came through the door and the kids with the drugs acknowledged him. He gave them an impersonal nod, and his gaze searched the balcony. When his eyes found mine, he strode my way.

"Are you okay?" His hands wrapped around my upper arms. He peered into my face. "Zoe?"

"Um, yeah." I shook out my head. Had I really just seen Albert? Maybe my hopes and fantasies were getting the best of me. "I just needed some air. Look at this great view, huh?"

Weston eyed me as if trying to decipher truth. I turned and faced the city. The sparkly lights stretched out in an endless weave, crisscrossing the black fabric of the valley floor. Protecting the valley, the rocky peaks of powerful mountains reached heavenward in leaping black shapes.

Matthias, where are you? Do you know that I saw Albert? Do you know he's changed? I hoped so, for Matthias' sake.

Weston's shoulder and arm brushed against mine, his warmth comforting. Real.

"I want to dance with you." Weston turned toward me. I felt his gaze examining me, and faced him.

The moonlight, partially hidden behind a bank of traveling clouds, cast his face in white. He inched closer and wrapped around me. Behind him, the group of kids laughed and whispered, and I was vaguely aware that they were talking about taking hits.

"Right here?" I asked.

He seemed totally focused on me, but when one of the boys let out a groan, he frowned. "Inside." Taking me by the hand, he led me through the glass double doors back into the warmth of the 37th floor where couples strolled. Some sat on couches, talking.

Music pounded from speakers, and the dance floor rocked and waved with gyrating bodies moving to the beat. Weston started jumping, so I did too. We danced through the crowd until we were on the dance floor.

Chase waved from the edge of the bouncing mass. I suppressed a chuckle at his attempts to dance. Each limb moved to its own internal beat, none of which coordinated with the pound blasting from the speakers.

But his grin was huge and he didn't seem to care.

When the next song filled the air, the whole room slowed. White and gold flashing lights shifted to soft pinks and reds in the shape of hearts, spinning in tandem with the romantic melody.

Weston pulled me close and I locked my arms around his neck. The tips of his hair fell around his face, moist with sweat from dancing, and his spicy cologne filled my head.

He smiled and held me closer.

I rested my head against his chest, enjoying the perfect evening. Through the crowd I caught Luke and Krissy swaying in each other's arms.

The sight brought a smile to my face. My gaze continued skipping those around us. Most faces familiar, all caught up in oozy happiness as they danced to the slow tune.

I saw him then—Matthias—a steady pure, white vision in the crowd. I stopped. I was astounded that no one else saw him but me.

Weston stopped, too, and followed my gaze. His grip around me tightened. *Weston sees Matthias?* As amazing as that miracle was, I needed to go to Matthias.

I stepped back. Weston's grip remained firm. I refused to take my eyes off Matthias for fear he would vanish before I had a chance to speak to him. I squirmed, and broke free of Weston, but he grabbed my arm.

"Zoe." The desperation in his voice boomed over the music, bringing my eyes to his. His carried fear. "You're safe with me," he plead. "I can take care of you."

"Do you… see him?"

He nodded.

"I have to go to him."

"Please don't." Weston held my gaze for a few tight seconds before freeing me.

I wove through the dancers; some had caught me leaving Weston alone in the middle of the dance floor, and their curious gazes now trailed me. I ignored them.

Matthias' smile gleamed. His aura was more brilliant, more commanding than it had been before, and the force reached out and brought me to him with such magnetism, my feet nearly floated over the hardwood floor until I stood in front of him. He was dressed in white, but not in his usual casual clothing. A sleek suit of the softest fabric—silken velvet— I reached out to touch it and he extended his arm toward the exit, gesturing for the two of us to go outside.

I glanced over my shoulder at Weston on the fringe of the dance floor, watching us.

Matthias' gentle gaze remained on me, wholly focused, creating that

194

solid feeling of absolute love deep inside of me. The doors to the ballroom were open, and he and I crossed through them into the lobby of the 37th floor.

I was so happy to see him. He radiated magnificently, I could not take my gaze from him. *You're so beautiful.*

I can say the same about you. He spotted the glass doors to the balcony, and once again held out his hand in that direction. I smiled at the irony that I'd just been in the same spot with his father.

Matthias held the door open, his blue eyes deepening as I passed him. My heart opened in my chest, the love and admiration I had for him overflowing into my soul with the calm, yet powerful current of an unstoppable tide.

The balcony was empty and we strolled to the iron railing. He never took his eyes from me to even glance at the view. My body flushed with his aura—more thrilling than I'd ever felt. As if my mortal body couldn't contain the potent sensation, I was ready to burst even without touching him.

"Zoe." The gentle melody of his voice wove in, filling any final voids. "You're the bees knees tonight."

"Thank you." The tingling racing through me from head to toe wouldn't stop. "Where have you been?"

"Let me look at you." His gaze swept my face, but not casually—this sweep was deep, studying. Memorizing. "Do you know I never went to a school dance?"

"You didn't? Never got asked? Girls who lived back then were lame."

He threw his head back in laughter. "You think so?"

"I know so. If I'd been alive, you'd never had a weekend night free and I would have made sure you went every dance."

Sassy bearcat.

I laughed.

"I could cut a rug back in the day." His gaze latched on something and I followed it. Weston. He stood inside the glass doors, hands thrust deep in his front pockets, eyes following our every move.

"Weston is not pleased with my cutting into your evening."

I tried my best to show Weston that I was not planning on ditching him for the rest of the night. I smiled and tilted my head at him. Pleading still hung in his eyes, and his body looked edgy.

"I told him I needed to see you. He was worried I was in danger." I watched Matthias' face for any change of expression. His pleasant grin remained unchanged. "I take it I'm not?"

He shook his head.

"Albert was here earlier."

No shock, fear or anger passed over Matthias' face or shone in his eyes.

"He looked different," I said. "He asked for my forgiveness."

Matthias' blue eyes deepened with flecks of sapphire. "Yes, Zoe."

"You've seen him?"

"Last night, I witnessed the change."

"So I wasn't imagining it. What… happened?" I asked.

"His heart changed. He wants to be a better soul."

"Wow. That's…" Extraordinary. But then I'd seen the difference in Albert myself. I guess I hadn't really believed someone like him could want to change. I didn't want Matthias seeing a drop of doubt in my soul about the miracle, so I averted my gaze but that was useless.

"You know as well as I that change can be instantaneous—if you want it bad enough."

I'd said those exact words to my mother. "It was you, wasn't it? What you did for me." Emotion rushed in passionate waves through my yearning cells. "Did he see the… *being* who came for you?"

Yes. His heart was touched. A miracle, Zoe.

"Was that God?"

Matthias' countenance pulsated with a strobe of blinding light—like his heartbeat was indelibly connected to it. "No."

You have your own guardian angel, I should have known.

The vibrant pulsing strobe within him melded seamlessly into his own stunning beauty.

"You finally have what you deserve," I murmured.

≥✦≤

196

"Pop's on the right path."

"So, you… haven't actually… talked to him?"

He shook his head. "A change of heart can happen instantaneously. The road to refinement… that takes some time. But I look forward to the day when he and I will be reunited."

That's wonderful. I stepped toward him, the need to savor and share joy through an embrace overpowering.

He stepped back.

A thread of panic dangled deep inside of me. His smile slowly vanished. His eyes held mine, unblinking.

"I can't touch you?" My voice scraped out. I reached for the cold iron railing to steady myself.

"I'm sorry."

My head emptied of pleas. My heart plummeted to my feet. I closed my eyes to hold back an onslaught of tears. The news left me blank inside.

"My refinement has placed me in a position that—"

"Don't." I held up a hand and forced my gaze to his face, scored with sorrow for the touch we could no longer share. *You deserve whatever has happened to you. I don't mean to diminish that.* Still, the longing inside of me only intensified as I looked at him, knowing I would never touch him again.

Not never, Zoe.

I turned, facing the city lights, hoping he wouldn't see the tears escaping my eyes, streaming down my cheeks. My shoulders buckled once, and I felt his aura press into my side as he moved closer. *I'll miss you.* The thought washed from my head with tears.

"Ah, Zoe. Don't cry. Please."

I nodded, and wiped my cheeks. The cool night air chilled my skin. I wasn't sure I could look at him without breaking into more tears. *Give me strength. Please. Please, God.*

Matthias' blue eyes seemed clearer, bluer. So pure. Like beautiful gem stones. I couldn't think of any words to say. My heart was overcome with grief. Loss. But it was unfair of me to revel in my own sorrow when he'd experienced miracles. He deserved better from me.

"This dancing I see here is—" He glanced around. "It's rather scandalous."

"It's called bear hugging," I sniffed.

"Bear—my. Hmm." The tempo slowed, the song melancholy but sweet as the chords rang out. Love poured into my body. I wanted to be closer. To bond. My longing grew, swelling in an uncontrollable rush inside of me. *I love you.*

Zoe. His right hand came in close to my cheek. Warmth, power radiated into my skin. Was I breathing? The world around us swirled away.

A far away look of resignation entered his eyes, penetrating me to my core. "I came to say goodbye."

I opened my mouth to speak but couldn't. If I hadn't been gripping the icy iron railing, I'd have crumpled to the floor.

"Zoe, that moment in the forest, I would have done anything to see that you were free of Albert's assaults. I—"

"Now you're not able to be with me anymore?" I broke in a choked sob. "You've been promoted or something, right?"

Matthias' face scored with compassion. "Please."

"Please what? Forget you? Forget the way I feel about you? I can't. I wouldn't want to no matter how much it hurts." I turned and walked away from him. On the other side of the glass doors, Weston stepped closer, as if sensing something was wrong. His hands anchored on the glass.

I crossed the balcony to the opposite end, trying in vain to outrun the inevitable. Matthias was there, waiting for me. His power and love wrapped around me. Another tear streamed down my cheeks, cooling against a wisp of breeze stirring the night air. Matthias cocooned me in light and comfort; comfort I didn't think I could possibly access, given the sorrow gouging me.

With tenderness, he reached out and his presence stroked my tears away even though our flesh never made contact. More tears followed, drawn out like poison from my soul.

Our last touch.

Not our last, Zoe.

Until I die.

Silence. Heavy. Unbearable.

I knew this moment would come. I have to remember the way you felt. I can't forget.

Precious moments fled by.

What if I can't let go? I wondered.

You can. You've got a fulfilling life ahead of you.

"I don't want it."

"I'll be waiting for you."

I reached for the impossible. Deep down, I was happy for him. I wouldn't take his father's change of heart away from him for anything, but I was devastated that meant he no longer would be with me.

The years ahead seemed as endless as the dark heavens. Would the pain ever go away? The longing? The missing?

I don't want you to hurt.

You should have thought of that before you offered to go in my place.

His blue eyes were earnest. "I love you," he said. His light scent scarcely breathed in and out of my lungs.

"Do you remember when Abria was in the hospital?" he asked. *You were afraid she'd remember the pain.*

You kissed her forehead and told me she wouldn't remember. My eyes flashed open. "No."

"I don't want to leave you hurting."

I shook my head. More tears fell down my cheeks. "I'd rather live with the memory."

Matthias' eyes glistened.

I braced for agonizing emptiness. But my soul filled with his love. I'd tried to hold onto him before. I'd thought my futile flesh could actually keep him here on earth with me. Instinct, maybe a final shred of fantasy or hope had my fingers fisting around empty air.

Stay.

Our eyes locked. Yearning sang through my soul and the driving melody twined with the resplendent hum of his aura. I braced for another beam of light to burst and carry him up. Matthias faded from my view.

TWENTY-ONE

I stood on an empty balcony. A chill raced over my bare arms, the back of my neck, but serenity resided in my heart. I wouldn't have given up any of my time with Matthias, even knowing that I'd spend my life missing him.

A light tap drew my attention. Weston stood inside, staring at me from behind the window, his palms spread on the glass in desperation. I drew in a deep breath and started for the door.

His gaze followed me tentatively, as if he didn't believe I was coming to him. We stood facing each other, the glass between us. The raw apprehension on his face, in his eyes, drew me to him. He'd been here for me, had faith in every thing I'd told him, loved me with in spite of it all. The need to embrace him pushed me to take the steps away from where I had said goodbye to Matthias.

Weston opened the door and warm air chased the chill from my skin. I stepped inside.

"Are... you okay?" he asked.

I nodded. "Yes."

"What happened?" Weston's gaze searched mine. His sincerity touched me.

"Matthias... said goodbye."

Weston's eyes widened. His gaze swept the empty balcony. A moment passed. Muted music from behind closed doors of the ballroom danced in the background.

He placed his hands on my shoulders. "Something happened last night, didn't it?"

"Yeah." Dazed, I stared off into the black night, trying to juggle conflicting emotions. "Matthias offered himself to go in my place and... now he's... he can't be here anymore."

"Are you sorry?"

I shook my head. Sad. Missing him. Empty.

But not sorry.

Weston's gaze shifted out the window at the vacant balcony. Time crawled by in an self-conscious silence. I was thinking of Matthias, and I was certain Weston knew that. His gaze fastened to mine and he embraced me. Mortal flesh, and mortal comfort lit my heart with a spark of peace.

I wrapped my arms around him.

Summer

The scent of barbequed hamburgers carried on muted gray smoke snuck in the open windows of the kitchen. The deck door was ajar and Dad stood at the grill, spatula in hand, ready to flip the sizzling meat.

Mom and I carried platters of buns, condiments, potato salad and a colorful array of cut vegetables outside to the wrought iron patio set where Krissy and Luke sat, holding hands.

"Are you sure I can't help?" Krissy asked.

I set down a tray of buns. Mom placed the round bowl heaped with chunks of oniony potato salad in the center of the oval patio table.

"You set the table," she smiled.

"And I folded the napkins," Luke put in. He held up a paper napkin, folded in a triangle.

Krissy's cheeks pinked and she nuzzled Luke. "Yes you did. They look good."

I positioned the vegetable tray next to the potato salad and plucked a carrot stick, crunched it. I pulled my cell phone out of the front pocket of my jeans for the time. Weston should be here any minute.

"How close are we?" Mom crossed to the barbeque and peered over Dad's shoulder at darkening rounds of meat.

"About five minutes," Dad said.

Abria bounced out of the open door and onto the deck, proceeding to climb on one of the heavy chairs. She giggled.

"Careful," Luke told her. "Little monkey."

Matthias had called Abria 'little monkey' more than once. I smiled, and saw him in my mind standing in Abria's bedroom—as I'd seen him so many times before—holding Abria in his arms. A shot of love warmed me, deep down.

Aunt Janis had adopted the pet name since Matthias had left. It was still

203

hard to hear it.

I'd forced myself not to count the days since I'd last seen Matthias. Each day, I'd ached. Though school, Weston and life had helped soften the perforation of missing him, many of my thoughts still carried some part of him: the unique blue of his eyes, the twinkle of his spirit when I stood in his presence.

I picked Abria up and held her against me. "Did you buy Abria those special wheat-free buns at the health food store for her burger?" I asked Mom, carrying my sister back inside. Changing the subject might help—even if only temporarily. Mom stood over the sink, washing cooking utensils.

"Yes, thanks for reminding me. They're in the cabinet. Get one out for her, will you please?"

I did, and Abria turned her head, uninterested in the specialty product. "Hopefully, she'll grow to like it," I chuckled. One of the things Mom and Dad had learned at the autism conference was that children with autism tended to improve behaviorally when they were on a wheat-free diet.

So far, Abria hadn't warmed up very well to the specially made foods. But she was working with a wonderful speech therapist—at the suggestion of one of the specialists—and learning to use words to communicate.

"I thought Weston was coming," Mom said.

The door bell rang. I grinned. Her right brow arched over a grin that mirrored mine.

I placed Abria on her feet, jogged to the front door and swung it open. Weston looked yummy as a chocolate bar in jeans and a brown knit long sleeved shirt that accentuated his sculpted form. His coffee-rich eyes sparkled and he smiled. "Hey."

I wrapped around him and breathed in his scrubbed-clean cologne, so freshly applied the scent dampened my nose going in. "Mmm, you smell great," I murmured.

"So do you." His face nuzzled deep into the curve of my neck. "Yum, hamburgers."

We laughed. I eased back and lightly slugged his arm. He shut the door and I held out my hand. "Hungry?"

His keen gaze swept me from feet to eyes. "Starved."

I led him through the afternoon sunbeams pouring in the windows and into the kitchen. He greeted Mom, who gave him a hug before she handed him a clear glass bowl filled with yellow cake and cream, layered with strawberries. "You're just in time. Take that outside for me, will you please?" She winked.

Weston nodded in good-mannered obligation and he and I went out on the deck. Abria stood on the same chair she'd tried to climb moments earlier, her gaze skyward, arms reaching.

Weston greeted Krissy with a nod, Luke with a handshake and then he gingerly placed Mom's trifle down on the table.

"Hey, Weston." Dad waved the spatula in greeting.

"Mr. Dodd." Weston left my side to join Dad. "How's it going? Looks good."

"Going good. Hope you're hungry."

"Very. Can I do anything?"

"We're about ready, I think." Dad's gaze flicked over Weston's shoulder to me. I couldn't keep the smile from my face, and felt insipidly in love, so I reached for another carrot stick and crunched, habit taking my gaze to Abria.

"Okay." Weston crossed to me wearing a huge grin, his hands diving into the depths of his front pockets.

"You look happy," I murmured.

"Dad came home today," he said.

I hugged him. "I'm so glad."

He reached for my hand and our fingers twined. "Me too. Mom's happy to have him back and when I left to come here, they were in their bedroom, talking. At least I heard them talking. Not that I was listening. You know what I mean." His cheeks flushed.

I nodded. "That's the best news I've heard in a long time."

"Ready." Dad announced, plopping the platter of meat down on the table.

"Up!" Abria squealed, arms reaching for the sky.

Mom came through the door and immediately grabbed her. "Why weren't you guys watching her?"

"We were," Luke said, then dipped his head sheepishly.

"She's fine, Mom." I pulled out a chair to sit and Weston moved in behind me, and his hand covered mine. He finished bringing the chair out and I sat. Weston sat in the chair next to me.

"Luke, bring Abria's highchair to the table, will you please?" Mom tilted her head in the direction of the kitchen.

Luke got up and went inside.

Dad found an empty seat and surveyed the bounty on the table. "Looks good. Mmm, my favorite dessert." His eyes sparkled at Mom. "Thank you."

Mom sent him a private smile that warmed me, then she sat across from him.

Luke dragged out the highchair and placed it table side, then hefted Abria into it and locked the tray in place. Abria grunted with protest, her frustrated gaze skyward.

I followed her eyes to the blue sky filled with billowing white clouds, tinted now with warm amber shafts of light as the sun slid closer to the western mountains. I never looked at the clouds without thinking of Matthias and Heaven. Knowing he was happy and safe in a place I looked forward to, but didn't long for like I had longed when he had been my guardian.

"Up!" Abria repeated, her hands straining.

Mom studied her with interest. "Do you think she remembers Matthias?" she whispered. Luke had yet to tell Krissy about Matthias, and the two of them were engaged in a chat.

Who could forget him? "I'm sure she does," I said. Another pang of familiar missing gnawed its way through my soul.

Dad extended his hands to his sides on the table top in invitation to join us all together for a word of prayer. The warm spring sun bathed us in radiant beams. We held hands and Dad bowed his head, sharing thoughts of gratitude.

My cell phone vibrated in my pocket just as Dad finished. Mayhem broke out as arms reached for meat, buns, condiments, salad and everything else. Chat filled the air. Abria continued repeating, "Up! Up!Up!"

I pulled out my cell phone. A text. From Britt.

i'm back. i wanna c u, zoe. is that ok?

It took me a few seconds to put aside the surprise of hearing from her.

sure.

Britt and I planned to talk later. I slid my phone back into my pocket. I wondered how she was, where she was in her life now.

Weston handed me a burger.

"Thanks," I said. "That was Britt. She's back," I kept my voice soft, so our conversation wouldn't be heard. But Dad was analyzing his barbequing job with Mom and Krissy and Luke were laughing over something.

"Up!Up!Up!"

Weston reached for the ketchup. He grabbed the bottle and squirted a blob on his hamburger meat. "You going to see her?"

"She wants to see me."

He finished dressing his hamburger and his eyes met mine. "She needs you in her life."

"Aww, thanks."

"It's true." He kissed my cheek.

"Up!" Abria, uninterested in the food spread on her tray, now tried to squirm to her feet, so she could stand in the high chair.

I took a bite of my hamburger and stood. "I'll take her," I said around a mouth of food.

Weston pushed his chair back from the table and stood, ready to help me. I shook my head. "Don't. It's okay."

"Thanks, honey," Mom said. "You can try sitting her in a regular chair."

We all knew that wouldn't keep her in one place.

I gathered Abria into my arms and walked the length of the deck with her. "What is it with you today?" I whispered into the softness of her ear. "Aren't you hungry?"

207

She arched away from me, her gaze locked on the pastel orange clouds passing through a sunset-washed sky. "Are you thinking of Matthias?" I asked, watching her face closely for any recognition to his name. She glanced at me for a split second. A rush of joy oozed through the open spaces where missing him gnawed.

"He's up there, watching over us."

"Us! Us! Us!"

I hugged her tight, a smile creasing my lips. I followed her gaze heavenward. "Ab-so-lute-ly."

A Special Thank You

Writing this series has been a wonderful experience for me, as I've taken many of the incidents in the HEAVENLY stories from my own family life. I'm grateful for the gift of writing, and that I can share this story with my loyal readers many of whom have, through their enthusiasm, spread the word about the books to the world. To them I owe hugs and friendship and a mention: Sadie Ann Price, Katrina Whittaker, Tammy Williams Owens, Melissa Silva, Lisa Sano, Aurora Momcilovich, Maria Cabal Gomez and Lynsey Newton to name a few. So many readers have connected with me and thanked me for opening their eyes to the curious and sometimes hard to understand world of those who live with autism. I'm pleased when lives are touched and grateful to have any part in helping others understand the difficulties and treasures living with the handicapped can bring, if we—as people—put aside our apprehension.

Thank you, reader, for sharing in my story.

Jennifer Laurens

ABOUT THE AUTHOR

Jennifer Laurens is the mother of six children,
one of whom has autism. She lives in Utah with her family,
at the base of the Wasatch Mountains.

Other Titles:

Falling for Romeo

Magic Hands

Nailed

Heavenly

Penitence

Visit the websites: www.heavenlythebook.com
www.jenniferlaurens.com

LaVergne, TN USA
03 November 2010
203398LV00002B/35/P